PENGUIN BOOKS

CAN'T QUIT YOU, BABY

Ellen Douglas (a pen name for Josephine Haxton) was born in Natchez, Mississippi, and grew up in small towns in Mississippi, Louisiana, and Arkansas. She was written five earlier novels and a volume of short stories. Her first novel, *A Family's Affairs*, and her collection of stories, *Black Cloud, White Cloud*, were each in turn selected by *The New York Times* for inclusion among the ten best fiction titles of the year. Her third novel, *Apostles of Light*, was nominated for a National Book Award. Her fourth, *The Rock Cried Out*, was written under a grant from the National Endowment for the Arts, and her fifth, *A Lifetime Burning*, received wide critical acclaim. She has also published *The Magic Carpet*, a collection of classic fairy tales retold, with illustrations by Mississippi artist Walter Anderson. In 1989, she received the fiction award from the Fellowship of Southern Writers. Ellen Douglas has three sons and five grandchildren. She lives in Jackson, Mississippi, and teaches one semester each year at the University of Mississippi.

Can't Quit You, Baby

ELLEN DOUGLAS

PENGUIN BOOKS

PENGUIN BOOKS
Published by the Penguin Group
Penguin Books USA Inc.,
375 Hudson Street, New York, New York 10010 U.S.A.
Penguin Books Ltd. 27 Wrights Lane, London W8 5TZ, England
Penguin Books Australia Ltd. Ringwood, Victoria, Australia
Penguin Books Canada Ltd. 10 Alcorn Avenue, Toronto, Ontario, Canada M4V 3B2
Penguin Books (N.Z.) Ltd. 182–190 Wairau Road, Auckland 10, New Zealand

Penguin Books Ltd. Registered Offices: Harmondsworth, Middlesex, England

First published in the United States of America by
Atheneum, an imprint of Macmillan Publishing Company 1988
Published in Penguin Books 1989

13 15 17 19 20 18 16 14 12

"Can't Quit You, Baby" written by Willie Dixon, © 1965 Hoochie Coochie Music (BMI),
administered by Bug/Arc Music Corp. All rights reserved. Used by permission. "Spoonful"
written by Willie Dixon, © 1960 Hoochie Coochie Music (BMI), administered by Bug/Arc
Music Corp. All rights reserved. Used by permission. "Back Door Man" written by Willie
Dixon, © 1961 Hoochie Coochie Music (BMI), administered by Bug/Arc Music Corp. All
rights reserved. Used by permission. "Built for Comfort" written by Willie Dixon, © 1963
Hoochie Coochie Music (BMI), administered by Bug/Arc Music Corp. All rights reserved.
Used by permission. "All the Things You Are" music by Jerome Kern and lyrics by Oscar
Hammerstein II, © 1939 T. B. Harms Company. Copyright renewed (c/o The Welk Music
Group, Santa Monica, CA 90401). International copyright secured. All rights reserved.
Used by permission. "I Got a Razor" written by Willie Dixon, © 1960, Monona Music
(BMI), administered by Bug. All rights reserved. Used by permission. "The Seventh Son"
written by Willie Dixon, © 1955, renewed 1983, Hoochie Coochie Music (BMI), adminis-
tered by Bug. All rights reserved. Used by permission.

This is a work of fiction. Names, characters, places, and incidents are either the product of
the author's imagination or are used fictitiously. Any resemblance to actual events or per-
sons, living or dead, is entirely coincidental.

LIBRARY OF CONGRESS CATALOGING IN PUBLICATION DATA
Douglas, Ellen, 1921–
Can't quit you, baby/Ellen Douglas.
p. cm.
ISBN 0 14 01.2102 1
1. Title
[PS3554.0825C3   1989]
813'.54—dc20   89–32774

In memory of Mathelde Griffin

Acknowledgments

I wish to acknowledge gratefully the assistance, through a generous grant, of the National Endowment for the Arts. Thanks, also, to Patti Black and Dan Denblayker of the Mississippi Department of Archives and History, and to Dr. William Ferris and his staff of the Center for the study of Southern Culture at the University of Mississippi.

As always, I am grateful to my family for their support and encouragement. For this book I want especially to thank Anna and Jim for being there, and Brooks, Ayres, and Kenneth for their patient reading and rereading and their invaluable advice.

"I can't quit you, baby, but I got to put you down a little while."
— WILLIE DIXON

ONE

T he two women are sitting at
right angles to each other at the kitchen table on a sunny
July morning in the nineteen-sixties. On the stove behind
them a pot of boiling syrup scents the air with cloves and
cinnamon. They are making preserves.

Did you know Wayne Jones died yesterday? the white
woman says.

The black woman looks pleased. Serve him right, she
says. She has a small sharp paring knife in her hand and
is peeling figs carefully, leaving the stems and white un-
derskin intact and dropping them in a bucket of limewater
on the floor beside the table.

Julia!

I hadn't told you I worked for him when me and Nig first
come to town?

These are beautiful figs, the white woman says. Almost
every one perfect. Not too green and not too ripe. She culls
half a dozen overripes and drops them in a trash bag.

Of all the preserves they make together, the two agree
that figs are the most delicious, the most aesthetically pleas-
ing. They go to a great deal of trouble to keep them whole,
so that in the jars they will swim in all their shapely beauty,
surrounded by cartwheels of golden lemon and curls of brown
cinnamon bark, in a sun-drenched syrup of unparalleled

3

delicacy. Separately their mothers or grandmothers must have taught them this recipe, for they did not know each other until they were grown.

I said I worked for him, the black woman says.

I know you did. That's why I mentioned seeing the obituary. I gather you didn't like him very much. The white woman bends down, bathes her hands in the limewater, and stirs up undissolved lime from the bottom of the bucket. You'd better keep washing the juice off your hands or it'll make them raw, she says.

He was a case, Mrs. O'Kelly, a case. Almost drove me back to the country. He had Wayne's Cafe then. Before he started running the school cafeterias. Remember?

Hmm? the white woman says.

What I could tell you about him!

Hmm? The white woman is deaf and wears a hearing aid, a tiny shell in her ear with a cord running down to the battery and receiver clipped to her brassiere strap.

Julia raises her voice slightly. I said, it was when he had the cafe. You know, they stayed open, until eleven, opened up in the mornings at six. Sometimes I was on the night shift—three to eleven, sometimes on the day shift—five A.M. to three—didn't matter which. He might come down and be waiting for you to open up and start coffee at five in the morning. Or he'd stay and close up at eleven. Didn't have to—me and one of the other girls could run the cash register and had keys. He was a damn crazy man—crazy for black women.

Such behavior is inappropriate even to Wayne Jones. The white woman does not wish to credit it. You mean he got after you down *there*—at the cafe? No.

Chased me around the table more times than once, Julia says.

There is no getting around in these stories of two lives that the black woman is the white woman's servant. There would have been no way in that time and place—the nineteen-sixties and seventies in Mississippi—for them to get acquainted, except across the kitchen table from each other, shelling peas, peeling apples, polishing silver. True, other black and white women became friends under other circumstances, but such friendships, arising out of political crisis—revolution—were rare. In this house the white woman had to choose to sit down to set the tone of their connection.

But—servant? Mistress? They would be uneasy with these words, and so am I. The servant might quote the Bible: And the last shall be first, Lord. Yes. As for the mistress, the sexual connotation might drift across her mind—she's still happy to be her husband's lover, his only mistress. Of anything else she'd avoid the implications.

So, let's settle for housekeeper and employer. Yes, that's better. And try for now to be absentminded about race and class, place and time, even about poverty and wealth, security and deprivation. Here, for example, are some situations that will not be explored:

The white woman—Cornelia—is driving Julia home from work. The latter is sitting on the backseat of the car (or the front seat. For the purpose of dramatizing a point either will do).

Cornelia is taking Julia to register to vote (or declining to take her, or Julia is declining to go) under the perilous circumstances of black registration in Mississippi in nineteen sixty-four.

Or they are listening together to the news of the assassination of John F. Kennedy. It is just past noon and Julia has been serving the white family's dinner. Now she is bent over the kitchen table, clutching her belly, moaning.

Try to be absentminded about all these neglected possibilities. You can't? You point out that by listing them I've included them? Ah, well, I didn't say it was possible. I said, *Try*. They have other, perhaps even more complex business with each other. And don't misunderstand. *They* weren't absentminded about these ludicrous and dreadful matters. To them race sounded the endlessly repeated ground bass above and entwined with which they danced the passacaglia (or, as it may sometimes appear, the boogie) of their lives.

As you will have observed, both these women have ancient names indicative of someone's interest, in the past of both families, in Roman history. Not uncommon in the nineteenth-century South. Remember the great Mississippi statesman of the Reconstruction, Lucius Quintus Cincinnatus Lamar? And how about Cassius Marcellus Clay—the first one, as well as Muhammad Ali.

After the custom of the time and place, neither Julia nor her husband Philip are called by their names among their friends and relatives. Philip is called Nig (I reckon because he works like a nigger, Julia said, when she and Cornelia had got well enough acquainted for Cornelia to ask), and Julia is called Tweet.

My grandpa called me Sweet when I was a little girl, she said the first day.

I think I'll call you Julia, if you don't mind, Cornelia said. It's such a lovely name.

As for Philip, she calls him Mr. Carrier. I certainly can't call him *Nig*, she said to her husband, and she said the same thing to Tweet, who said, Fine. Philip said nothing. He is a man of few words, at least in Cornelia's house.

When Julia came to work for Cornelia in nineteen fifty-five, she was thirty-five and Cornelia was thirty. Cornelia and her husband had two children. Julia had lost two babies and she had two grown stepdaughters now living in New York and California.

Every weekday morning at nine-thirty Julia appears at the door of the room where Cornelia prefers to hold court. Cornelia is an accomplished cook and the kitchen is her throne room. Most mornings when she has finished breakfast she sits in the kitchen planning what she will cook that day and listing what she needs to cook it. Julia, when she arrives, is usually bearing a gift. In summer it may be tomatoes from her garden or a spray of blooms from her neighbor's flowering pomegranate or a handful of ragged robins snatched off the ditch bank on her way to work. Sometimes, especially in winter or in rainy weather, the gift may be something insubstantial, plucked out of the air or out of the past—a piece of advice about human behavior. On a disastrous new romance in her neighborhood, for example: He turned out to be a jicky man and a jicky woman ought not ever take up with a jicky man. A verse from the Bible. Or she fills the house with song: Every time I feel the spirit moving in my heart, I sing. Or, sometimes, measuring out the salt and baking powder: Spoonful, spoonful, spoonful. One little spoon of your love is good enough for me. Or she tells a tale out of her life.

At the beginning when Tweet produced a tale (often long and complicated, with an ambiguous moral or circumstances that seemed unacceptable to Cornelia), she, Cornelia, listened with a distant courtesy—condescension, even—that might have put off a less committed storyteller. But Tweet talked on. Cornelia sat or stood, peeling figs (or beating or mincing or fluting or folding in or stirring up or rolling out), and Tweet talked on. Later, it was as if the tales had washed over Cornelia like small lapping waves, subsiding into themselves and vanishing.

Today Tweet's gift is Wayne Jones.

Yeah, he was after me, she says. I was good-looking then. Didn't get these bad risings scarred my face until I was nearly thirty. My skin was smooth. Never did have good hair, but you got to admit even now I got good legs. And I always had these unusual eyes. Make people look twice.

Tweet has large eyes with long lashes. The irises are two-colored—concentric circles, the inner blue-black, the outer a pale blue—and the white is not white, but faintly tinged with a blue as pure as the sky. No one seems to know what causes this curious phenomenon. Some people find her eyes unnerving—as if she might be looking at you twice, once with the inner circle, once with the outer—but Cornelia thinks them beautiful.

That was nineteen and forty-five, Tweet said. I didn't tell Nig. Wasn't nothing he could've done. Just make him feel terrible. I had to handle it myself. She dipped her hands in the limewater and washed the fig juice from them. What'd he die of?

What's that?

I said, What'd he die of? Is your battery going dead, Mrs. O'Kelly?

Cornelia took the tiny battery case out of her shirt pocket, shook it, and twisted the wire connected to the earpiece. Bad connection, she said. Cancer. Everyone dies of cancer these days.

You going to die of cancer if you live long enough.

Or something, Cornelia said.

He had a black cancer eating at him back then. Cancer of meanness. Cancer of woman-craziness. That long ago. You think you can make yourself die of cancer?

Make yourself? Cornelia shook her head.

I might have wished it on him, Tweet said. You could say I tried to. Hated him enough to.

It's a waste of time and energy to hate people, Cornelia said. I don't hate anybody.

Hmm, Tweet said.

I just don't, Cornelia said. Really.

Now Tweet is humming, then singing softly a snatch of an old song: . . . twelve o'clock they killed him. Glad to see him die. . . .

What's that?

He's a white man, Tweet said. And I'm working there. Comes up behind me. Puts his hands on me. There would be others there to see it. Ugh. She shrugged him off. Had that thin mouth, lips no wider than a straw, like a gray slit in his face, turned up at the corners in a mean kind of smile. Gray. He was gray. Reckon he had lead poison? I worked for a lady once had lead poison. She raked their two piles of peelings into the center of the newspaper that was spread on the table, rolled the paper up, crushed it as fiercely as if she had Wayne Jones rolled up inside, dropped it in the trash, and laid out fresh paper. You got a God's plenty of figs, she said.

You'd better put your hands down in the limewater again, toughen them up, Cornelia said.

8

One night, everybody else is gone, he chases me around the kitchen like he's loony, Tweet said. He's going to rape me. No doubt about it. I run past the big sink, pick up a meat cleaver off the counter, and in a minute I'm backing through the swinging door into the cafe where the light's still on, anybody can see in from the street. That changes things. He's suppose to be respectable.

It come to me then what to say to him. I can't quit—can't give up the job. I need it. Mr. Jones, I say, if you don't leave me alone, I'm gonna tell your wife, you hear? I'm gonna tell Mrs. Jones. (I knew her—she used to come in the cafe every day for lunch. She's OK, you know. I liked her pretty well.)

He looks at me with that gray smile and just shrugs his shoulders and I back through the cafe towards the front, carrying the meat cleaver. Don't forget to bring that cleaver when you come to work tomorrow, Tweet, he says. That's a good cleaver.

I might bring something else, I say. I got a .22 pistol at home.

Ah, Tweet, don't *be* like that, he says and laughs.

I ain't thinking about shooting him, of course. I wouldn't shoot a white man.

Two days later he's after me again. I'd made up my mind when I said it about telling his wife and I went out to her house that afternoon, soon as I figured she could've got home from work. Caught the bus out there. It goes in two blocks of their house. So I went. She's home. I knew for sure she was there and he was down at the cafe that shift—called them both, they answered and I hung up.

Well, Tweet! she says. (She's glad to see me.)

Poor thing, I'm thinking. Married to that . . . Tweet shrugged. Plenty like him. I know that's the truth. She looked at Cornelia. Then louder, I say, I know that's got to be the truth.

Cornelia nodded absently.

I knew she'd be puzzled over me being there at her house

9

five-thirty in the afternoon, so I jump right in and tell her I need to talk to her about something serious. I'm not scared, Tweet said. No, I'm not scared. I'm mad. If it don't do me no good, if it gets me in a mess of trouble, still, I'm going to tell her.

It's about Mr. Jones, Mrs. Jones, I say. About me and my job and Mr. Jones. I look at her and she begins to shake her head and wave her hands in front of her face like she's waving off gnats.

She would never believe you, Cornelia said. Or never admit she did. You should have known that.

Tweet grinned, wiped her paring knife and tested the blade against her thumb. That wasn't the way it went, she said. You know what she says when that waving off gnats don't stop me from speaking? I can't do nothing about it, Tweet, she says. I can't help it. You got to make allowances for him. He's just *like that*. Yeah. *He's just like that*. Pitiful, ain't it, Mrs. O'Kelly?

Cornelia nods, I don't believe it, she says. Julia, I just don't believe it. But of course she does.

I stayed on another two, three months at the cafe, Tweet said. Kept the cleaver handy. He got after somebody else. Then I got a job in the kitchen at the community center. Worked there until nineteen-fifty.

The funeral is at two-thirty tomorrow afternoon, Cornelia said. They're probably waiting for their daughter to get here.

Are you going to bake them a cake or something?

Cornelia shook her head. I don't know them that well, she said.

Cornelia is a woman, rare in our time, who has not spent any part of her life alone. Early on, even when her husband was away, there were the children; and when their second child was grown and gone, wherever she and her husband went, they went together. She has never found her way alone into or out of a metropolitan airport or flagged a taxi or spent a night alone in a hotel. None of these facts seem remarkable to her nor have they seemed so to her husband. She has not been fearful or stupid or unresourceful, and she does not think of him as playing the heavy male. They are companions. And she hasn't been useless. She's raised her children and worked as a partner in their successful bookstore in the small city where they live. That is the way her life has happened and, in her passion for him and her commitment to her household and her work—children with straight teeth and straight backs and straight A's; gleaming silver, polished mahogany and walnut surfaces; towels and sheets in ribbon-tied stacks on the shelves; books in their places, old bindings mended, new ones dusted; a sunny kitchen with a crown roast of lamb in the oven and a génoise cooling on the cake rack; files and inventories orderly, customers happy—she has not asked a question, has only said occasionally, reading in the morning paper of some new catastrophe: My God, we're fortunate.

Even her deafness, closing in slowly in her twenties and thirties, she has treated as a trivial annoyance. Hearing aids had been perfected as if at her command. And her best vision of herself—her will, perhaps—required her to present herself with grace and skill; she seldom seems to misunderstand the muttered phrase or to lose those last words spoken so softly at the end of a sentence. True, she misses fleetingly the old days early in her marriage when she and John used still to dance to the tunes of the forties—"Begin the Beguine" and "All the Things You Are" and "In the Mood"—and is sad, though she never says so, that, although she feels the beat, wants to dance, the music is all but lost on her, skewed by the powerful amplification of her hearing aid. But it may be that, like an oriental potter, she believes that nothing should be perfect—the precious flawed pot set in the place of honor at the tea ceremony. Or perhaps that her deafness is the guarantee of good fortune.

Such women as Cornelia—sheltered women—would have

11

been the commonplace of her mother's generation and class. In her day, as everyone knows, upper-class girl-children had nursemaids or nannies or mammies, depending on where they lived. At five or six they went to private or public schools or had governesses, depending on how wealthy they were. At fifteen they went with properly brought up young men to properly chaperoned parties and dances. At twenty-two they married and had husbands and children and servants. Their cooks lived in or came to fix breakfast before the husbands left for work, but after the housemen (often the cooks' husbands) had slipped in at dawn while the family was still sleeping to lay and light the fires and carry out the ashes.

This way of enjoying life was possible in smallish cities and towns in the South even for people of "moderate means" (as we used to say) until a few years ago, because black servants could be hired for sweatshop wages and because public schools were almost as exclusive as private schools. Blacks went to their own schools—and not for long. Country boys—poor whites—dropped out by the time the girls were old enough to look at them with desire. The Jews were "just like us"—might as well have been Presbyterians. After all, as enlightened people often said, Jesus was a Jew.

Yes, until now—until her middle age (not always, but ever since the day she married), everything in Cornelia's life has gone extraordinarily well. It's as if she was born under a lucky star, as if a fairy godmother bestowed on her the gifts of beauty, brains, and good luck. My darling, we're so lucky, she says to her husband again and again from year to year, reading of tornadoes, fires, floods, hearing of the death in battle of beloved sons, of whole families killed on bloody highways.

True, her mother used to remark that Cornelia loved her husband too much, that it was unseemly still to be "in love" after so many years, but her mother was always a jealous woman. And it does not appear that this excessive emotion (if it is indeed excessive) has flawed the family

12

facade. The children seem to have sustained no injury from Cornelia's attentions to their father. Both are grown, whole, intelligent survivors, not only of ranking second in their mother's regard, but, thus far, in nineteen sixty-nine, of the perils of the nineteen-sixties. Her father is still healthy and independent in his condominium near Mobile; her mother died at a suitable age without pain—lifting the leaf of a stuffed artichoke to her lips, saying, Delicious! John's parents were killed so early (in an automobile accident) that they still seem young—arrested living in their early forties, shadowy figures who were snatched away through no bodily failures of their own—and who might have been troublesome (although I don't think Cornelia would ever allow this thought to cross her mind) if they had lived.

And Cornelia still has a blue-eyed, fresh-faced beauty, looks nearer thirty-four than forty-four. Her thick chestnut hair is untouched by gray and her pale skin marked lightly by time and weather. Being fair and sensible, she's always, even as an adolescent, been cautious about overexposure to the sun.

Until now. She isn't a fool. She knows, of course, that no human luck lasts. But she and John, she says to herself, even though he is eight years her senior, have a good twenty-five years ahead of them, time enough to sail and fly, to swim and fish, to enjoy the grandchildren who will soon be coming along, and then time enough (although she would never express herself in such sentimental terms) to hold hands and gaze into the falling darkness, teach themselves finally to welcome the night.

Cornelia over the years has considered herself a listener. Another woman might not have time for Tweet's gifts—for the tales of childhood, the snatches of song, the handful of ragged robins. But from the beginning Cornelia, kneading dough, fluting a piecrust, cutting carrot curls or radish rosettes, has never by a word or gesture betrayed the boredom, the condescension she sometimes feels, her rejection of the moral code that Tweet's stories sometimes imply, her doubts about the verity of some outlandish set of events. She accepts the tales like the flowers that she sticks in a jelly glass and sets in the window by the kitchen sink and forgets.

Can one be a listener if one is deaf? What if, as sometimes happens, one simply does not hear? Techniques must be acquired, for example, to make the speaker comfortable. Cornelia is an expert at watching while she listens. She wears an alert, intelligent expression on her face and has a rich stock of responses which serve a general purpose and enable her to navigate around the mounds of silence that sometimes rise like unexpected shoals and sandbars in the rush of words that batter at her hearing aid, tear along the fragile crippled auditory nerve. These skills are useful at work and at cocktail parties and garden-club meetings where no one wants to be importuned to repeat, boringly to repeat, what everyone else has heard.

Unlike many deaf people, she has not solved the problem of her own occasional boredom and confusion and isolation by becoming a nonstop talker. She takes pride in her ability to keep everyone comfortable—whether or not she has heard and understood. And she takes pride, too, in her own silences.

She takes an even more complex and powerful pride in her relations with her intimates. The fact is, she thinks, people sometimes drop their voices so that she will *not* hear. Her children, her friends, her father take this advantage so for granted, they are scarcely conscious of it—even her beloved husband may respond at the dinner table to a question from one of the children in a voice so low she cannot make out what he is saying. He doesn't mean to, she says to herself. She says nothing to him—to them. She never never asks anyone to repeat himself unless she is sure what was said was meant for her. She never says: What are you talking about? Never says: Speak a little louder, please. Never says: What?

14

Except to Tweet and people like her who are—yes, say it—purveyors of services of one kind or another, that is, who in Cornelia's view must be heard, who depend, at the least, upon her direction, but often, too, on her advice, her justice, or her generosity.

And then, sometimes, out of her own need, Cornelia abandons both listening and appearing to listen. She lays aside the tiny packet with its dangling wire and flesh-colored earpiece, or clicks a switch and closes out the world. In the pool where she swims laps three times a week; in the garden, immersed in the repetitive swing of gathering and dropping beans in a basket; pregnant and sitting alone with the sun on her back, the pressure of a light wind against her cheek, feeling the beat of blood and breath, the silent moving presence of the child under her heart—at these times she lives for a while in a silence that does not strive either to hear or to give the appearance of hearing.

I was raise by my grandpa, Tweet said. Raise by an old man—older than most grands. That's partly why I'm like I am. You think about it.

You mean . . . ?

I mean he was in the *Civil* War. He's got a *federal* pension. So that makes him—even if he was only a boy—that makes him old, old when I was born. Let's see, Mrs. O'Kelly—if he was born in . . . ? He's got to be full-grown before the end of the war, even if he started out a boy.

Don't you know?

Tweet shook her head. He never would talk about it. I never got him to say why he went—how he made up his mind it was the thing to do—or where he fought or how he got wounded. Not one word. And looking back, I see he had his reasons for that. People got their pensions taken away, or never got em. Less said the better. But anyhow, he must have been grown-up by the time it was over. So he's—add it up.

Well, if he was eighteen at the youngest when the war was over, that would make him—let's see— thirty-eight in eighty-five, fifty-eight in nineteen-five, eighty-eight in nineteen thirty-five—but that's impossible, Julia.

Can't help if it's impossible, it's true. He died in nineteen and thirty-five, when I was fifteen years old. You see, he wouldn't have been more than eighty-eight, the way you calculate. But he was older than that. Close to a hundred.

But I mean, it would be impossible for an eighty, eighty-five-year-old man to be raising a child.

Well, he was lively to the end. Just shrinking. All those years, he was getting a pension for being a wounded veteran—didn't have but three fingers on his left hand and a stiff leg. But he could ride a horse, follow a plow. I can hear him, see him now, talking to his mule, singing. He talked different to every mule he had. And sang: Wake up, Rosie. Tell your midnight dreams. Yeah. And like that. He was partial to the cane fife and the drum. Sang them old blues. Like this: That's all right, baby. You gon need my help some day. He'd walk down the furrow, throw one leg out a little, sing till he'd have the mule keeping time. On horseback, he'd favor his bad leg, kind of reach down and work the stirrup over his foot—but he could ride without no trouble. And during the Depression he managed better than most. He was the one had money coming in when nobody else did. Yeah, he's my welcome table—on this earth.

But what I'm talking about—why I'm like I am. Suppose you raise by an old man. Suppose he's peaceable. Not one of these old men beats children. Little bitty fellow. Shrunk up to nothing time I was ten. I was big as he was, my arms stronger than his. Nevertheless, I respect him. I know he's got power. But he don't want me to be afraid of him and I ain't. I live all my childhood in a house where I ain't afraid

16

of nobody—nothing but ghosts and baby chickens. That makes a difference.

Ghosts and baby chickens! Cornelia is putting dough through her pasta machine, once for each lump at each setting and then through the blades. Tweet is loading the dishwasher. The kitchen smells of crushed mint and garlic, of simmering fresh tomatoes. Cornelia stops and glances at Tweet to see if she is serious. Julia? she says tentatively.

Little bitty chickens so soft, they feel like they ain't got no bones, Tweet said. And ghosts! Evil out there. I be a fool not to know that. She continued: Most girl-children need to be afraid—afraid of white men, white women, white kids. . . .

Would you be afraid of *me*, if . . . ?

But Tweet went on. . . . afraid of brothers, uncles, daddies, mama's boyfriends, mamas, even. Not me. I'm with my grandpa and nobody else. And another thing. He wants me to be independent—knew he'd be gone time I was full-grown, so he taught me to be cautious, foresighted, taught me to stand on my own feet.

Oh, I thought he was the most powerful man in the world, Tweet said. When I was a little bitty girl, I thought he knew everything and I knew he meant to teach it all to me. I listened. I watched. Taught me to make a split oak basket, rob a bee tree, skin a catfish, look in a mule's mouth and know how old he is. Taught me to milk a cow, ride a horse, build a pump to store potatoes and pumpkins in the wintertime.

A pump? Cornelia said.

Yeah, you know, like a root cellar, only it's a hole in the ground set in a high spot with straw and all over it. We had us a root cellar under the house, matter of fact, and later on it prove useful. But after it flooded in nineteen and twenty-seven, he never did use it again, not to store in.

He could remember years, Tweet said. What happened in every year, and the name of every mule he ever had.

17

Yeah. Well, the truth of it is, most of that ain't been much use to me. But other things he taught me, like to watch my money—he could count and read numbers without no difficulty, if he couldn't read letters. To speak up for myself. And he was powerful! I remember when we'd go up to town on a Saturday to tend to his business, we'd stand by the side of the road out in the middle of the country—all you can see is road and fields and turnrows, nobody around but us. It looks like to me all he's got to do is raise his arm, he can make a bus appear to take us to town. It's magic. We're out there and all of a sudden he's got his arm up and here's a bus coming down the road. He's done called it. Yeah, I got nothing but respect for him. But just the same I ain't afraid of him.

But Julia, where were your mother and father? Why didn't you live with them?

Well, Rosa and my daddy never did live together. She had me, see, when she wasn't but fourteen. You know, Rosa and me more like sisters than mama and daughter. My daddy took advantage of her and then went off. Yeah, like the song says, he was a back-door man. When the rooster crow, told him it was time to go. And afterwards, there she was, got me. How could a child like her look after a baby?

Her family was cropping up there on the creek, needed her in the field, and then they moved to a new place, took her along. I was two or three. So the old man, my daddy's papa, says, Leave that baby with me. I'll raise her up for you. Of course, they know it's an advantage for me. He had the pension check coming in, he owned a little piece of land up there—farmed his own land. So they give me to him and took Rosa and went.

They wasn't all that far off—over in Buchanan County—and every so often her and her mama would come around —help us get the crop in, bring me clothes and hair ribbons, clean the house good, help him work his garden, put up vegetables. They kept up with us.

Yes, Tweet said, I was born lucky—like you say you

18

was. The bad luck started when my daddy came back, and that wasn't until I was fifteen years old.

So here they come, Tweet said, getting off the bus down on the road where the turnrow stops. Guarantee my grandpa didn't summon *that* bus. We sitting on the front porch, him and me. It's fall, early November, but one of them sunny days makes you feel so good. . . . Porch faces south, catches the sun, and when it's warm like that, he sets up in his old split-oak rocker, stretches out his stiff leg, says it helps his rheumatism. He hears the bus stop—his hearing is still sharp, but he can't see nothing the last few years of his life except light and dark. People like shadows to him. He makes em out moving when they pass by a window or a door.

Who getting off the bus, Tweet? he says.

Ain't nobody I know. A man and a woman I never seen before, and they coming this way.

Well, he says. He's inclined to say, *Well* and then stop and think a minute before he says anything else. What they look like? he says.

I study them. They scuffling up the turnrow. It's been a dry fall, turnrow's ankle-deep in dust and about the color of old dry cow skulls been out in the sun two, three years.

He's got on cowboy boots, I say. (I hadn't ever seen any *real* person wearing cowboy boots before. Only in the movies one or two times when he took me to the show on Saturday afternoon, sit way high up in the air next to the roof and see Tom Mix, Hopalong Cassidy, and so forth.) Got him a cowboy hat, too, I say. It's black, wide, shade his face so I can't see him too good.

What you say, girl? Hit's a white man?

Nahsuh, I don't mean they white.

Well, by now they coming closer, maybe a hundred yards off. She all dress up, I say. I'm use to being eyes to my grandpa, describing everything he wants to know about. She got on these ankle-strappy green shoes, high heels and stockings.

Hmmm, he says.

Big green hat with a red flower on it and a flowery dress.

Hmmm.

They carrying grips and coats. Reckon where they going? Ain't nobody up this turnrow but us.

Long about then he sees us, stops, puts his grip down, commence to wave his arm and yell. Papa, he says. Papa, that you? Took and waved his hat. I saw a gold tooth gleam in his face.

Me, all right, my grandpa says to me. Who else it's gonna be? I been right here for sixty years and more, ain't I? Ever since I first crop this land in eighteen and seventy-six.

I told you, Tweet said to Cornelia, he's a little bitty shrivel-up old man, didn't I? Mouth fell in, because he don't keep his teeth in for nothing but corn on the cob and fried chicken. So he's sitting in his rocker. Got on this old World War One army overcoat use to belong to Mr. Lord. You remember them coats—heavy and khaki-colored and big-skirted?

Cornelia nodded. I've seen pictures of my father wearing one, she said.

Well, he's wore his so long it seem to me sometimes it has done become his skin—soft and wrinkly, same color he is. He lays it against the chair back or pulls it around him to keep off the wind and if it's after dinner he takes out his teeth and puts them in a saucer on the porch railing and he'll set there like in his nest or like a cat under a window, just taking the sun.

Now he stretches hisself up, throws off his coat. Seems like right in front of me he commence to get bigger. Like, sitting there in that chair, he look up at the sky with them eyes can't see nothing much in this world, and then he retch up and pull down size and strength from somewhere up there. Turn *darker*, seem like. Head set up straighter and taller on his neck. Hand me my teeth, Tweet, he says, and I give them to him and he puts them in.

Tweet, he says, low-voicey, you and me might be getting some trouble here. You keep your mouth close with these peoples, lessn you spoken to. Understand? Be polite, but don't answer no questions. Do like I tell you and keep your mouth close.

So this black cowboy hollers out again, Papa, it's me.

Who is he, Grandpa? I say.

That's your daddy, girl, my grandpa says. Ain't but one in the world calls me Papa, and that's him. Commence to chant low: Lord have mercy, he's singing, Lord have mercy on a bad-luck soul. Yeah. Looka yonder at what I see, Alabama Rosie, she's comin after me. Then he laughs. But it's a cold laugh, Tweet says.

At this point in Tweet's tale, it may be that Cornelia, in a lapse from her usual punctiliousness, let her eyes wander absently. It's inventory time and she needs to go downtown early. Or it may be that there was housework to be done and the morning half over. In any case, Tweet had long since finished loading the dishwasher and wiping the kitchen counters and Cornelia was arranging the last strands of fet-tuccine on the drying rack. Tweet broke off. Thought he'd outfox us, she said. My daddy, I'm talking about. She looked at the clock. Work to be done, she said, and left the kitchen.

After a while over the drone of the vacuum cleaner, she raised her voice. Meanest man I ever seen, she sang. Ask him for water, and he give me gasoline. . . .

If he hadn't said that right then, hadn't warn me, things might have gone different. Even with the warning, I was dazzle. I want a dress like hers, and shiny shoes. And her skin, her hair! Eyes like diamonds. Teeth that shine like snow. She was a light-skin woman, browny-red hair, all soft and wavy. Lord, I couldn't stop looking at her. My grandpa would let me go down the road to Glen Burnie once in a while and get my hair straighten, but I never did have good hair.

Come to find out, of course, it was a wig.

They come up on the porch and she walks right over to where I'm standing backed against a post, halfway scared by what my grandpa had said, and she says, You must be Julius' girl.

Yeah, that's right. My mama had name me after him. Nemmine she didn't see him again after she got me. Reckon she was still hoping when she name me.

Ain't you the prettiest little thing, she says, standing right up next to me, and it seem like my hand was going to raise itself up and touch her hair, but I remembered what my grandpa said, and I didn't move, just said, Thank you, ma'am.

Papa! Papa! He's got grandpa by the hand, acting like he's going to kiss him or maybe pick him up out of the chair and carry him off.

Good evening, Julius, Grandpa says. That's all. But his voice is like two rocks scraping against each other, and maybe my daddy heard the roughness in it.

You axing yourself what I'm doing here, where I been all this time, he says, and I'm going to tell you straight off.

I ain't axing myself nothing, Grandpa says. I ain't ax myself nothing about you since nineteen and twenty-one.

He lets go of Grandpa's hand and walks over and looks at me, puts his hand on my head and kind of tips it up so he can look in my face. Gold tooth shining. He's got slanty eyes and a scar on his left cheekbone like he might have been in a knife fight. And he's *old*. Hair gray. I didn't have no idea my own daddy would look so old—my mama being so young. But if you stop to think about it, he would have to be old, probably up in his fifties, if he was the son of my grandpa. I feel his fingers on my scalp, through my hair— cold. His hand is cold like he's been handling ice.

You my own dear daughter, he says. My onliest child. Looks back at Grandpa. Spit image of Rosa. (I'm about the age of my mama when she had me.) Where's Rosa? he says. You can tell by the way he moves around and all, he still don't realize my grandpa can't see him. He's kind of acting for my grandpa's benefit. He puts his cold arm around me, pulls me up against him, and I'm looking down at them high-heeled boots with vines stamped all over them, pointy toes and funny-looking kind of curved-under heels. I just keep looking down at the boots, feeling his arm around me and wanting to pull away, but not wanting to be impolite.

Come here to me, Tweet, my grandpa says, like he could see how I'm feeling.

Calls her Tweet, huh? my daddy says. Where's Rosa? he says again.

I squirmed out from under his arm and went over by my grandpa and he pat my hand, like to settle me down. Then he says, Rosa told me she done had a letter from you in nineteen and twenty-six. She still where she was then, over in Buchanan County. Married now.

Ain't that fine, my daddy says.

I reckon.

A lot of things happened since nineteen twenty-six, the lady says.

I want to tell you where all I been, what all I done the past few years, my daddy says. I had bad luck and good luck. I made me a little money. I even got me some teeth. He points to the gold in his mouth. So now I come home because I wants to help you out.

Hand me my cane, Tweet, my grandpa says. He had knock it over when he was reaching up, making hisself tall just before my daddy come. He stands up. I reckon y'all better come in the house, he says, and I put the cane in his hand and he starts in. My daddy stands there looking at him with them slanty eyes—the way he moves the cane along, not to help him walk, but to feel the floor, like for rough places, and he says, You don't see so good, Papa?

23

I sees well enough, my grandpa said, and he reached out and took hold of the doorknob without groping and walked in and walk straight over to the fireplace and sat down in his armchair. He call to me. Bring my coat in, Tweet, he said.

I went and got it and started in. My daddy grab me by the shoulder. He's blind, ain't he? he says. Ain't that pitiful?

He sees pretty good, I said.

They had brought presents, Tweet said. Yeah, they was slick. Brought me a pair shoes with high heels, dime-store beads and bracelets and like that. My grandpa couldn't see them, but he took them in his hands and felt them and didn't say nothing. Brought him presents, too. Walking stick with a brass tip. Pair gloves with wool linings. He says, thank you, and tells me to put the gloves in the chifforobe.

They sit home with us that first night. He (my daddy) explains to Grandpa whereall he's been at, why he ain't been home or even wrote us a postcard.

I couldn't read it if you had wrote it, my grandpa says.

Well, but Tweet here, she could've read it to you, he says. You goes to school, don't you, Tweet?

Some of what he told us was probably true, Tweet said. It was the Depression, remember. Hard times. He was out of work a long time, he says, even been locked up in jail, but it wasn't no hanging crime. He was ashamed to let on how bad off he was. But now things are different, he's married, got a good job. I wonder about that, because he looks so old to me, but I'm just a child, maybe he's not old as he looks. He puts his arm around the lady and says, This is my wife, Papa. My wife's name Claree, come from Alabama. She works in a beauty shop up there in Akron, Ohio, where we met. Her whole family lives up there now—Mama and three sisters—good people. Her and her sisters brought her mama up from Alabama to see after her.

Yeah, ain't nothing like family, Claree says. Family got to stick by one another.

They . . . Tweet broke off. Something I keep on wondering about, she said. What did they say to themselves? I say: What did they tell themselves? About coming, I mean. When I'm mad, thinking about what all happened, I see them sitting down together, talking. And she says—I hear that sweet low voice—We needs to go take care of that old man. (How old you say he is? He ain't long for this world.) You needs to make your peace with him and you needs to look after your child. Ain't that right? I say to myself that they fixed it between them from the beginning to come and steal the money and the land howsomever they could do it— nemmine the rest of what happen. But then I say, no, that's not the way it went, not what they told themselves they was doing. People don't say: We're bad, going to do evil. They come down south to see his papa just like they told us. Maybe he needs somebody to see after him. Maybe they ought to take him up to Akron, Ohio, with them and see after him up there. And me, too. Or maybe send me to Rosa, if they worked it out that far. Nothing wrong in that, is there? And then, what was my grandpa's would naturally be theirs. They wouldn't have to talk about it. That's just the way things supposed to be. I'm a child, can't take charge of land and money. And looka here—they didn't know it, but he's blind! But then, he's so stubborn. Don't know what's good for him. The stealing and all happened accidentally, so to speak, and from what started out as good intentions.

Cornelia was arranging flowers on the kitchen table. She snipped off the stem of a blue hydrangea blossom, struck a match, and singed it. Stealing is stealing, Julia, she said firmly. You can't steal by accident.

Well, Tweet said. I s'pose.

Right is right and wrong is wrong, Cornelia said. She placed the hydrangea, nodding and glowing, in a celadon bowl already overflowing with color—sea green bowl, green leaves, white and rose and blue hydrangeas, rose and lavender crape myrtle. That's just exactly right, she said.

So that goes on a few days, Tweet said. Not long. They not patient people. It's boring out there in the country. And it could be he really had a job he was going back to—had just so long to accomplish all he could. But mainly, I think it was boring. My grandpa naturally didn't have no car. Nearest place for socializing was the commissary on Mr. Lord's place and that was three miles down the road. Glen Burnie is seven miles off and ain't much there. We did have a radio—we'd got the rural electric by then—and he told me, Tweet, you need to listen to the radio, find out what's happening in the world. Don't make no difference to me— I be gone before long. But you need to find out all that can be useful to you. Mainly, though, I listen to the music. He was the one would listen to the president on his fireside chats and the news and all.

Did I say it was November? Yeah. Not long after Halloween. You know, our people not much on Halloween, Tweet said. Or at least they didn't use to be when I was a child. Children going around pretending like they scaring grown people and grown people acting like they scared. Didn't nobody have time for that foolishness. Too much real evil, too many real spirits to be afraid of. Tweet leaned across the kitchen table, her dark scarred face close to Cornelia's smooth white one, the bowl of flowers between them. The dead live, she said, gazing with those strange blue eyes, concentric circles of blue, bluish whites, into Cornelia's eyes. The dead stay in the place where they die and their power is in that place. She continued to gaze at Cornelia, who snipped off a rosebud and loosened and rearranged the flowers in her perfect arrangement. Power for good, Tweet said. Power for evil. My grandpa's soul is in the furrow by the turnrow where he died. When I'm feeling strong enough to bear it, I can go down on the edge of the cypress brake by the turnrow where he lay down, and he is with me. I'm afraid, but nevertheless I go. I lay a flower in the furrow. Sometime—maybe next year or the year after —his soul might move on, but now it's still there. More than once he has spoke to me.

But Julia! Cornelia stepped back, folded her arms across her breasts and shook her head, *No.*

Tweet laid her finger on her lips and looked away as if she were listening for her grandfather's voice.

He speaks to me, she said again. I make myself strong to listen. I know I need to listen, to give way to him. I have to be strong to give way.

Embarrassed by this foolishness, Cornelia picked up the bowl of flowers, turned away, and carried it to the living room where she set it on the coffee table. Tweet followed her. He's been known to sing, she said. Not so long ago I hear him singing this: Roberta, don't you hear me calling you? You don't answer like you used to do. Sang it all the way through. Ain't that a strange song for him to have sung? Reckon he's still thinking about days when he was young —days I don't know?

Cornelia moved the bowl slightly, wiped an invisible ring from the table.

Sometimes he talks about being dead, Tweet said. Tells me I still got to learn to die. But I tell him I can't help it, I ain't got time for that right now. I tell him it's OK for him to talk about learning to die. If I live to be as old as him, I got another forty years to enjoy myself before I start in practicing.

But anyhow, nemmine about that, what I'm saying is, we—our people—don't have time for these play-like ghosts. These dress-up children that go around begging for candy. Begging! Ghosts don't beg. Might make you beg. But maybe he and she been gone from the country so long, they done forgot all about the power of spirits. Think they can use it and not be harm by it.

More than one time, Tweet said, I seen lights in the cypress brake down from our house. My grandpa told it there was gold bury back there in the brake—gold from Civil War times. He says they was a white man made his fortune selling our people and when war come along, he bury his gold back there. Devil waiting on him when he come, shape of an alligator. (I ain't so sure I believe the devil goes into an alligator—my grandpa had some notions. My own belief is the devil didn't have to go *into* no alligator. He could just point him in the right direction.) Anyhow, whether or not he was in the alligator, he ate that man—I mean the alligator did—at least people told it that they kilt one (I reckon if the devil was in him, he had done left by then) and he had a man's leg inside of him, rubber boot, trouser leg and all, and my grandpa says he seen it. And other people seen him (the white man that sells slaves) going back in the swamp and he never come out. Time I was born, people for sixty years been going in there looking for gold. But nobody never found it. More than one time at night I seen lights in the cypress brake, right where my grandpa point out to me he had went in and buried the gold. Devil's guarding that gold, that's what my grandpa would say to me when I saw the lights in the cypress brake. Devil's still in there, Tweet. You keep out of there.

Yeah, and more than one time I been walking down the turnrow when night is just coming on, light's uncertain, seen a man pass by and he raise his hat to me. I look around after he pass and ain't nobody there. It's a white man, too. Ain't no living white man in this world would've raise his hat to me. It was the devil.

Julia, Cornelia said, those lights in the cypress brake— that's fox fire. It's . . . it's chemical. The old tree stumps rot and something in them—phosphorus—makes . . .

Tweet shook her head stubbornly. . . . nothing about no fox fire, she said. And you ain't explain about that man I saw on the road disappeared. Evil. The world is full of evil.

Cornelia was rolling and folding dough for puff pastry during this conversation. She wrapped the dough in waxed paper and returned it to the icebox with a shrug. I just don't believe in ghosts, she said. And evil? People do evil things because they want to—they *mean* to. Or maybe nobody taught them better. Evil is in people, not the devil.

It's all the same thing, Tweet said. Inside or outside, it's all the same thing.

I think Halloween might've reminded Julius and Claree about ghosts and all, Tweet said, because it was after Halloween that they come. Or maybe the first time it happen (what I'm fixing to tell you about) was real and they seen how they could put it to use. Anyhow they commence trying to scare me and my grandpa. Like I said, a week or more had gone by. They'd been talking a little bit and a little bit more about us going up north with them or either them staying and helping us. They safe enough talking about us going north. They know they're not going to budge my grandpa off that place where he's been since eighteen and seventy-six. Not unless he is out of his head. But seems like to me maybe they use the going north talk like a crowbar, to pry my grandpa loose—threaten him with it, so he'll agree for them to stay with us. Is that what they started out wanting? And how long? If they bored, how long was they intending to stay? And what was they intending to do? Anyways, every time they say this or that about staying and helping us, he answers more or less the same way.

Y'all need to go talk to Mr. Lord, he'll say. You want to make a crop down here? Likely he's got some land he'll go on shares with you.

And they hadn't got the nerve yet to say they want to stay in the house with us, take charge of his money and his land. But they would've got bored with that, too. . . . Howsomever, they continue to go on about how concern they are over my grandpa's health and his eyes giving out, saying he needs somebody—needs *them*—to be close by, looking after him.

And every time, he says, I got Tweet. Setting up in his armchair close to the fire (weather's getting colder), setting up tall as he can, he says, I got Tweet.

Tweet ain't nothing but a child, needs looking after herself, my daddy says. He puts his cold hand on my arm, looks at me, smiles like he loves me.

How come your hand always so cold? I ax him one time. You makes me shiver.

Circulation to my extremities is poor, he says. Doctor says my pressure is low. Ain't got enough blood. I needs to eat plenty of red meat.

Tweet ain't no man, Claree says. Can't see after your business.

She do well enough, my grandpa says. I see after my own business.

Yeah, but your eyes ain't so good as they used to be. (That's my daddy talking.) You getting along in years. . . . And they go on with one thing and another about how he needs help, and every now and then he says, I got Tweet.

S'pose she takes up with a man and goes off, my daddy says one night. What about that? She's getting to be a woman. Or can't you see that? He looks at me like a man looks at a woman, touches my hand, and Claree grins at him, says, Watch yourself, darling.

They're doing other things, too—like he has done fix the fence where it broke down, making hisself useful. She goes up to town on the bus, gets some goods from Penney's, makes us some new window curtains. But my grandpa ain't move from his position. They hadn't found out if he's got a will or a bank account or, if he don't, where he keeps his money. On up towards December and they still hadn't found out.

Did you know? Cornelia asked.

No, Tweet said. He hadn't ever told me or nobody else. And I wasn't no kid. I was thinking about it—not before they come, but as soon as I begun to smell where the wind was blowing from. Wind blowing from back by the privy,

30

from the ravine where we drug the mule died that fall, from over yonder cross the creek where you see the buzzards wheeling.

I listen to them talk about Grandpa's business and about him being blind and old and helpless and all, and I was afraid—never had been afraid before like that—afraid of living people. But I couldn't get him by hisself to find out —to ax him if he want to tell me anything, ax him what I ought to do. Seem like they taken turns keeping an eye on him. He couldn't go out on the porch to the washbasin unless one or the other of them was looking out the back window at him, waiting for him to come in.

Not many places in a three-room shotgun you can hide money. You can put it in a chest—that ain't hiding. You can plaster it up under the wallpaper. That would be the first place anybody would look. You can raise up a board or a brick in the hearth and hide it under the floor. . . . I see them everyday, looking—at the floor, the ceiling, the walls. Like I can almost hear them axing each other: Where is it at, where is it at? And they look at me. Do I know? Where is it at?

Well, and something else, too. Did he have a will? People like us, you know—people like him, can't read or write— not many would trust a lawyer to make them a will. Might leave it to themselves—lawyers, I mean. But on the other hand, my grandpa ain't your ordinary person. He's a disable veteran of the Civil War—I mean, on the side of Lincoln. He's got a federal pension. And it looks clear to them by now, I think, that he wants me to have his place. I'm the one he cares about—the one cares about him.

And if he had a will and if he left the place to me and if they could find the will and tear it up, then everything would be my daddy's. But I didn't know none of that. All I knew was I could see them looking around: Where is it at? And I could see my grandpa getting tireder, setting up straight in that armchair, answering them with, *I got Tweet*.

There must have been somebody he could trust, Cornelia

said. A neighbor, a relative. What about old Mr. Lord? He was an honest man. Didn't you tell me your grandfather's land was right next to his?

Yeah, Tweet said. Fit right into his, like a slice out of a pie. Would straighten out his line if he could get it.

Well, next day or two it all bust open, Tweet said. Evil out there in the dark, in the cold, knocking on the walls, scratching on the roof like frozen tree limbs. I'm feeling worse and worse, yeah, scareder and scareder.

I'm coming home from the store just about dark one night and I see the lights moving in the swamp. Run all the way home and find my grandpa all wrap up in his army coat, sitting in front of the fire, sleeves crossed over his breast, tails crossed over his legs. I'm trying to catch my breath, breathe easier. I didn't want to scare him. I said to myself, scared as I was, I wouldn't tell him about the lights. He's got enough on his mind.

Fox fire, Cornelia said firmly.

How come, if it's fox fire, it's moving? I ain't never seen a rotten stump get up and walk.

He starts in talking right off, Tweet said. Tweet, he says, quick now, I needs to tell you . . .

I look around, don't see either one of them. Where they gone? I say.

Nemmine that, he says. They gone. Now listen. It's on my mind I want you to have this place, Tweet. Tweet, he says, I have done wrong by you. Ain't never made no will leaving it to you. Want to know the truth, I thought he was dead. Been nearly ten years since Rosa got that letter from him, and nobody all that time heard nothing from him.

Now, listen, he says, us got to get to town and make me a will. Because that's what he's here for—to get all I got

—and I'm going to keep him from it. He draws a breath, pulls his coat close around him like for comfort. Also the money, he says. We got to see about the money.

What money, Grandpa? I say.

Don't speak, he says. Listen. We ain't got much time. Sat'dy morning we going to catch the bus, go to town, see Lawyer Quinn at the bank and get it fix up.

How we going to get away from them, Grandpa?

Ain't going to have to git away. It's in my mind what I'm going to tell them. Now, listen, as to where the money is. . . .

Maybe he thought he wouldn't last until Sat'dy. He wanted me to know right then. And I want to find out. But that was when the door commence to rattle and seem like the wind blew down the chimney, puff the smoke all out in the room and I seen a flapping outside the window and heard a noise—what did it sound like? You never lived in the country, did you? Sound like a woman crying, like a dog whining, like a panther screaming, all the same time. Then sound, screech, like a rabbit when a fox bite its neck, break its back.

I forget all about not wanting to scare him, forget about the money, everything. Grandpa! Grandpa! I'm hollering. Grandpa, I saw fire burning, lights moving in the brake. Grandpa, the devil, he's out there.

Door shaking and rattling. My little grandpa turn as gray as ashes on the hearth, but he pull me to him, three-fingered hand digging into my arm sharp as a bird's claw. Wrap the skirts of his coat around me and draw me in close. I put my two arms around him, kneel down before him, lay my head on his breast.

Yeah, Tweet, ain't going to die right yet, he says, sing-song-like. Hmmm, Tweet, ain't going to die right yet. And when I do, Lord, the devil—raises his voice, Devil, he ain't going to take me. No.

I can feel his heart thumping like it's jumping up to get out of his mouth. Door keeps rattling, shaking. Hold on here, Tweet, he says. Yeah, hold on. I'm not sure if he means hold him back from death or if he means he'll protect me if I hold onto him, but I keep my arms tight around him.

Well, the wind dies down, fire begins to draw, he sets back, we let go of each other. Hush, now, he says. Listen. The money . . . he says, whispering, and then the door flies open and they come blowing in, eyes popping, panting. She's kind of halfway like she's crying or praying—clasping her hands together, looking up, green hat all blowed sideways, wig turnt crooked.

Oh, Lord, she says, oh, Lord God, something turrible going on out there. Y'all hear that turrible noise? You ever heard such a noise before? Me and Julius had done gone . . .

Coming back down the road from Martha's house, my daddy says. See this light moving out there in the swamp. I say to myself . . .

First thing come into my mind, she says, somebody must be out there. I say to Julius: Somebody out there, Julius. Reckon they after your papa's money? Reckon he got it buried out there?

My grandpa sets back, motions me to stand up.

And then we hear that screaming, my daddy says. I say to Claree: I don't know about no money. Sound like something after my papa and Tweet. Us better . . .

We come running, she says. Cut across the pasture, tore my stockings. She waves her hand at her legs—shoes all dusty—but I didn't see no tears in her stockings.

Turrible screaming, my daddy says. Ain't no human man out there, I say to Claree. If hit's money buried out there, the devil after it.

My grandpa pulls himself up straight in his chair, grips the arm, leans his back against the straight back of the chair. He has done got strong and dark in the face again and he gives them a dark look. Ain't no money of mine out there, he says, and it looks to me like he's talking to the chimney as much as he's talking to them. Maybe he's telling the devil he ain't buried no money. Take every penny I got for me and Tweet to live. How I'm going to bury money? He looks at me and he looks at them. You might have heard about that white man bury his gold out there during the Civil War, he says. You ever heard about him, Julius?

Yassuh, my daddy says.

Ain't nobody ever found that money, my grandpa says. They used to tell it that's what the devil seeing after out there.

Next night, Tweet said, it was the same thing. But this time they at home with us. Me and my grandpa sitting by the fire, she's in the kitchen washing out her stockings (she has three pairs of silk stockings besides the ones she says got tore up) and he (my daddy) has just gone back to shake down the fire in the kitchen stove for the night. It's one of them big old iron stoves, Tweet said. Burns wood. At night you shake down the fire and bank it, so there's a bed of coals in the morning, easy to start it up again.

They're moving around—I hear the firebox door creak, like he's opening it—when it happens again: screeching and flapping at the side window, smoke comes puffing out into the room, and like a thump. Might be somebody jumping on the roof. Front door rattles. Back door bangs. Seems like for a second I seen a face outside the window—white, holes for eyes, black hole for a mouth, and like a white hand scratching at the glass. I begun to yell.

Hush, Tweet, my grandpa says. Hush. He set like a bird, head cocked, listening.

Then (but not right away—maybe half a minute passes) they come running up into the front of the house, first her and then, in another minute, him. She's hollering, What's the matter? What's the matter? And then after her my daddy comes—lays his cold hand on my arm. You OK, Tweet?

he says. You OK, Papa? Something turrible going on out there. But we here. We take care of you.

My grandpa squinch himself down in the chair, turn his face away from the face of my daddy, reaches out towards me. Tweet, he says. I need to go lay down. Git me the chamber. I ain't going to the privy tonight.

My daddy looks at Claree. Papa poor old heart ain't going to stand much more commotion like this, he says.

Come along, Tweet, my grandpa says.

Old as he is, he is still a modest man before me, Tweet said. I give him the chamber and then wait in the front room until he calls me. Then I go in to help him with his nightclothes. He never would show hisself to me naked. I help him off with his shirt—unbutton the buttons—and I pull the nightshirt over his head and turn down the bed and help him in—it's a high old bed with a step made out of a box for him to climb up on—and he lays down and I turn my back to him while he pulls off his pants, and then I put the quilt over him.

So in a few minutes he's laying there under the quilt that he told me long ago his mama made, all stripes and squares like the rungs of a ladder, blue and orange and green and lavender and black. He's got the quilt pull under his chin, his hands laying on the outside, his gold wedding ring on his finger.

Untuck that bottom corner, Tweet, he says, like he always does, if the corner tucked in. So I untuck it. That's so all evil can pour out the bottomest strip that runs to the edge of the quilt, and won't none be left in his bed.

Expressionless, absentminded, Cornelia listened and did not listen.

He's laying up in bed, little as a monkey, and he looks at me and closes one eye and winks. He hadn't ever winked at me before in his life. Then he spoke out real strong, so my daddy could hear in the front room, and called to him and Claree to come in, and they did.

36

Julius, my grandpa says. He fold his hands on top of the covers, looks at one of them and then the other. My time is coming and I know it, he says. I have done live a long time in this world. (He's acting very solemn, but he had winked at me.) I got in my mind I want to do right by you, you being my onliest son in the world, and by Tweet here and by any chirren you and Claree might have.

He takes a deep breath. The truth is, Julius, he says, I have done thought a long time that you was dead. So two years back—in nineteen and thirty-three—I made me a will leaving this place to Tweet, and, naturally, like I told Mr. Quinn at the bank, since Rosa is Tweet's mama, she would be her natural guardian and would look after her, if I was to die. But now, he says, here you come with Claree and I see I got to change things. Ain't right for Tweet to have this place if you alive, I say to myself. You are my son. So it's in my mind I will go to town on the bus Sat'dy and go to the bank, where Lawyer Quinn is keeping my will, and tell him to tear it up.

He close his eyes like he's real tired. Then he open them and say, I'll make me a new will and leave this place to you, but listen here to me, Julius, I expect you to do right by Tweet. He looks stern. I know you, Julius, he says. I know you likely to sell this place. You ain't no farmer, never was, and never will be. You got to live by your own lights. But you suppose to do right by Tweet. All right? You see she is look after.

Papa, I swear I and Claree are going to do right by Tweet, my daddy says. And she can come stay with us if she wants to, or she can stay with her mama. You haven't got anything to be concern about. Would I have come back here, trying to help out you and Tweet, if I didn't mean to do right by her?

That was Tuesday night, Tweet said. So us all go to bed and commence waiting for Sat'dy. Didn't hear no more panthers crying, and the wind die completely down.

So far, telling you about Cornelia, letting Tweet speak for herself, the narrator of this story has maintained his—or rather, her—anonymity, even though she's occasionally made herself free to comment on Cornelia's silences and to speculate about her character. But now, as Tweet talks on, I begin to wonder what you take for granted about this taleteller. I am honor bound, I think, to call your attention to her. I want you to believe her, but there are pitfalls in the path of her narrative that I must make you aware of. You may have assumed that she is a white woman. But perhaps you've not yet thought how difficult it is for her to be true to her tale.

She begins, as every storyteller does, with the illusion of freedom. Whose story will she choose to tell? It's her prerogative to decide. But then she finds herself drawn, only dimly knowing why, to these particular sufferings and triumphs, to this human world. It's as if she has some buried connection with these lives, a connection she must explore and understand. But then, she may misunderstand. And besides, she has the power to distort, if she chooses to exercise it. She must resist the temptation to satisfy her sense of how Tweet and Cornelia *ought* to behave; must resist the need to keep herself comfortable.

Perhaps she can find someone more detached, more objective than she to tell us now about Cornelia. I call up faces and voices she might hide behind. A man, perhaps. An author who is a black lawyer with an extra Ph.D. in psychology. Or a soft-voiced, steely-eyed black grandmother. Or an elderly single aunt of Cornelia's who is wise and dispassionate.

But I would still be here, wouldn't I?

I encourage myself that, although it is difficult, it's perhaps not impossible for the tale-teller to rise above her limitations, escape the straitjacket of her own life. Just as Tweet tries, truly tries to give the gift of truth about her life to Cornelia.

As for Cornelia, who says so little about herself, she's not faced with this difficulty. For her, it's as if everything is already sorted out, as if she dances over a polished floor, skis on a summer day over the steely bright surface of a calm lake under a blue sky piled high with cumulus. She won't lose her footing, she's sure of it. She won't find herself sinking into the dark water among slimy cypress knees and alligators and alligator gars.

The tale-teller, though, can't be a dancer, a skier—she has to drive the boat, to pull the skier behind her. She has to make you see Cornelia and begin to understand her.

Curious, I had no problem with your seeing Tweet— her round face, pitted and scarred by the risings she spoke of; her wide, powerful nose; her hair, thin and skimpy (Never did have good hair.); her legs, dark brown, slender, muscular and shapely, built to escape Wayne Jones and the devil; and her eyes—mysterious concentric circles of blue.

So, now—Cornelia: Do you notice that she stands slightly swayback, as if she's lifted her shoulders like a queen ready to receive the heavy, ermine-trimmed mantle she must wear to the coronation? Do you see the tensing of her neck muscles, as she resists the impulse to turn her head slightly, refuses to favor her good ear? Do you see her as she accepts Tweet's gifts of flowers, ripe pomegranates, baskets of persimmons glowing orange in the October sunshine, her tales of tribulation and triumph? She smiles. She has a wide-lipped, generous mouth that resists what seems to me its nature—the impulse to irony and tolerance and sorrow— a mouth that refuses to turn down, that *always* wears a kindly smile, a gracious smile, the blind smile of a deaf woman.

Tweet I see not only in her middle age but as a smooth-skinned adolescent, her round face with still a trace of childishness in the uncertain chin, the plump arms (her grandpa's darling), but in her eyes, already, shrewdness and resolution. And I see her as a passionate lover, an outraged woman, although I'm not yet sure where the tales of her life will lead us.

Shall we try to see Cornelia, too, in her youth? What was she like as a young girl, before she became mistress of her household, purveyor of génoises, fig preserves, and home-made pasta? Should I choose sixteen as the illustrative age? No. Begin when she is nine.

It is a rainy Easter morning. She is too old for the fool-ishness of eggs and rabbits, not yet old enough to care about her appearance. She is dressed for Sunday school, standing in the middle of her bedroom. She wears white socks, Roman sandals, and the short-sleeved dress of pale green pongee with an intricately smocked yoke (not a new dress—only common people wear new dresses on Easter Sunday) that the maid has laid out for her.

Her mother comes into the room with a heavy tread: Al-ready overweight, she will get fatter as she gets older. She has a peach-tree switch in her hand. Cornelia has done something—something dreadful—or surely on Easter morn-ing her mother would not be holding a switch. (Perhaps she lost her temper and struck her younger brother, or even spoke impudently to her mother.)

Then—I can scarcely bear to write it—Cornelia's mother is switching her legs—*hard*. She feels the sting of the blows, looks down, sees red welts rising on her legs, a drop of blood furrowing down (she has thin skin to go with that lovely chestnut hair), looks up, sees the fury on her mother's face. She stands without moving, her hands hanging loosely at her sides, a kindly smile on her face. She is too old for this punishment, is embarrassed at her mother's failure of judgment. Her face—it's as if during the switching her face acquires its poised, grown-up expression. She is in control and she intends to stay in control. This absurd occasion is something first to ignore and then to blot out.

And her father? He is not at home—perhaps not even in the city when this—I suppose one might call it a nonconfrontation—occurs between Cornelia and her mother. Father is often away, although it's true he always brings presents for everyone when he returns.

I want to remember when I am thinking of Cornelia that every act in a human life has layer upon enfolded layer, not only of imagining, but of circumstance beneath it. One can account for any act by circumstances opposite to those one has just adduced. The mille-feuille—the risen and browned pastry from Cornelia's oven—is the product of mixing water and salt and flour and rolling it out and covering it with bits of ice-cold butter, folding, pressing, and rolling it, chilling and then rolling and folding it again and again, and then subjecting it to 450 degrees of heat. Extreme heat and extreme cold. Stress and rest. Does the heat produce the pastry, or the cold? The relaxation or the tension of the gluten? The fat or the water? The salt or the flour?

Cornelia would say that these are absurd questions because there are no *this* or *that* answers in the world of puff pastry. And she would find no connection with her own behavior. Human beings, she might say, are not made in ovens and iceboxes.

After that night, Tweet said, whilst they waiting for Sat'dy, I'm waiting for my grandpa to get a chance to talk to me, tell me his true purpose. They ain't so watchful now. Figure everything is coming to them without no more trouble. But I'm watchful. I can't sleep hardly. Looks like my grandpa getting littler and littler. He gets up later, goes to bed earlier, spends his days in his chair, humming a tune, dozing off with his old coat over his knees to keep his legs warm. I feel like he is becoming somebody else, trying not to bother me with it.

As for them, they have took over the housework and feeding the chickens and all, but still they go everyday down to Mr. Lord's store to pass the time with the people there, leave him at home by hisself.

I'm going to school everyday like I'm supposed to. On Wednesday they be home from the store time I get back from school—it's a two-mile walk—but on Thursday they're not there. When I come in, my grandpa is waiting for me, setting in his chair in front of the fire, his cane by his side, his army coat across his knees.

Tweet, he says, they went to town this morning, must've missed the bus coming back. Don't take off your coat, he says. We going to the cypress brake. He gets up, puts his coat on, takes his cane in his hand.

It's cold now, sure enough. Almost to December and we had a hard frost the night before. Leaves are mostly down —but not the cypress needles, because they stay late. Evening drawing in. It's coming to the shortest days of the year. Time I walk home from school, it's most four-thirty and the sun is behind the cypress trees, lighting them up all bronzy, like they get that time of year, light like in a big church coming down slanty through the leaves and across the tall slanty trunks.

I'm afraid. We walk over the needles and our feet don't make a sound. We like ghosts. I can see where we headed, down into the cypress brake where, last spring, it was all covered with water—but now it's hard ground, because it's been so dry all fall. Down towards where sometimes I see the lights moving. I'm afraid. Tweet paused. Partly, maybe, it's the trees with their knobby knees sticking up through the needles like pieces of giants' legs. Partly, so quiet. Like the trees holding their breath, waiting for dark. And I know, in the spring, when the water's up, me and my grandpa could come in here in a boat if we want to and there would be catfish and widemouth and crappie and bluegills swimming in amongst the knees—and buffalo and alligator gars big enough to swallow a whole litter of puppies if you was to throw them out there to drown, and alligators, too, and cottonmouths hanging off the branches, dropping into the water, skimming along, coming towards you and then veering off. Where they all gone?

Are you watching which way we going, Tweet? my grandpa says.

And I say, yassuh, but I hadn't been, so I look back and I see the slope of the land, and above the brake the roof of our house that sits back on a ridge a little way behind the cornfield.

I'm afraid, grandpa, I tell him. I don't want to come back in here.

Ain't far, he says. He stops a minute, breathing hard like he's been running. Don't take much to tire him out. I'm going to show you where the money is, he says then and he draws a breath and starts walking again, feeling with his cane. Now hush, he says. I'm counting my steps.

Don't want no money. I didn't. I had change my mind.

Hush, he says. Ten steps more. Walks a little way and stops. Puts out his hand to the left and lays it on the trunk of a cypress tree. Turns to his right and counts his steps a little way more and comes right up against a big old hollow cypress tree—still living, but with the inside all hollow and a hole so big at the bottom, you can walk in without bending your head.

I practiced until I'm sure I can find it, he says. Come inside.

No, I say. I don't want to go in there.

But he takes my arm and pulls me in. We got to hurry, he says, and he points up and shows me how you can see light out a hole maybe fifteen feet up, higher than the water ever comes. This the tree, Tweet, he says. Nothing to be scared of. Devil don't come out only at night, unlessn you

43

messing with something you ain't suppose to be messing with, and this is mine. He smiles at me. Devil's busy with that white man's gold. He ain't studying us.

I know he's making that up to make me feel better. The devil thinks all the gold in the world suppose to belong to him.

But my grandpa goes on talking. Start from the big cypress tree that stands at the edge of the brake directly in front of us house, he says. His voice echoes and seems like they's also a buzz inside that tree. I can't hardly bear to stand there and listen, but he's still holding hard onto my arm. Walk ninety-two steps, he says. Not far, you see, Tweet. Not far. You don't need to be scared. And you don't even need to count steps, because you can see this hollow tree off to your right, soon as you get in a little ways. And this is where the money is at.

I think he must be getting so old he's crazy, because I know you can't keep money or nothing else in a hollow tree that it's under six feet of water during half the year.

Let's us go home, Grandpa, I say. I'm cold, and it's getting towards dark, and besides, they might be coming back if they caught a ride from town.

Look up, he says. What do you see?

I see that hole you showed me.

Look on the other side, right opposite to the hole.

Now my eyes used to the twilighty light in there, I see there's a great long piece of honeycomb hanging down from the side of the tree and below it I see pieces of board nailed, leading up to it.

Hit's a bee tree, Grandpa, I say. And now I know that's what the buzzing is I been hearing. Bees all clinging together like they do in the wintertime, flipping their wings to keep the hive warm.

All right, he says. Now you seen it. We going back home. On the way I tell you. It was like even after he had showed me, even knowing he needs to tell me, he couldn't hardly bear to let his secret go, wanted to keep it just a little bit longer.

He'd been saving his money little piece by little piece a long time, he said. Started after he got the land paid out in nineteen and twelve. Used to be, when he was younger, he said, he always felt like, if he had to, he could protect it, and so he kept it at home. But then his sight begun to go and he begun to feel his age, and that was when—been about four years, he said—he decided to hide it, and he thought and thought and come up with the bee tree. Hit's in a piece of pipe stopped up with beeswax, he says, and it's strap right up against the tree next to the hive and they have done built hive all around it. Them steps you saw, that's how you can get up to it. I put them there like I had climb up and rob the hive. Time come, last year, I had save up enough to put another little piece of pipe up there and I did.

Now, he says, you know about it and when something happen to me, you can come down in here and get it.

Ain't nothing going to happen to you, Grandpa, I say. And if it do, I can't come in here by myself. Because I knew I wouldn't.

But he don't pay no attention to what I say, just goes right on talking. You got to be sure nobody sees you come, he says, and you got to bring the smoker, so you won't get stung. You know how to do it.

Ain't nothing going to happen to you, I say again, and then, Maybe you wrong about them, Grandpa. Maybe . . .

He doesn't say nothing.

Next thing, I'm lying on my pallet wide awake. You got to know ain't but two beds in the house—my grandpa's in the middle room and in the front room the bed where I sleep. They have took my bed and I been sleeping on a pallet on the floor in my grandpa's room. Sometimes he snores, wakes me up, but seems like even his snore has got quieter the past few days. That ain't what wakes me up. I wake up from a dream of us—me and my grandpa walking along the turn-row towards the highway. Cold. The wind blowing from the north and under my feet I feel the mud in the turnrow stiff with frost. Tweet, I got to catch the bus, he says. Let's us hurry up because here it comes. Tail of his coat flapping in the wind.

No more than that, but I wake up scared. You can dream a true dream, Tweet said, and it will stay with you all your life. She paused and Cornelia said absently, Hmmmm.

I'm lying there scared and sad, and then I hear a car on the road, car doors slamming, voices outside calling good-night, somebody—a woman—singing. They had done caught a ride back from town. Come in stumbling and talking loud. They're drunk, I reckon, too drunk to worry about waking us up.

I hear them moving around in the front room. They light the light. Door closed between us room and theirs, but I can see the light come up under the crack. And now he must be throwing wood on the fire and I hear the poker scraping on the hearth, and they're still talking and laughing. But my grandpa is sleeping, I know, because I can hear his little snore. I'm surprise he hasn't woke up.

And then I hear the singing again—and it's her. She's humming in a deep voice, beautiful voice. Not loud: sometimes it goes down almost to a whisper, sometimes sounds like a sad cry, or it goes up high, puts me in mind of that panther we heard; but it carries and I can hear every note. I lay there astonish. I hadn't ever heard her sing before.

And now I hear her stepping around, too, and it seems like she must be dancing and he must be beating like on a drum or something, because somebody is keeping time for her. And then she commence to sing again and he answers her. This is what she's singing. I know it well, because I have heard it more than once on the radio, Sat'dy afternoons, when they play the blues and like that.

46

> Darling, did you bring me any silver,
> Darling, did you bring me any gold?
> Baby, did you bring me anything
> Keep me from the gallows pole?

He answers her, scratchy-voiced, talking more than singing:

> Baby, done brought you some silver,
> Darling, I brought you a little gold,
> Baby done brought you everything I got,
> Keep you from the gallows pole.

I keep hearing her feet, like she's dancing, and somebody —one of them—beating on something, and I creep out from under my covers and slip into the closet in the space next to the chimney, slip in amongst the clothes hanging there —mine and my grandpa's—careful to be quiet, not to knock against the shotgun and the rifle I know are back in the corner, leaning against the wall; and at the back of the closet, where I know there is a knothole—you can see into the front room—I wait until I see light and I put my eye to the hole and see her. She's in front of the chifforobe (got a mirror door), she's done taken off her clothes and she's dancing for him, fire crackling, light from the fire on her skin, light from the bulb hanging down in the middle of the room (still swinging a little bit) throwing her shadow around on the floor. I told you she was a light-skinned woman? The fire makes her look all shiny and bronzy and she has taken off her wig and her hair stands up short and spikey. Shakes her bosom, turns around, and with the mirror I can see both sides of her, front and back. She's dancing towards him and he's laughing.

Darling, I done brought you everthing I can rake and scrape. . . .

Clearly Cornelia does not wish to hear this explicit description. Nor, perhaps, does she wish to reveal her reluctance—her revulsion—to Tweet. To reveal, after all, is to

47

admit—to reveal oneself. Does she surreptitiously turn the tiny knob that lowers the volume in her hearing aid? I believe she does. In any event, Tweet, caught up in the memory of those strange moments in her life, continues.

. . . turns around again, holds her bosom up in her hands, comes towards him. Oh, it was a strange thing for me to watch, young as I was, living all my life in the house with nobody but my grandpa. I couldn't take my eyes off them. He's beating on the hollow brass bedpost with his shoe, sitting on the side of the bed, naked, too, gray hairs on his chest scraggly and thin. He reaches out to her and she dances away and I see that he is—manly-like. And she's still singing. This time, it's *Papa*.

> Papa, you bring me any silver.
> Papa, you bring me any gold?

And then he's beating on the bedpost with his shoe, saying in a scratchy, trembly, old-man voice: Yeah, I brought it. And she dances up to him and bends over him and sings: I thought it. Shakes herself in front of him, and dances away. Daughter, I brought it, he says.

Yeah, Papa, I thought it.

And she mocks my grandpa then, Tweet said. She picks up his cane from where it's leaning against the chifforobe and dances around the room, naked, bent over like him, throwing out one leg to the side, like he does when he walks. Gold, she says. Gold. And now they are both laughing, and he grabs ahold of her and pulls her up close to him.

I see them mock my grandpa and a red rage comes over me, standing there in the cold and dark, with the smell of my grandpa's clothes all around me. I lay my hand on the barrel of the gun leaning against the wall beside me and I know it's loaded like it always is. I could kill them. I want to kill them, make them disappear. But seems like then he—my grandpa—lays his hand on my shoulder, says, Nemmine, Tweet. Hang on here. You ain't suppose to do that. And when I look again they have done turnt out the light, and I hear the bedsprings commence to squeak like they most usually do every night since they been in there.

Tweet was silent for a while. Then she began again. There wasn't no harm in most of that, was there? she said. They're living like a natural man and wife—singing, dancing before the glass, taking their pleasure. It was only them mocking my grandpa that made me mad.

She is speaking in a low voice, meditatively. Cornelia does not say, What? Does not ask her to speak louder.

Still, Tweet said. I'm cold, cold. I creep out of the closet and crawl back under my covers, shivering, and I lay there a long time before I sleep.

As for the grandfather, what has he been thinking? What is he planning? I see him night after night lying in his high old bed under the laddered quilt his mother made, the bottom corner, with its passageway for evil, hanging to the floor. Like most old people, he sleeps lightly, wakes early. From the moment, weeks ago, when he heard Julius's voice shouting, Papa, it's me, he has been thinking. He is afraid—afraid for Tweet's future, although I doubt he is afraid for himself. He is probably ready, or almost ready, to move on.

But even though he is old and wise, I believe he has made a mistake. He has lain in bed night after night planning and discarding plans. I'll go to town, he thinks, and make the will. Julius won't know what I put in it. I'll leave it with Lawyer Quinn and I'll put in it that Rosa is Tweet's mama and for Lawyer Quinn to send word to her whenever I die. Then, when I leave the office—he's beginning to doze— then . . . The fire spurts up and crackles and he rouses, hears a log break apart.

But suppose Julius goes with me, he says to himself. Suppose he puts on like he's got to help me, me being blind and can't read. He might do that. Then, how . . . ? Or here's another way it might be a mistake. If he doesn't go with me, suppose he thinks he's got to keep on seeing after me, even with the will, to keep me from going back and changing it again. He and Claree might stay—they might never leave.

Or . . .

Night after night he lay there under the quilt, and on Sunday night, the night before the panther screamed for the first time, tired to death of thinking, he decided that he and Tweet would go to town on the bus on Saturday, with the excuse that he had to cash his pension check. If he tries to go in the bank with me, he thought, mess with my business, I'll face him down. Ain't none of his business to help me.

But on Monday he changed his plan. Something in their voices, something in the panther's human scream, set him thinking again. I'll take Julius with me, he thought, and I'll make the will with him sitting right there. I'll explain to Lawyer Quinn that Julius has got him a good job, a new wife, that Tweet's always been with me, a child to me, and I got to look after her, make it legal for her to get the land. And when we finish, I'll tell him and Claree to go on their way. They ain't got nothing further to gain from me, nothing. Yes. That's the way to do it.

Perhaps all he thought was: This is the way to get rid of them once and for all. But into his dreaming mind there may have drifted the possibility that for land and money his son might kill him. That if Julius believed himself to be the beneficiary, the temptation would be more than he could resist. Is that the deep, almost unacknowledged reason why he fixed on this final plan? Lying there, he decided that if Julius knew he had nothing to gain by his father's death, then he would go away. Yes, I believe this is what he thought, or dreamed, drifting into sleep.

But how is it that he penetrates thus far and no farther into his son's character? That he knows, if he is going to get to town—get even so far as the end of the turnrow to flag the bus—he has to deceive Julius; knows that much and yet, finally, refuses the knowledge that Julius might kill, not just him, but Tweet, too. Does he think, perhaps, that after all it's time for him to die, that the temptation to kill him is no great sin, and add, But not Tweet. He wouldn't hurt Tweet?

Or is he seduced by admiration for his own ingenuity, forgetting everything in his satisfaction at the thought of Julius's frustration when he, still powerful in his blind old age, reveals in Lawyer Quinn's office his true intentions?

And what happened between them—how many years ago—what coldness or failure on his part, what rejection on Julius's that has brought them to this pass?

One thinks of the father in Hansel and Gretel. Remember? How the father accedes to the wicked stepmother's urging and with her leads the two children deep into the forest and leaves them there to die. In the fairy tale there is no explanation other than the parents' poverty. Children who hear the story never ask: What kind of father would do such a dreadful deed? They *know*. No one says: Why would the children go back to their father? The need for happy endings precludes such a question. The tale-teller says only that the wicked stepmother is dead and that the father, who has grieved every day for his lost children, rejoices at their return. Can I sort this out with regard to Tweet's family? Here we have a father and a son—a son who is father of a daughter. And, of course, a wicked stepmother. I think neither the old man nor the child asks these questions. The grandfather does not say to himself: How can I thrust him out into the cold? He does not say: Would he kill me? Worse, would he kill his own daughter? Could he dream of such dreadful deeds? Julius, if he says anything to himself, if he contemplates a murder, may say: But it's time for him to go. He's stayed too long. Or: It's suppose to be *mine*.

As for Tweet, she doesn't know, any more than Gretel did, why her daddy and Claree are what they are. She only knows, as she said to Cornelia, that there is evil out there. Inside or outside, it's all the same.

But I doubt, if she fills her apron pockets with the witch's gold, that she will take it home to her daddy and her stepmother.

Now what? It's Saturday. Julius has left Claree waiting in a cafe on Blaze Street while he and his father and Tweet consult with Lawyer Quinn. The will has been made. The three of them are standing together outside the bank.

Julius, I hear the old man say, you bound to know, once you think about it, that I ain't now and never has thought for one minute that I would leave my land to you. You know it. He does not look at, cannot see his son, who stands in the weak December sunshine with his fists clenched in his pants pockets, two knots straining against the cloth.

Julius is trying to smile. The long scar slashes, ashy gray, across the darkness of his cheek almost to the corner of his mouth. It's true, as Tweet said, that he looks old. But his gray hair is strong and vigorous, springing from above his bony forehead in short crinkled curls.

Julius is strong. That's what Tweet thinks. And he's mad. She sees his rage in his clenched fists and his smile. She is still afraid.

Leaves whirl up out of the gutter on a gust of warm wind and blow against their legs.

You have tore through my life like a piece of tin roofing whirling around in a tornado, the old man says. Except for dropping off Tweet, you ain't done nothing but damage since you was old enough and strong enough to go against me. No way I could let you take this child's inheritance from her long as I'm a breathing man.

And he takes my hand, Tweet said to Cornelia, tells me to come on, and we start off down the street towards the bus station. Seems like he's marching to a tune, you know, like "We Are Soldiers."

My daddy follows us. Papa, he says, I'm going over to Blaze Street to get Claree.

Go ahead, my grandpa says and keeps marching. I'm stepping along beside him, marching with him. Music in my head. Yeah. We are soldiers of the cross. She laughed. That's a Dr. Watt. The saints'll conquer though they die. That's us.

I ain't going to hold it against you that you prefers Tweet to me, my daddy says. I see she's a big help to you.

My grandpa doesn't say nothing for a minute. My daddy catches up and keeps on walking beside us. Then my grandpa says, Julius, you and Claree needs to get your things together and go on back to Akron where you got a job and she got a shop. Y'all well able to look after yourselves.

My daddy must've already had in his mind what course he's going to follow. He lays his hand on my shoulder. Seems like to me the cold in his hand must go all the way up to his brain. Y'all don't need to worry about me and Claree, he says.

My grandpa keeps on walking.

You got the right to do what you want to with what belongs to you, Papa, my daddy says. Claree and me ain't going to have hard feelings towards you just because you leave your land one way instead of another. You're right. We got to go back to Akron, I got to go to work, she's got to tend to her business and her mama. But we always ready to help. You need us, you call us.

I thank you, my grandpa says, and keeps walking along very deliberate, still holding my hand.

I'm going on down to the cafe, get Claree, my daddy says again. We'll see you and Tweet tonight.

Time we get on the bus, my grandpa is so tired, he ain't hardly able to step up on the step. I stand behind him, put my arms around him, step up with him, kind of lifting his legs with mine. He's muttering all the time: OK, Tweet, hit's OK, Tweet, and when we sit down, he puts his hands in his coat pockets, balls up, closes his eyes, and falls asleep.

Skip all the time after I get him home, get his supper, settle him in bed. It's the next day before they turn up, and by that time, Sunday afternoon, he's feeling stronger. They pack their things, don't say much, and after a while whomsoever brought them down comes back in an old piece of Model A Ford, picks them up, and they're gone.

Seems like the air feels lighter around my ears. The house gets bigger. I take up my pallet and fold it away, change the bed in the front room. I don't even mind putting up the chickens and slopping the hog, I'm so glad they're gone.

It's one of them warm December days and I help my grandpa out on the porch and he sets in the sunshine awhile, getting his strength back. Well, Tweet, he says, looks like maybe you won't have to rob the bee tree after all, not for a while, anyways.

Towards four o'clock the wind comes up in a hurry and it commence to turn colder. He ax me what the sky looks like, tells me I better be sure we got plenty of wood in, the weather's fixing to change, and sure enough on the radio at five o'clock they say a cold front's moving in. It snowed all night that night and Monday morning it was down to eighteen. The news says no school today.

How did they do it? Tweet said. They're used to cold weather up there in Akron, I reckon. Eighteen degrees and snow might seem like nothing to them. She shook her head.

We stay inside, close to the fire all that day, listen to the news, she said. I put on my grandpa's boots and go out once to slop the hog, feed the chickens, bring in wood. At that time we didn't have no cow. Mule's got plenty of hay, can see after hisself.

How did they do it? I go over and over in my mind from time to time how it could've been and I don't have no sure answers. Weather was so bad: Commence to snow again late Monday afternoon, and it was still snowing when my grandpa woke me up in the middle of the night. It puzzles me how they or anybody could have come and gone. All I can think is they must've got the borry of that old car for a couple of hours—or took it without anybody knowing.

The way it happen, best I can remember, my grandpa waked up first, pull me out of bed, says, Hurry up, Tweet, got to get out of here, house is on fire. The room was full of smoke. I'm sleeping heavy, I reckon, but I wake up, commence coughing and choking, and I remember him pulling me out of bed. Crawl, he says. Hold your breath. Git down low and come on.

And we crawl, him half dragging me, under the smoke towards the front door. Door's locked or blocked, we can't get out. He's coughing and choking and so am I. He must've known in a second what's happened. Hold onto my coattails, he says, don't stop for nothing. We getting out of here. It's hotter now, smoke heavier, he doesn't even try to make it to the back door, too much fire in there.

We're crawling across his room and then I know I'm not crawling; it's like I'm dreaming that he's dragging me along with that little three-fingered bird claw of his. I hear his breath, harsh, I feel him slap me, and I rouse up and it's like I can't give up before he does. Feel the heat, smell it burning my hair, hear it in my hair, like the sound of water sizzling on a hot stove. I commence to crawl again and I'm trying to hold my breath much as I can and then he's pulled the rug off the trapdoor in his own bedroom, lifted up the door, and we stumble down into the old root cellar, hadn't

55

nobody thought about since the nineteen and twenty-seven flood except to raise the trap now and again and throw down some poison for the rats. He pulls the trap shut after us and we're scrambling across the root cellar (ain't more than four feet deep). Help me here, Tweet, he says, and we push up the little slanty outside door and we're out under the sky in the snow, fire shining on the snow, makes it look like clouds in a sunset. We stumble around to the front and in the firelight I see the washstand always sits on the front porch. It's pushed up against the door.

Yes, Tweet said. I seen it with my own eyes. Then, in a minute fire shoots up, roof caves in and the walls topple in on top of the roof. Heat so strong on my face, I back off, cover my eyes, hardly feel the cold in my feet.

The ground is deep in snow, snow up over my ankles, and I'm in my long-sleeve flannel gown that Rosa made for me and he's in his nightshirt and overcoat. I see he's got on his boots and someway he's grabbed my shoes and brought them along.

Put on your shoes, Tweet, he says. I think us better go on up the road to Martha's house before we freeze. And I lean against him, shivering and crying, and wipe my feet off on the bottom of my gown and put on my shoes.

No use crying, child, he says. Tears just freeze on your face, and he takes off his overcoat and wraps it around me. Sing, Tweet, he says. Sing. Keep us going. So I commence "We Are Soldiers."

Did he see the washstand? Cornelia asked.

How could he? Ain't I told you he don't see nothing but light and dark?

Cornelia shook her head. Maybe you didn't see it either, she said. Everything must have been confusing for you— the smoke and the fire. Were you badly burned?

No, Tweet said. My hair and eyebrows singed. Face blistered a little bit, but mostly it was the smoke. We was still choking on all that smoke. So, anyhow, I commence singing and then I take his coat and put it around both of us, one side over his shoulder and the other over mine, and we start out walking, stumbling and uneven, what with his stiff leg and the snow and all. I'm guiding him, because of course he don't have his cane. We hadn't got very far along the turnrow when he stops. Whoa, he says. Whoa, Nelly. That's a mule we used to have. Now listen to me, Tweet, he says, and do what I say. I can't walk all the way to Martha's, tired and cripple as I am. It was the first time I ever heard him call hisself cripple. Quickest way for you to get me some help is to go on. You can run. Git on down there and fetch them back for me. He pulls his coat off his shoulder. Do like I say, he told me. Take my coat and put it on and go. One of us has got to get help.

I'm crying again. Can't take your coat, Grandpa, I say.

Yes, you can, girl. Yes, you can. I be all right.

Grandpa, I say, I . . .

Go on, he tells me. I'm going to walk back to the house, stay right there close to it, where the fire will keep me warm, and he turns around and starts walking. Hurry up, he says. You want to help me, hurry up. Now, go on.

And I take his coat and put it on and button it, tails dragging in the snow, and I commence running. Look back once and see him headed towards the house, slow, throwing his leg out a little bit like he always did. Didn't have no cane to feel his way ahead of him, but he was walking along slow and steady. He stops once, hollers after me, Sing it, Tweet. Sing it.

I run as well as I could to Martha's house and got them out of bed. Snow had got all inside my shoes and time I got there, seem like my feet was made of stone.

So Martha's husband, James, saddled his horse and went back. But when he got there, my grandpa was laid out in the furrow of his cornfield there by the turnrow, and he was dead. It seem like, James said, he hadn't fallen down, he had laid down on his back, closed his eyes, straighten his legs, folded his hands on his breast. Much as to say, It's OK, Tweet. I'm just going to take me a little nap.

57

Later on, the day after the fire or the day after that, when Rosa got here, I heard the people ax, Is Julius coming back for the funeral? Rosa says she thinks he's on his way to Akron on the bus. Down to Mr. Lord's commissary some people say they saw him Sunday afternoon, him and Claree, and he said they was leaving. That's all we knew for sure.

I *say* that's all we knew for sure, but *I* knew how it must have been.

Wednesday Rosa went down to the commissary, used Mr. Lord's telephone, and called Claree's people in Akron, but they hadn't got back yet. She told them the funeral was set for Sunday. On Thursday he called up, talked to somebody down there and sent us up a message to Martha's house, where we was staying. They couldn't come back for the funeral, he said. They had done spent all their money. Tell Rosa, he says, how grieve he was. Getting on the bus, he'd had a feeling he shouldn't go. And what about Tweet? he says. Poor little Tweet? Was she OK? Did she get burned up in the fire? And whoever it was told him I was all right. Praise God for that, he says. We can rejoice over that.

What about the washstand? Cornelia said.

Nobody saw it but me. I thought about telling and I didn't. What would happen if I told? In those days things like that—among our people, I mean—nobody paid attention to it. The word of a nigger child and no evidence? The sheriff wouldn't even have looked into it. Not worth the expense. And the fire? 'Twasn't even in the paper. Nothing but a nigger shack up on Sandy Creek and one old man dead, should've been dead twenty years ago.

I thought hard, thought about the money and the land, and I come to the truth. My daddy wanted me dead, too. Didn't just want his papa dead. It wouldn't do him no good until I was dead. I thought about Rosa. I knew I wasn't going back to Buchanan County with her, leave behind what my grandpa had left me. It was mine. But mainly I thought

58

about my daddy coming back and I was afraid. I had to decide quick what I was going to do.

So I got married.

Didn't have to look far, Tweet said. Nig was farming forty acres over on Mr. Lord's place. I'd known him all my life. If I ever thought about him before that, I reckon I thought he was an old man—he was twenty years older than me. But of course that didn't make him but thirty-five. His wife had died—her and the baby—in childbirth the year before. He already had two girls by her. He was known around our part of the county as a steady man, a worker. Maybe not smart, but steady, quiet, always done the right thing. After my grandpa got feeble, he was one of the men would come around sometimes and lend us a hand.

I hadn't noticed it before, Tweet said, but he was good-looking—stocky, slow, but strong as a horse. Built for comfort, like the song goes, and not for speed. And he was light on his feet (Come to find out he could dance.) and, well, you know what he looks like, got them big eyes and even now, old as he is, good skin. If I'd been listening at the time when people mentioned him at church and all, I would've known he'd always been after the women. His first marriage didn't change that and—she looked sideways at Cornelia— neither did his second. But he had a way about him that made me feel easy. At my grandpa's funeral he cried. I noticed that. Well, I said to myself, I'll chance it.

Afterwards, back at Martha's house, I looked straight at him and didn't drop my eyes and I think he knew well enough what I had on my mind. He come to see us again the next day.

Rosa stayed on. Wasn't nothing settled yet about the farm or about me, although I suppose she must've thought I'd go back to Buchanan County with her and we'd come later and settle about the land. She might have had in her mind that we would rent it or they would come back and farm it with me. I didn't wait long enough for her to begin to talk about that.

So Nig come and kept coming. He would drop in and sit by the fire with us everyday. Rosa knew him well. They was close to the same age, had growed up on the same place— Mr. Lord's. It might be she saw right off what I was thinking about. But she never was one to say much. She's somewhat like you—reserve. I used to think sometimes—still do— she don't know *how* to talk about what's happening, what she's thinking. She's that still.

Fourth day Nig come, he cut his eyes at me and when he left I follow him out on the front porch. Cold out there. Snow still on the ground, piled up on the north side of the house where the sun don't strike, icicles hanging from the porch roof a foot long. All my clothes burnt up and I'm wearing a dress of Martha's that's too long on me, old sweater of Rosa's out at the elbow, standing on the porch shivering, us looking at each other. My grandpa always used to keep me in nice clothes, but nothing left of that. Nothing but my nightgown and shoes and his old coat. It's not clothes that's going to count now. Nig looked at me and looked at the floor and looked at the icicles. He might have been thinking: How can I court this scrawny little girl in this draggly old ladies' dress and sweater? But I didn't give him time to think more than one sentence.

He opened his mouth like he was about to speak and I spoke first. Mr. Nig, I say, you can see I got a problem here. This here land my grandpa left me, I can't farm it by myself. I needs a man. And you got problems, too. You need some help with them chirren. It's in my mind if we got married, it would go a long way to solving both us problems.

Well, he said.

I had took him by surprise. Put me in mind of my grandpa, the way he said, Well.

60

But it didn't take him no time to make up his mind. Yeah, he says. I think that's what us ought to do.

Went to town the next day for the blood test and got married three days later. Afterwards I told him about Julius and Claree and the washstand.

Now, Tweet, he says, you know that couldn't be.

I know I seen it, I said. But it won't do them no good to mess with me now.

I didn't tell him about the bee tree.

T W O

Unlike Tweet, Cornelia has
never seen her life as a series of adventures. How has she
seen it? Earlier I wrote that she stood erect, slightly swayback, shoulders high, as if she might be waiting to receive
the ermine-trimmed mantle she would wear to her coronation. Does she then see herself as a queen? Not necessarily. To carry oneself in a regal manner, to accept the
responsibilities and perquisites of one's position, is not to
see oneself anyhow. It is rather to act. And Cornelia is one
of those people, so baffling to the writer (who is always,
compulsively, examining character and circumstance, cause
and effect), one of those people who draw back, almost as
if it might be a sin, from examining the causes and consequences of their acts. She does not say to herself: Now
what should I do? any more than, swimming, she asks herself, What now? before she takes the next stroke, turns her
head for the next breath; or any more than, in the old days,
dancing with John, she *thought* a step. Perhaps she fears
that if she did—think a stroke or a step—she might find
herself sinking, falling.

This is not to say that the behavior of such people brings
them success or failure, or that their lives are happier or
more miserable than other peoples' lives, only that they live
in a particular way. Their lives would have to be shattered,

65

the water in their quiet pools turned to undertow, for them to think of changing.

You can see that writing about someone like Cornelia imposes its own restrictions. I am unable to record for you what she says about herself during those long hours she and Tweet spend companionably together. She says almost nothing about herself. To her it is almost unthinkable to speak to anyone, even herself, of her feelings, her childhood, her intimate life with her husband, even her children's lives. Such confidences are not simply trashy, dishonorable (an old-fashioned word still very much a part of her vocabulary), for her they are scarcely formulable.

I am left therefore with surfaces, with scenes.

Again I am drawn to a scene with her mother, this one happening several years after Cornelia is grown and married.

They are sitting together in Cornelia's living room over a game of double solitaire. (When Mother visits, Cornelia stays home from work to entertain her.) People who don't exchange confidences, don't talk of meanings, have, after all, to pass the time with each other, and Cornelia and her mother often pass their time together playing cards. During the card games they talk, it's true, but they exchange recipes instead of confidences, they speak of events rather than meanings, they speculate on the motives of politicians and pastors, never of parents and spouses.

This day, however, is an exception. Something has moved Cornelia's mother to a genuine revelation.

What brought about Mother's uncharacteristic gesture of intimacy? Perhaps the security of Cornelia's warm living room, the recognition that her child is safe in the harbor of matrimony? I doubt it. Mother has never liked John or thought him a suitable husband. Perhaps, then, she feels the desire to be known, to become friend as well as parent to her grown child? Hmmm. Questionable. In any case, this is what she says:

I took the two of you (Cornelia has a younger brother) and went home to Mama. Tacky. Disgraceful. But I did.

66

Cornelia does not interrupt. In the course of this account she does not ask the question that would spring instantly to my lips: Why? She never finds out why her mother left her father, and for a long time after this particular afternoon she does not even ask herself. If John—to whom she probably repeated the conversation—had pressed her at the time, she might have said: If she wanted to tell me why, she would have told me.

Anyhow, uninterrupted, her mother goes on. It took me a few days to gather myself together and tell Mama what I'd done—it was summer and she thought I'd come for an ordinary visit.

She puts a king from her deck in an empty space, lays down her cards, smiles across the table at Cornelia. Cornelia lays down her cards, too. Double solitaire requires both players to play continuously as fast as they can. The object of the game is to go out first.

We may have been sitting together like this over a game of double sol, Cornelia's mother says. Remember how your grandmother loved solitaire? How she would cheat to finish out a game when she was playing by herself—and then tell you she had cheated?

Cornelia nods dreamily. Well, she says, she couldn't conceal it from herself, after all, could she? So why not tell it?

I told her I'd left him—that I was not going back, Cornelia's mother says. That I couldn't—I wouldn't. I remember she'd put down her cards when I started talking. I can see her sitting there studying the cards, not looking at me. But finally she looked up, put her attention on what I was saying.

My dear, she said, don't think for a moment you can come home to *me*. I've raised my children. If you leave him, you'll have to make a life for yourself and your children however you can.

I suppose I didn't say anything, Cornelia's mother continues. Anyhow, Mama went on: Look at me, my dear, she said. How could I help you? I'm sixty-four years old. I have just enough money from your father's insurance to take care of myself. But that's not the point. The point is: *You* married him. You chose a life with him of your own free will. Now, if you want to change your life, it's your business, not mine.

What could I have said? So (Cornelia's mother picks up her cards) I went back to him. What else could I do? He never even knew I'd left him. She riffled the deck and the diamond in her engagement ring (a Tiffany setting—it had belonged to her husband's mother) glinted in the firelight of Cornelia's cozy living room. I thank her for it, she said. She was absolutely right.

Cornelia does not want to hear this. She does not. But she doesn't dare turn off her hearing aid. Her sharp-eyed mother would see that surreptitious movement in an instant.

Yes, I thank her. God knows how our lives—your lives, too—would have gone, if she'd opened her house to us, backed me up.

She pushed back her chair from the table, thrust out her small foot in its high-heeled, glove-leather pump (she's always been vain of her small feet). I'd have been standing behind the counter at Rosenstein's on *these*, she said, working for Jews, selling piece goods to people like me. Instead, I did well by you children—by us all. Look at you. She glances around the room—books in their places on the shelves, pictures in silver frames, the soft glow of lamplight falling on the intricately patterned carpet, the polished wood. Who would have thought in your teens . . . ?

Cornelia says nothing.

You were such a peculiar child, my dear.

Maybe you shouldn't have had children, Cornelia says. Hearing herself say this has a curious effect on her. She feels a mixture of fear and exhilaration. It's as if someone else has spoken, someone for whom she has no responsibility. She says it again. Maybe you shouldn't have had children. Sometimes it crosses her mind, hearing her own voice through her hearing aid, that someone else is speaking.

Whose voice is that, slightly distorted, metallic, fuzzed by a shaky vibration?

Oh, *children,* Mother says. Children should be kept in bureau drawers until they reach their majority. They're monsters until you break them in.

No, Cornelia says. No, Mother. Ours—John's and mine —are not monsters.

I'm joking, of course, my dear. Can't you take a joke? She lays down another king in an empty space and Cornelia, too, picks up her pack.

This scene wrings my heart. So much is left unsaid or somehow skewed in the saying. It can't be true, can it, that grandmother would have shut the door against her daughter in that desperate hour? That Cornelia's mother is *grateful* for this harsh lesson in rejection?

And why, why does she tell Cornelia this tale now, so late? Does she think she hears (in spite of what she occasionally refers to as Cornelia's *inordinate* passion for John) the groan of creaking timbers in their marriage? Is she covering her flanks? *Don't think for a moment that I'm available. I've raised my children. You and John will have to work out your problems for yourselves.*

And then there are, of course, all the complex things about the lives of women that Mother just touched on when she extended and admired her own expensively clad and aristocratic foot and mentioned the loathsome possibility of clerking at Rosenstein's. Did grandmother and mother take for granted that their husbands would have abandoned them after a divorce—would not have supported their own children?

But not us, Cornelia would have said. Not John. That will never happen to us.

In any case, it appears that Cornelia's mother, out of her own nature and experience, whether from cowardice or from her knowledge of their three characters, would not risk an ultimate test either of her mother's love or of her husband's conscience or of her own capacity to survive. And now she wants Cornelia to know about this piece of their past, and to know that she was right.

Cornelia smiles at her mother—a distant, faintly embarrassed smile. I remember the expression on her face and the switch against her bare legs that rainy Easter morning so long ago.

Cornelia grew up in a time and place that (in her mother's view, anyhow) presented more than the ordinary hazards in the way of reaching successful maturity—the haven of a suitable marriage—the hazards being the possibilities, in rising order of their catastrophic significance, of, one, marrying a rich but unsuitable man; two, marrying a poor *and* unsuitable man; three, dying of scarlet fever or a burst appendix; and four, worst of all, bearing a child out of wedlock.

The time and place—the period of the second World War in a small southern city with nearby air bases and army camps—made hazards one, two, and four particularly threatening. One could not, of course, speak of them except obliquely—recounting the fates of unfortunate maidens— one talked instead of what is and isn't done. Cornelia's mother, Mrs. Wright—almost no one calls Mother by her given name—was more than ordinarily inflexible in these matters. Other young girls went out with soldiers—surely, at the very least, with officers—on "blind dates," or with only the most tenuous introductions—at church perhaps, or at a USO dance. But Cornelia's mother had heard horror stories of supposedly respectable men—a major, even— who married impressionable young girls and were found later, when questions of allotments arose, for example, or of where to ship the effects, to have wives and families elsewhere. She required Cornelia to limit her engagements to men who brought letters of introduction from relatives or acquaintances in other cities.

How could her mother continue to exercise this control? She could not, for long—and shortly she did not. Cornelia was only nineteen when she burst through the walls and married. She was far too strong and self-willed to accede in maturity to her mother's wishes.

But there is something in her character that to begin with worked against defiance. She has always had a sense of the appropriate thing to do. She waits until the time is right to assert herself. One doesn't get into quarrels with one's mother at sixteen or seventeen about matters over which parents have always had a proper control. At eighteen one tests the water, and at nineteen one says what one is going to do and then, in the face of whatever opposition, does it.

Other things, too, contributed to her mother's successful domination of her adolescence. She is a reader. She has lived absorbed more deeply in the lives of Elizabeth Bennet and Dorothea Brooke, more concerned for their difficulties than perhaps she has ever been for her own. And she has always been—reserved, as Tweet would say. She was never the kind of young girl who attracted boys, who knew how to flatter and flirt, to keep herself surrounded by suitors. Or perhaps she did know, she simply did not choose to act. She seemed unaware—no matter that her reserve included intelligence and resourcefulness—of the power of her own beauty, her sexuality. I see her, unconscious of the picture she makes, leaning her chin on her hand in the open window of her room in the classic pose of the dreaming young girl, looking down into the shady street below. Her book lies on the floor beside her, her brush on her lap. The window faces south and she has been brushing out her hair in the light of the morning sun. Sunlight glints off the strong copper threads of her hair and softly illumines the childish curves of adolescent flesh that mask the strength of chin and cheekbone and slightly aquiline nose. She has the profile: (Where have I seen it?) the heavy graceful curls lying like marble on her broad forehead; the fine thin nose with a slight dent in the bridge, between her wide-set eyes; the lips pressed so firmly, yet sensitively, against each other; the chin with its almost-invisible cleft. Not the purity of Praxiteles, but something later, touched by Rome with the knowledge of the nature of power. Yes, she is beautiful—and strong.

Cornelia and her family live in an old two-story late-Victorian house with an octagonal tower clad in fish-scale shingles hooked on at the side. The first story of the tower is a solarium; the second, because of its awkward shape, Mrs. Wright has never liked and she uses it for storage. The third, windowed to the east and south and surrounded by a captain's walk, Cornelia has chosen for her room. What could be more romantic than the sight of a young girl sitting in the morning sunshine in her tower bedroom brushing her hair? But there is no one to see. The young men don't ride past the house, yearning for a glimpse of her. She is too—serious. Too lacking in small talk, too direct, too quiet. And when she does speak, she has too formidable a vocabulary. She has had only one male friend during the years of her adolescence, the son of a family both suitable and wealthy who moved to their city from New Orleans because the father has interests here that for a time need closer supervision. The boy is quiet, shy, doesn't fit easily into the "crowd" that ignores Cornelia. Perhaps that's why he and Cornelia gravitate toward each other. In any case, he shares her love of the outdoors and of guns—yes, she's a good shot, too—takes her out shooting or walking in the woods, says she's like a boy—never complains about discomfort and is a tireless walker and doesn't talk too much. That may not be at all what he means. Sometimes, balancing across a log in some ferny ravine, he jumps down into the mud, takes her hand to help her over. They take turns throwing clay pigeons for each other and I see her leaning against a fence post at the edge of a pasture, looking exceedingly happy. She releases the bird and then, instead of watching it, turns to look at him, his long graceful body and curly brown hair, the patch of rosy cheek resting against the stock as he squints down the barrel and leads the bird.

But then Mother says something favorable about him, *approves* of him. Or perhaps she goes to call on *his* mother. Afterwards the friendship cools and then, in a year or so, he is gone.

How can I tell you accurately about Mother? In fairness to her, I should say that I don't like her, so my report may be distorted by personal bias. There she sits in her solarium while, above, Cornelia dreams in the sunshine of her bedroom window. Mother is already overweight—looks like a fat spider, with her swelling body and hairy arms and legs. Her face is caked, in the style of the forties, with too much pancake makeup which does not conceal incipient wrinkles and is crusted in the crease of her double chin. By the time she dies so happily, fifteen years after Cornelia's marriage, mumbling, How delicious! over her stuffed artichoke leaf, she will have sprouted a crop of chin whiskers and will be grossly fat. Serve her right, as Tweet would say.

I dislike her, though, not because she is fat, but because she is a limited provincial snob, because she has concealed Cornelia's beauty from her, because she seems to me to hate her daughter's sexuality, to be jealous of her happiness.

Here is something she did when Cornelia was fifteen. She sent her out to her first real dance (saying, You look lovely, my dear), dressed in a hideous bile green moiré taffeta evening dress with awkward three-quarter-length sleeves, an ill-fitting, long-waisted bodice that hid the tender curves of her young body, and a wide taffeta sash with a huge bow at the back. It was an outfit that Lewis Carroll might have dreamed up to keep Alice a little girl forever.

No matter that she was light on her feet and ready to learn, no one danced with Cornelia. No one broke in. Dance after dance, every muscle in her body stiff with anguish, she endured the sweaty hand of her miserable, stumbling date against the bedraggled bow at the small of her back. At intermission he feigned a bellyache and took her home.

You're an awkward dancer, my dear, Mother said the next day. But you have other assets.

After that evening no one asked Cornelia out for a long time—a year, two years.

Mother would be outraged at my version of this occasion. She bought Cornelia's dress at the best shop in the city. The material and workmanship—and price—proved its suitability. Maybe she can't see Cornelia. She sees instead the expensive dress walking across the floor of the Elysian Club, eyed, not by the young men lounging against the walls and clustered by the bandstand, but by chaperons—women who will encourage their sons to court and marry such a dress.

And Father? Father isn't there. Father seldom goes to such affairs. He prefers to loaf comfortably in the study at the University Club, to look vaguely at Cornelia next morning and absently inquire whether she had a good time; to raise and spread the morning paper and shield himself from his family.

If she had allowed herself such thoughts, such intimations of emptiness, Cornelia might have seen herself as an echoing void around which her parents' lives seemed inexplicably to revolve.

After high school Cornelia began to attend an acceptable local "finishing" school. But then the war came and everything changed.

During those years there were so many men available, so many homesick soldiers yearning to spend an evening in a real house, to gaze quietly and peacefully at a real young girl, to dance, to picnic, to lie on the grass and hold hands—thousands of them, tens of thousands—it was inevitable that some would come along with proper letters of introduction, would not notice or care that Cornelia was reserved, that she neither flirted nor flattered. She was female. She lived in a real house. That was enough.

At first none of these young men particularly moved her. Perhaps, to begin with, stepping into the arms of one stranger after another, she held herself as rigidly as she had in the arms of the unfortunate lad who had taken her to that first disastrous dance. But again and again she went out with them, because, as everyone agreed, it was the seemly, the charitable thing to do. She dreamed, sleep-danced her way through evenings at the officers' clubs, the cadet clubs, even the USO (removing the diamond ring she had inherited from her grandmother, lest someone think her guilty of displaying her wealth).

Yes, she began to hear the music, began to dance, almost in her sleep. One soldier after another was delighted to teach her the steps—presented himself with hungry eyes and pulsing body, as if he were saying, Me, me next. I haven't much time. She whirled across the floor to "Beer Barrel Polka" and "Two O'clock Jump," dipped and swayed to "Begin the Beguine" and "Solitude," learned in her sleep to dance the Big Apple, to peck and shine and truck.

No one knew her. No one expected anything of her. No one cared what she read or what she was wearing. No one knew Mother. The beat of the band drew everyone to the floor and Cornelia, speechless and dreaming, joined the dance.

And then, in time to the music, perhaps, she felt her dream begin to be broken into, not particularly by any one soldier, but by the whole army of them—so young and hopeful in their clumsy GI shoes, their regulation haircuts, clean ears sticking out from cropped skulls, uniforms crackling with starch. They reminded her—yes, that was it, the source of the faint stirring, the pain under her heart—they reminded her of her seventeen-year-old brother, away now at a suitable military school, who—there was no denying it—might soon be following them to unimaginably deadly and faraway places: Guadalcanal, Guam, Eniwetok;

El Alamein, Monte Cassino; Omaha Beach, St. Lo, Bastogne. . . .

Then, one night at the air base officers' club, whirling round the floor, spinning like a top to Glenn Miller's "In the Mood" from the jukebox, she saw the man for whom she would defy her mother. A lovely man with blue eyes and a lock of lank black hair falling across his forehead, a man with a still, watchful face and a body that seemed to her, even in the first brief moment of glancing at him, charged with energy.

If Mother had been there, he might have passed her first tests. She would have observed that he wore the glamorous disguise of crushed pilot's cap, campaign ribbons, and battered flight jacket, and even more glamorous, the tiny brevet of the RAF on his right breast pocket. He spoke standard American English with a faint trace of clipped British precision. His manners were the manners of an officer. But, of course, she would have thought, all these, even the manners, may be precisely that: a disguise. And it is true that underneath, almost obliterated, like the vanishing lion's head on an old silver teaspoon, were the hallmarks that announced his true provenance.

Mother had the magnifying glass with which to make them out.

But Cornelia had only the faintest passing interest in his uniform, his ribbons. She was looking at *him* standing in the doorway with his cap in his hand, watching—her; and later, sitting at the bar alone, still mostly watching her. He ordered a drink, but scarcely touched it. Now and then someone came up and spoke to him, diffidently, almost as if paying homage, and he responded absently, nodding and smiling.

Cornelia had come to the club with a young major who was the cousin of a cousin, a West Point graduate and an army brat, clearly on his way up. In the course of the evening she maneuvered him into introducing the captain with the RAF brevet and after the three of them had had a drink together, John asked her to dance. His hand on her back was sure and she relaxed against him, easily followed his light step. He asked if he might call her and she said yes.

But I've forgotten your last name, she said.

O'Kelly, he said. I'm from New Orleans. But I've been away from there a long time.

The next day he called. Without telling her mother where she was going, she went to meet him at a local nightclub. She stayed out without reporting where she was until long past midnight.

She had seen him first, she told him afterwards, had noticed him sitting at the bar in the club, so withdrawn and self-contained. He'd been a challenge. But he said, No, he had seen her earlier that same day. Walking in the neighborhood, he'd passed her house. I like to walk in town, he said—to watch the children, I suppose. I miss seeing children. And the houses. I like looking at all these old houses—shingles like snake scales, lace paper lattices. When I was in England I went to see all the castles and keeps and . . . He broke off. I saw you sitting in the tower window, he said, brushing your hair like Rapunzel.

She laughed and touched the shining copper threads. It's not long enough for you to climb up, she said. But if Mother has anything to say about it, you might need to.

Already she was direct, her intention forming.

It turned out that he was a certified hero. (This she found out from the West Point cousin of a cousin.) He'd flown three years with the Eagle squadron, had survived the Battle of Britain with seventy-five missions to his credit, had been shot down twice while he was picking up his trace of a British accent. Now, back in the American Army Air Corps, he was an instructor, teaching other young men to avoid death as he had.

But it was not, or not mainly, the glamor of his calling or the charm of his Black Irish face—high wide peasant cheekbones, blue eyes and black hair—that drew her to him. No. He was alive. She'd never seen anyone so alive.

77

And his touch—just the touch of his hand against her back as he guided her across the dance floor had brought her to life.

As for him, I think, it must have been not only the glamorous sight of the princess at her tower window but her reserve, her inability to flirt and flatter, her directness, her very dowdiness that drew him to her.

When she came in that first night and her mother asked where she'd been, Cornelia shook her head vaguely and said, With a friend. And when her mother said, Who? Cornelia said, Mother, I'm nineteen. It's ridiculous for me to have to answer to you for where I am and what I'm doing every hour of the day and night.

The battle was joined. Mother would not relinquish her power. She would not.

But where was her father? Whose side did he take? I have to report that Father did not join the battle. He was and is a gentle, uncombative man who abdicated his power to his wife early in their marriage. Cornelia looked once or twice to him for support, but he dropped his eyes and retired behind his newspaper. She looked no more.

Mother met John, I think, before Cornelia was quite ready to introduce him. He came unannounced one afternoon, knocked at the door, and when the maid answered, asked for Cornelia. Mrs. Wright, in the solarium, heard his voice and came out, pacing along the hall with her slightly spraddled, fat-legged walk, stood for a moment behind the maid, and looked him over. She knew instantly now where Cornelia had been disappearing to almost daily for the past couple of weeks.

The maid gave way to her mistress. Cornelia is asleep, Mrs. Wright said. It was the first excuse that popped into her head.

I was walking in the neighborhood, he said. I told Cornelia how much I like to walk around old neighborhoods, look at the trees and the old houses. . . .

She inclined her head stiffly.

It's a relief after looking at barracks and airplane hangars all day and all night, he said. Dirt streets. Cardboard buildings . . .

Clearly she was waiting for him to leave.

I'm John O'Kelly, thirty-third squadron, he said, taking off his cap. Cornelia and I met at the Officers' Club a couple of weeks ago.

By this time she had heard more of him than she needed to pass judgment. Her ear had picked up the ghost of a diphthong in *dirt* and *Thursday* and *thirty-third*, as unerringly as her eye would discern the minutest hesitation among forks at a dinner party. And *O'Kelly*? Brooklyn? Irish Channel? Shanty boat Irish! is what Mrs. Wright heard in that vanishing *oi*. Probably Catholic, she thought, with an inward shudder.

But by now Cornelia had heard his voice and was running down the stairs. John! She took his hand and drew him toward the door. I'll be back shortly, Mother.

Wait, her mother said. And then, Cornelia! But the screen door slammed and they were gone, almost running, almost dancing, down the oak-shaded street, laughing as if there were . . . laughing at me, she thought. Laughing at *me*.

She wouldn't be heard shouting after them like . . . like a fishwife. There was a pressure in her chest, a pain under her heart that might be the warning of a heart attack. With a groan audible all over the house, she sat abruptly down. When the maid came hurrying through the pantry door (she'd been eavesdropping), she slipped on one of the small oriental rugs that lay like islands along the polished floor. Catching herself, she stumbled against a table, and a porcelain lamp came crashing down.

Mrs. Wright, sitting spraddle-legged on the fiddleback Empire chair by the Sheraton card table with its silver card tray and Sevres urns painted with scenes of lambs and shepherdesses, clutched her heavy breasts with both hands, groaned again, looked at the fragments of her lamp scattered across the floor. You're fired, she screamed. You clumsy

. . . stupid . . . *nig*. You're fired. If you show your face
again in my house, I'll . . . I'll have you arrested.

Cornelia dreamed that night of her mother. In the dream
she and her mother have set out driving to the bakery to get
a beautiful round golden caramel cake and bring it home
for all the family to share. Rain is falling heavily in the
dream. The car skids into the deep mud of a flower bed
which turns out to be quicksand. The car is sinking rapidly.
Now, while Mother is standing on the hood of the sinking
car, Cornelia, without being aware how she got there, is
safe on firm ground. Frantically she screams for her mother
to step ashore—to save herself. But the car is sucked under
and Mother is up to her neck in black mud. Throw me your
coat, she calls, and Cornelia takes off her heavy winter coat
and, holding on to the collar, throws the skirt out toward
her mother, who grabs it and tries to pull herself to the
bank, the edge of the flower bed. Now Father, too, is in the
mud, pushing and heaving at his wife, as Cornelia pulls and
Mother sinks deeper and deeper. Her mouth and nose slip
below the viscous black tide. Cornelia reaches out and seizes
her hair, but it is a wig and comes away, leaving a bald,
veined and mottled scalp over which the blackness closes.
A few bubbles rise sluggishly and burst with loud plopping
noises. Cornelia and her father look at each other. We did
the best we could, he says cheerfully, and climbs out of the
mud.
    Cornelia woke up. If I'd slept a little longer, I would have
sent someone to call the fire department, she assured herself,
and drifted off into a dream of John.

In the course of the next two weeks Cornelia's mother dis-
covered that John was indeed precisely what she had judged

him to be. His alcoholic father had drifted all his life from one job to another (night watchman, ferryman, parking-lot attendant) and his mother, between babies, had taken in sewing to supplement the family income. Both (fortunately, Mrs. Wright might have said, if she'd been able to think of anything fortunate about John O'Kelly) had been killed in a wreck in their early forties, leaving seven children (of whom John was the third) to be scattered among older siblings and aunts and uncles for the duration of their childhoods. John was eighteen. He was a man, able to look out for himself. At least, I can hear her saying to Father, planning this unthinkable wedding, the parents can't come.

John made not the least effort to conceal his background from Cornelia or from Mrs. Wright. I think he was a true democrat, unconscious to begin with that anyone might consider him—unsuitable. Perhaps he had never had occasion to think about suitability. He'd been busy surviving—had spent the past five years thinking about how to do his job and stay alive. He spoke of his parents, of their poverty. When he said that his mother had taken in sewing, Mrs. Wright again came close to having a heart attack. The ghost of a smell drifted unbidden to her nostrils, the smell of houses where food congeals on dirty dishes in the kitchen, while women with lank and unwashed hair bend over sewing machines, and diapers, still faintly ammoniac even after washing, dry on racks before gas space heaters; where children with crusted nostrils toddle through drafty rooms and the smell of poverty is like the smell of death. She recalled coming home after delivering the Junior League's Christmas baskets, hanging out her coat to air, washing her hands, saying to her husband with a shudder, Anyone can keep clean. *Anyone.*

John, making what must have seemed to him the obligatory moves that a man makes in order to seem less threatening to the mother of his lady love, expressed his interest in and admitted his ignorance regarding antique tables and oriental rugs. He stretched out his long legs as he talked and tilted back in one of the Empire chairs. Mrs. Wright rolled her eyes heavenward.

Tilt down, John, Cornelia said. Those old chairs fall to pieces if you look at them.

He spoke of having joined the Merchant Marine after his parents' deaths, of long idle weeks at sea when he'd read and stood his watch and read and read, of jumping ship in England in 1939 and joining the RAF. They would take anybody, he said. They were desperate, you know—and I'd always wanted to fly. Two things got me in. I'd been a Boy Scout. Can you believe it? That's the English for you. Maybe they thought I was an Indian scout or something. But that was the only thing I could think of when they asked if I belonged to any organizations. And I could take pictures. Got one of my advanced badges in photography. Scouting was one thing you could do in my neighborhood that didn't cost anything, and the scoutmaster had a pretty good camera and donated the film. . . . So . . . He shrugged. That's the way it happened. I was an enlisted man and a photographer at first. Took reconnaissance pictures. And then later, of course, they sent me to flight school.

What will he be when he takes off his uniform? Mrs. Wright said to Cornelia that night. I'll tell you what. Nothing. Nothing! No background, no education, no prospects. He'll probably end up being an airline pilot (comparable in Mrs. Wright's lexicon to being a train conductor).

Cornelia smiled. She had already seen John without his uniform and she liked what she had seen.

Catholic! Mrs. Wright wailed. Catholic! Nobody is Catholic except the vegetable man.

Mother, you're living in the past, Cornelia said. There isn't any vegetable man.

I forbid you to go out with him. I absolutely forbid it.

Cornelia looked her mother in the eye. I intend to marry him, she said calmly.

Mrs. Wright said that this marriage would take place over her dead body.

How will you stop me? Cornelia asked reasonably. I don't have to have your consent, you know. I'm almost twenty years old.

Rage gave way to pleading. That's exactly what I'm talking about, Mrs. Wright said. You're a child. This is the first man who has ever paid the least attention to you. You're carried away, you've lost your head, because *at last* somebody has asked you for a second date.

Cornelia's face quivered. But she said no word to indicate whether or not this thrust had wounded her.

Of course he knows we have money, Mrs. Wright said. Why else . . . ?

Cornelia turned and left the room.

Father was in his study across the hall from the solarium while this conversation took place. When he came out, he announced that business would take him the next day to New Orleans, perhaps for a week, perhaps longer, and he went upstairs and packed his suitcase. The following morning after breakfast he put on his hat and took up his bag. I'll be staying at the Roosevelt as usual, he told his wife. If anybody wants to use my car, I'll leave the keys in the ticket office. He patted Cornelia on the shoulder, smiled regretfully at her, and departed for the station.

Still locked in combat, Cornelia and her mother scarcely noticed his going. Each retired to consider the next move.

Mrs. Wright began to organize the resources at her disposal. She could go to John's squadron commander. Didn't commanding officers have to grant permission to soldiers in wartime before they could marry? Surely she had heard that somewhere.

Well, yes, under certain circumstances, the commander of the thirty-third squadron said to her over the telephone when she called. If he were an enlisted man and we were overseas—in Borneo, for example—and he wanted to marry one of the natives. But since he's an officer and they're both citizens . . . unless . . . uh . . . how old is your daughter, Mrs. Wright?

Mother stared deeply, as if in a trance, into her bedroom wallpaper where huge scarlet roses nodded in orderly rows and leafy vines twined over half-hidden lattices. Seventeen, the wallpaper said.

Seventeen, she wailed. Oh, she's only seventeen. She's been swept away by his uniform and, oh, she's not old enough to know what she's doing.

Still, he said, I'm afraid seventeen is old enough in this state to marry without parental consent. I can, of course, advise. . . . But . . . I think you should talk to our chaplain. He's better equipped to deal with these problems than . . . And perhaps to your own minister? Meanwhile, I'll just shift your call over to the chaplain's line. All right?

In the brief interval before the chaplain picked up his telephone, Mrs. Wright recognized that a lie about Cornelia's age would very quickly be found out. She's nineteen, she said to the chaplain, but she is completely inexperienced. Oh, I hate to say this about her, but she's always been an awkward child. She's never had any attention from men, she's wholly unequipped to . . . And now this . . . this person . . . this *creature*. . . . I know he is considerably older than she, and . . .

Captain O'Kelly is an outstanding officer, Mrs. Wright, the chaplain said.

In the meantime Cornelia, upstairs in her bedroom, has been thinking over her situation and now, in the middle of this conversation, she knocks at her mother's door and comes in.

Something has come up, Mrs. Wright said abruptly into the telephone. I'll talk to you later. I'll call you tomorrow. Thank you so much. And she put the receiver in its cradle.

Mother, Cornelia says, I'm sorry you're so distressed about John and me. I don't want us to quarrel. But I'm serious, you know. I *am* going to marry him. If it weren't for the war, we could put it off. We could wait long enough for you to see that everything is going to be all right. Cornelia stands very straight as she speaks. Her hair is pulled severely back, but tendrils escape around her fine broad forehead. She seems to have grown taller and older in the brief interval since she left her mother's room, looks almost ready to become a true Roman matron.

I don't think you realize how much difference the war makes in peoples' decisions, she says. We can't tell, you know, when he might be transferred, sent overseas. We just can't tell. Still, I don't want to upset you. We'll wait a little while, all right? A month? Six weeks? We can safely wait six weeks, I think.

Safely! Mrs. Wright wails. Catastrophe number four on the road to a suitable marriage swims before her reeling brain. You're not . . . ?

I mean, surely he won't get orders to go overseas so soon. Surely he has another few months here. I mean, considering how many combat missions he's flown. And . . .

Pregnancy having been eliminated as the cause for this marriage, Mrs. Wright begins to plan her next move, scarcely hearing the rest of Cornelia's words, already saying to herself: I've been too hasty. I should never have approached the problem at so low a level. Who knows where that squadron commander sprang from. And the chaplain. He's probably a Baptist. Or God knows what strange denomination. It's even possible he might be a Jew.

Mrs. Wright has never known a clergyman outside the Episcopal church who measures up to her standards of birth and breeding.

Yes, she thinks, as Cornelia's words echo faintly in her head. If I could get him transferred . . . sent overseas . . . But who?

Of course!

In the evening she spoke on the telephone with the father of the young major who is the cousin of a cousin.

I can't, my dear, he said in that commanding voice that seems to come to generals with rank. I cannot monkey with transfers at that level. It's against my principles.

But you're a general, Mother said. You're a general, Arthur. You can do anything you please. And I'm absolutely certain it's the right thing, not just for Cornelia, but for the Air Corps. You don't want your young men to get a reputation for carrying off innocent inexperienced children like poor Cornelia. The tears rolled down her fat cheeks and her voice quavered. Cornelia is getting ready to ruin her life, she said.

Well. He sighed.

Shanty boat Irish! she hissed. Catholic! Why do you give these people commissions?

We didn't do it, he said plaintively. It was the British.

Arthur!

A war is going on, my dear, the general said.

I know, she said. That's the cause of this whole dreadful mess.

Very well, my dear, the general said. I'll see what I can do.

Upstairs Cornelia, standing on the captain's walk outside her bedroom, leans against the banister and gazes into the starry night. The ginkgo tree that grows beside the tower moves and whispers in a light wind. The time of year is early autumn, and already the tree is beginning to shed its yellow hair. She imagines John climbing up through the rough branches, sitting opposite her with his back against the trunk, smiling at her, reaching out his hand. He is her very self, she says, murmuring his name, and she feels his touch on her breasts, his hand against her back, drawing her to him, his lovely firm flesh on hers, and he seems to ride through her veins like a horseman, breasting the river of her blood. The night is charged with his presence.

The general did indeed intervene in John and Cornelia's lives. He called up John's records and looked them over. He decided that seventy-five combat missions were enough for any man; he would not have on his conscience sending this young officer back into combat, not even now, late in the war, with the skies over Europe less deadly than they had been a year, two years ago. Instead he would attach him to staff somewhere, make him an aide to some faraway general. That would suffice. The orders came down with signal rapidity. Within a week John learned that he had been transferred.

But such things, after all, follow a routine with which generals seldom concern themselves. Automatically, with his transfer, he would get two weeks leave. He would then proceed to a port of embarkation and there he would await his turn for a place on a plane.

So it turned out, Mrs. Wright's intervention precipitated the crisis it was meant to prevent.

After all, Mother, Cornelia said, we can't wait. John is going overseas.

Mrs. Wright gave a groan of anguish. No, she said.

Yes, Cornelia said.

She did not stay in the solarium to discuss the matter

further. She would let her mother simmer while she and John went out to buy the ring and the license and have their blood tests. Later Mother would be calmer. But Mother did not get calmer.

Can I make you believe what happened next? Such things do happen—or in this case, they did. That night, after Cornelia was asleep, Mother labored, with silent steps, moving slowly, stopping now and again to quiet her heavy breathing, up the stairs to the tower. At the head of the stairs, in the small vestibule, were two doors, one into Cornelia's room, the other opening on the captain's walk that surrounded the tower. Quietly she turned the keys, first in one lock, then in the other. Inside her room Cornelia slept peacefully on, a patch of moonlight moving slowly across her bed, the breeze from her open window lifting the muslin curtains and the strands of her copper hair. Mother took the keys from the doors, put them deep in the pocket of her robe, and retreated as quietly as she had come.

What could she have thought this rash act would accomplish? Did she seriously believe she could keep Cornelia a prisoner? My own view is that she did not think at all. Out of rage and outrage she acted. Picture her now, the deed done, sitting downstairs in her bedroom, her fat fingers, her very toes and the insteps of her little ungulate feet swollen with rage against this rebellious daughter and this upstart Irish lover. There is a smile of satisfaction on her face. She is so pleased with herself that she cannot sleep. She lies down in her bed, smiling, continues to lie there, waiting for the night to pass.

In the morning, laboriously, she climbed the stairs again and sat quietly down in the chair that stood against the wall in the vestibule. There she would wait until Cornelia waked up—she didn't, after all, want the neighbors to hear Cornelia calling down from the captain's walk for someone to come and unjam her door. She sat, arms folded on her bosom, feet side by side, and filled the tiny room with her bulk and the power of her resolution. She *would* triumph.

Inside, Cornelia rose early, went into the small bath adjoining her room for her morning shower, and dressed, before she knew she was a prisoner. She tried her door and found it locked, then stepped through the long window opening onto the walk and went around to try the other door. As soon as she saw that it was locked, too, she knew what had happened. She sat calmly down in her easy chair by the window and said nothing, even when, a little while later, she heard her mother in the hall.

Outside Mother begins to be restless. The morning is passing. Cornelia gets up and goes to the bathroom and Mother hears her steps, hears the toilet flush, hears her return to her chair, snap on the radio.

Cornelia?

Cornelia does not reply.

I know you are awake, Mother says. I hear you moving around in there.

Cornelia says nothing. Her book is on her lap and she is looking down at it, but she is not turning the pages. The sound of music fills the room.

Mother gets up and stands close to the door, speaking firmly to its heavy panels. I want you to have time to think, my dear, she says. I am doing this for your own good. She speaks louder. Turn the radio down, she says.

I have wired your father to come home, she says. (She has not.)

I am having the police look into this man's background, she says. We know absolutely nothing about him.

Cornelia flushes and sits up straighter, then relaxes. She's listening to the music: "You—are—the—promised kiss of springtime. . . ."

In a few minutes her mother goes slowly, heavily down

89

the stairs. Is it possible she has made a mistake? What should she do now? Well, to begin with, she can't let the child starve. She'll have the cook prepare a tray. But then, of course, she'll have to get it to Cornelia without letting her escape.

At eleven twenty-five Cornelia steps out of her bedroom window onto the captain's walk and stands looking up the street. Within a few minutes John appears, driving up the hill toward her house in his old prewar Chevrolet. He parks his car, gets out, and looking up, sees her there as he first saw her the day they met. Rapunzel, Rapunzel, he says. Let down your hair.

She smiles at him and watches as he walks closer. Such a light, ballet dancer's walk he has.

Will you come down? he says. Or shall I climb up?

She really has locked me in, John, she says as soon as he is near enough for her to speak without raising her voice. Isn't that absurd?

You've got to be kidding.

She shakes her head.

John is a practical man. Are you hungry? he says. Have you had any breakfast?

Under the circumstances my appetite is poor. She continues to smile down seraphically at him.

Mrs. Wright, at that very moment, is in the kitchen directing the preparation of a tray.

What shall we do? Cornelia says. Her voice and stance are carefree, as if the challenge is one to an ingenuity in which she feels complete confidence.

Have you been bored? John says. Have you anything to read?

She giggles. I've been thinking about you and listening to the radio, she says. I haven't been the least bit bored. And yes, I have plenty of things to read. But how are we going to get me out?

John looks at the tower and the captain's walk and ginkgo

tree. It shouldn't be too much trouble, he says. Pack some clothes. I'll be back shortly.

While Cornelia moves about her room, opening and closing closet doors and drawers, packing a suitcase, Mother climbs the stairs again, cautiously inserts the key into the door to the captain's walk, unlocks it, sets down the lunch tray, hastily relocks the door and then knocks at Cornelia's adjacent door. My dear, she says, I've put a tray for you on the balcony. I don't mean for you to go hungry. I just want you to think about the consequences of your acts. I just want you to have time to realize what you are doing.

Yes, Mother, Cornelia says, and Mrs. Wright is almost certain she hears a giggle.

Cornelia, this is not a laughing matter, she says.

Cornelia says nothing. On the radio someone is singing "Lili Marlene."

Are you hysterical? Mother says.

Cornelia turns off the radio. No, she says. I was thinking of Rochester's mad wife and how long he had to keep her locked up. But that's no laughing matter, is it? After all, she set fire to the house.

You're clearly in no condition to make a serious decision about your future, Mrs. Wright says.

Cornelia's voice, muffled by the intervening door, sounding deliberately portentous and hollow, follows her mother down the stairwell. 'St. Agnes' Eve,' Cornelia calls to Mother. 'Ah, bitter chill it was. The owl, for all his feathers, was a-cold.'

The child is clearly hysterical, Mrs. Wright said to herself. Should I . . . ? No. . . . No! I'll hold out. I won't call a doctor. (How serious is her blunder? She dares not even ask herself. But now—what can she do? How embarrassing, how humiliating to have to explain it to a doctor.)

Meanwhile Cornelia, who by now was quite hungry, stepped out on the balcony, brought the tray into her room, and ate a hearty lunch.

Within an hour or so John O'Kelly was back with his own suitcase, a length of rope, a piece of light chain, a drill, screws and a screwdriver, and a pulley.

A careful and methodical man, he climbed up the ginkgo tree, carrying his tools in a small bag. He drilled screw holes in the tree trunk and attached the pulley.

Why are we bothering with a pulley? Cornelia said. If you tied the rope to a limb I could just swing hand over hand.

It would be riskier, he said. I thought first about an extension ladder but I couldn't find one long enough. He put the rope through the pulley and tossed one end over to her on the captain's walk. Now, try the banister. Is it sturdy? It won't break under your weight, will it? Are you sure?

No, it won't break. See, here at the corners, it's reinforced. Mama always worried about our falling off.

OK. Now I'm going to throw you the chain, he said. Fasten it around the banister. See the catch there at the end? Now put the end of the rope through a link. That's so it'll slip easily. OK? Now put the end of the rope through your suitcase handle and then coil it up and throw it back to me. Now. Send your suitcase across.

He detached the suitcase and retied the rope. Now, he said, are you afraid? Do you want me to try it? Are your hands strong enough to hang onto the rope while I pull you across?

No, I'm not afraid, she said. No. And yes, of course. I've been climbing trees and swinging on ropes all my life.

All right, then, he said. Let's go.

She climbed over the banister, sat down on the outside ledge, took hold of the rope with both hands, and eased herself off the ledge.

Now she's dangling thirty feet above the yard, high over the yellow carpet of ginkgo leaves. The limbs shake, leaves fall around her in a golden shower, and John draws her steadily across.

Did you bring the license? he says.

Of course.

Below, Mother has heard their voices and now she comes out on the porch. Can the voices possibly be drifting down like the voices of ghosts from the ginkgo tree? She looks up, and there is Cornelia above her head, floating, as it seems at first, or, like a soul in the very moment of being translated to heaven, arms stretched up as if in ecstasy.

Oh, please, Mother says. Oh, please, don't. Wait! Go back. I was hasty. I was. I'll . . . I'll unlock the door.

But it's too late, Mother. Too late to plead. Too late to call the chaplain or the general. Too late even to avoid gossip and scandal. An interested neighbor is standing on her front porch, gaping at this curious spectacle.

THREE

I ever tell you about how me and Nig made up our minds to move to town? Tweet said. It begun on Christmas Eve nineteen and forty-two. By that time we was farming on shares with Mr. Lord. I tell you about that? And we made a good crop that year.

No, Cornelia said. You didn't tell me about that.

Hmm, Tweet said. Well . . . She's begun, but now she can't decide whether to go on or not. There are some things she talks about openly with Cornelia and others that she speaks of guardedly or not at all. It amazed me, for example, to hear her speak so openly of Wayne Jones's outrageous behavior. How could she be sure a white woman would listen tolerantly? The answer, I think, is that she did not care. She had her requirements of herself and of an employer: She *would* speak about certain matters. If she got fired, she got fired. She'd always been able to find a job when she needed one.

On the other hand, she hasn't spoken yet of the sequence of events that led to the loss of her grandfather's farm. I'm not sure it will be through her, even if she knows, that we find out what really happened. She must be angry with herself—ashamed—because she didn't succeed in keeping the land. She is vain—not of her beauty, but of her resourcefulness. And besides, she may think it would be too hard on

Cornelia for her to tell this story. The implications might damage their friendship. Cornelia, after all, didn't steal her land. She may not even believe that, given the opportunity, Cornelia would steal from her, although, hmmm . . .

But a scene pops into my mind that I think must—just because it popped into my mind at this moment—have a bearing on Tweet's reservations (not on either of the reasons I've mentioned, but on other even darker feelings). It's the day after Martin Luther King's assassination. He's dead, murdered, a bloody hole blown through his chest as he stood in innocent conversation on his motel-room balcony not so many miles from the city where Cornelia and Tweet live.

Tweet has not come to work this morning and she has not telephoned. The city is everywhere under a pall of sullen silence. Black children stay home from school. White kitchens are empty. Assembly lines grind to a halt. Garbage is not collected, chickens not picked, trucks not loaded. Cornelia gets into her car and drives through streets where black men stand in hostile clusters on the porches of houses where radios and television sets mutter the news again and again. She is paying a bereavement call. She knows that King's portrait hangs in the place of honor over the mantelpiece in Tweet's living room.

She parks her car, gets out, and walks briskly up the sidewalk toward the stoop. Next door at a window a dark and threatening face appears and disappears. Across the street three men stand silent together. One spits deliberately into the open ditch at his feet. Cornelia, however, sees none of this. She looks neither to left nor to right.

Now she and Tweet are facing each other in the half-open doorway. The face Cornelia sees might be, not Tweet's but Rosa's—older, ravaged, stoic, expressionless, but still, somehow, pulsing, heavy with silence.

Cornelia doesn't think: She's not going to ask me in. She speaks. It's awful, Julia, she says. Awful. I came to tell you . . . She puts her hand on the doorknob, moves the door gently back against the pressure of Tweet's presence, steps in. I'm sorry, she says. On the wall over the mantel, King looks down at them. Tweet cannot nod. She turns away and shakes her head, as if to say, What do *you* know about it? I'm sorry, Cornelia says again. But she dares not reach out, dares not cross the two paces that separate them.

They stand, Cornelia empty-handed (she's come in such haste, she's forgotten her purse), in the middle of the tiny cluttered room, Tweet looking away, staring out the window at the blank gray peeling wall of the house next door. Cornelia looks distractedly around her at overstuffed chairs, a sofa piled with not-yet-folded wash, a glass-topped coffee table littered with ashtrays, old bills, magazines, a Bible, discarded jewelry. There is a barrette, a twisted ropelike circlet in a pin tray, a pair of earrings and matching necklace on top of a stack of magazines. In the chimney opening that once housed a coal grate a gas space heater glows and pulses as if even on this April day there must be a fire against the encroaching chill. The room seems to Cornelia to be airless, as if the heater has sucked in all the available oxygen. The mantel above, like the coffee table, is piled with possessions —boxes of shotgun shells, three shoe boxes stacked on top of each other, strands of Mardi Gras beads and a net bag filled with doubloons that Cornelia remembers bringing back from New Orleans, a green glass vase filled with artificial flowers, photographs of Rosa and of Tweet's stepdaughters, Cynthia and Charlene, at various ages. Cornelia has been in Tweet's house many times, has sat and visited in this living room, but now she gasps at the stifling air, feels the walls closing in on her like the walls in "The Pit and the Pendulum." She stares at the barrette on the coffee table, gleaming like a round gold target, like the bauble a hypnotist uses to subdue his subject's will, under the light from the standing lamp at the end of the sofa.

I'm sorry, she says.

And then, thinking that she may be ill if she doesn't get out into the fresh air, she stumbles out of the house.

But Tweet was talking about Christmas nineteen forty-two, about Mr. Lord, about settling up.

In those days in the South most black people (and some white) farmed on shares with white landowners; Tweet and Nig were farming on quarter shares. That is, Mr. Lord furnished seed and fertilizer and credit at the commissary, and after the crop was sold, Tweet and Nig got a quarter of the money, minus the commissary bill.

He'd sold the crop, Tweet said. We knew that. But he always was slow to settle up. Never would until up in December. He hated to part with money. But now it's come up to the twenty-third. If anybody's going to town, buy shoes, a present for their mama, something to put on the table besides side meat and black-eyed peas, tomorrow was the last day to do it. I been getting madder and madder all week. Nig would say, Now, Tweet, he always settle up. We going to get our money. He ain't never been known not to settle up.

We're sitting around the fire that night, the twenty-third, and Rosa and her kids and her husband are there.

Cornelia knows well enough what Nig's house looked like, like a thousand tenant houses she's driven past all her life: tin-roofed, board and batten sided, three rooms in a row you could shoot a load of buckshot through from front door to back, a chimney between the front and middle rooms and a smaller one at the back, beds and chairs and tables crowded in, wall-to-wall. She knows, because Tweet has told her, that she and Nig and his two daughters shared the house and that Rosa and her husband, back at Sandy Creek and working for Mr. Lord now, lived next door in one exactly like it; and that both yards were crowded in spring and summer with the plants that Rosa loves and has taught Tweet, too, to cherish: ragged robins and four o'clocks and hollyhocks and sunflowers and daffodils and prince's-feathers; daylilies and hydrangeas that Mrs. Lord rooted for them; zinnias and marigolds and a climbing Lady Banksia on the fence and a Paul's Scarlet in the corner. And that behind the houses fig and peach and persimmon trees flourished and the vegetable garden was laid out in neat rows and fenced against the chickens.

But now it is December. The landscape is gray. Only a row of collards and one of turnips show green in the garden. Everyone is inside around the fire.

Tweet goes on with her story: I ain't going to put up with it, I says. No. No way.

You want to lose me my job? Rosa says.

She wouldn't let him fire you, I tell her. Where she's going to find a cook like you closer than Philippi? She won't put herself out to fire you.

It won't do no good, Rosa says. Nothing going to make him hand you your money till he wants to.

Next morning comes, Tweet says. Rosa goes to work. Our house is across the road from Mr. Lord's and I can see everything over there: See his fine brick house, the trim just painted last year, with the carport, so you don't get wet when you come home in the rain, and the barns and tractor sheds set back behind a locust windbreak, so nobody has to look at them, and, a little way off to the south, the pond they keep mainly in case there's a fire the fire department can pump water out of it. On the pond, ducks swimming and four or five geese they keep just for looks, and a boat drawn up on the bank if anybody wants to go fishing.

I'm up early, standing in my front room, looking out the window, and before eight o'clock I see him come out and get in the car and drive off. Maybe he's going to town to get the money—he always pays off in cash. I wait, and along about ten-thirty here he comes back. But he doesn't stop by the carport and ring the big bell—that would be a sign for everybody to come to the house, he's going to settle up.

I've waited long enough. I put on my coat and my old boots that I wear to slop the pigs and cross the road to his house and go around back and knock on the door. Naturally, since it's the kitchen, Rosa answers. She cuts her eyes at

me, shakes her head. Go on home, Tweet, she says, low
voicey. I look past her, see Mrs. Lord at the kitchen table
rolling out cookies—they got a crowd of children and grandchildren coming in. She looks up, says, Come in, Tweet.
Don't stand there letting the cold in, and I come in. I'm
looking at Rosa.

I needs to see Mr. Lord, I say.

Rosa acts like she doesn't hear me, turns around, commences running water in the sink.

Rosa, would you call him? Mrs. Lord says. My hands all
flour. (She's like you, Tweet said. Always polite. Likes to
cook. Makes an excuse if she ax you to wait on her.)

Rosa looks at me like she's gonna cut my throat, goes on
out of the kitchen and in a minute, here he comes. Done
put on his bedroom slippers. Top button of his pants un-
buttoned and his little round belly poking out over his pants.
Got the morning paper in his hand. I know he ain't planning
to go out again no time soon. Well, Tweet, he says, Merry
Christmas. Merry Christmas to you and Nig. What can I do
for you?

How we going to have a merry Christmas, Mr. Lord? I
say. That's what I come over here to ax you.

What's that? He's still smiling. Hitches up his pants,
grinning at me like Santa Claus out of that round, rosy-
cheek baby face. He's fat on Rosa's cooking, scalp shiny,
like he's so rich inside, oil pops out of his head.

Mrs. Lord don't even look up. She's got her mind on the
cookies, all cut out in stars and trees and Santa Clauses for
the kids to decorate. She crosses between us like we ain't
there, slides the tray in the oven, looking pleased with
herself.

I say it again: How me and Nig or anybody else going to
have a merry Christmas when you ain't settle up? How we
going to buy us a turkey? What we going to give one another
for presents—a stick of stove wood? What we going to use
for wrapping paper?

Now, Tweet, he says, you got credit at the commissary. You know that.

Ain't no turkeys at the commissary, I say. And I might want to buy my presents at Sears and Roebuck instead of the commissary.

Business complicated this year, he says. Takes a while to get everything straight.

I done run out of time, Mr. Lord, I say. I want me and Nig's money.

He looks at me and shakes his head. Ain't got no money yet, he says. You can't get blood out of a turnip.

Rosa's still got the water running, like she's trying to wash us all down the drain. She turns it off, dries her hands. You hush up and go on home, Tweet, she says.

I'm standing there trembling. Seems like the air has got heavy. Like I'm inside a drum, somebody pounding on the outside until my head's about to bust.

Tweet was silent a moment. She rubbed the soft vulnerable spot behind her ear where the jawbone hinges to the skull, where an ice pick will slip in without resistance and kill a man. Somebody need to kill him, she said thoughtfully. I would've done it, if I could get away with it.

Cornelia shook her head, *no*. She wants to leave, not to hear this. Maybe John needs her downtown. But she stays, listens.

Yes, Tweet said. I'd like to've seen the blood come busting out of that fat belly after I stuck him. She raised her voice, as if to make sure Cornelia heard her. I would have stuck an ice pick in his belly, behind his ear, she said.

Julia, you don't mean that. Not really.

Tweet shrugged. Now I'm walking home, she said. It's beginning to snow. Flakes float down, melt on my face. Seems like I take big steps. I step over the road with one giant step. From over by the barn I hear Nig calling. Tweet, he's saying. Now, Tweet, Calm down, Tweet. Where'd he come from? Rosa must've called him. But I *am* calm. I'm at our house now and I go to the kindling barrel on the porch beside the firewood, all stack neat against the wall. On the wall above the barrel, the hatchet hanging on two nails. On the window sill the file. Nig keeps all his tools right—the hatchet's got a good edge. I take it down and go in the kitchen and get me a handful of chicken feed out of the sack and put it in my pocket. Then I step over the road again and I'm in the middle of the yard hollering.

Come on out, Mr. Lord, I say. Come out. I got anything to do with it, me and Nig going to have us a Christmas dinner.

I see Rosa in the kitchen window. She's like she always is when people get mad. She's gone way in the back of her head, who knows what's back there, won't come out. Mrs. Lord peeping over her shoulder, sees me and that hatchet and disappears like she thinks I'm coming in after her.

Mr. Lord comes out the kitchen door, rosy cheeks, still in his bedroom slippers, holding up his pants. He don't step down off the porch. Now what you want, Tweet? he says.

I'm going to get me a goose for me and Nig's Christmas dinner, I say. I always been partial to goose. Dark meat—but it's got a good flavor.

Goose? he says, like he ain't never heard the word.

Yeah, get me a goose. I start across the yard towards the pond. Geese and ducks see me coming, start paddling in towards the bank: Quawk, quawk!

Now, Tweet, he says, sticks his paper under his arm, commences to button his pants. You settle down, you hear, he says. Ain't no sense in this.

I don't say a word.

Tweet, he hollers, I'm going to call Nig. He looks like that little Frenchman ain't but nine days old. Stuck his finger in a crawdad hole. (You know the song?)

Don't need to call him, I holler back. Look over yonder by the barn, peeping out from behind them locust trees. He's over there, ain't he? Because I knew he had been

104

watching the whole thing. So Nig, when he knows Mr. Lord sees him, he starts on across the yard towards me.

Now, Tweet, he says. You needs to come on home.

But I keep walking. Don't mess with me, Nigger. I'm going to get me this goose or know why.

He stops. All of them scared of my hatchet.

I stand there by the pond and start clucking and them fool ducks and geese come swimming up and I take the corn and scatter it. I've fed them plenty of times, they know me well enough to come up close. And when the fattest of the young ones waddles up and gets near to my feet, I reach down, grab her by the neck, squawking, flapping her wings, lay her against a stump, and Whack! she's dead before she knows what grabbed her.

I'm all over blood, and she's flapping and flopping like she's still alive, blood spouting out of her neck, head laying on the ground with the bill opening and shutting like she's still squawking. Mr. Lord has done retreated into the kitchen, looking out the door.

Now, Tweet, he says. You more than welcome to that goose. You take her home and enjoy her, you hear me? Nig, you take Tweet on home. She don't hardly know what she's saying, much less what she's doing.

But Nig stays a safe way off. He knows better than to mess with me.

Tomorrow I'm coming back, I say. Get me a pig.

I didn't have nothing like that in mind, of course, Tweet said. We got pigs of our own.

But that was the end of the country for Nig and me. I made up my mind we'd go to town soon as he settled up, and we went. Nig was scared to go. Everybody said, ain't no work in town. Mr. Lord said, Nig don't know how to do nothing but farm. You and him be back before planting time, begging for a crop. And I'm going to give it to you. Not for you, Tweet. But Nig's a good worker.

Nig found him a job at the Gypsum Company before

January was out and he's been working there ever since. Slack times he never gets laid off like most. It's true he still works like a nigger. They call him sometimes, two, three o'clock in the morning to take a shift, they know he'll always get up and come. He'll work in the cyclone without complaint, breathe that smoke when the trash catches fire, come home with his skin all full of gypsum splinters like a million little bitty cockleburs, I'll spend an hour helping him scrub and picking them damn splinters out with the tweezers.

She paused here, as if expecting a comment from Cornelia, but Cornelia said nothing. Like Mrs. Lord she was absorbed in the task at hand—stirring, rolling, turning, cutting out.

One of these days, they don't do right by him, they better look out, Tweet said. I'm liable to take my pocketful of corn, go down there, chop their goose's head off.

But what happened after Grandfather died? Why, in nineteen forty-one, were Tweet and Nig sharecropping for Mr. Lord instead of working their own land? That's the story Tweet can scarcely bring herself to tell.

Do you recall her saying that Grandfather's land fit into Mr. Lord's place like a slice out of a pie? That he would have loved to straighten out his line? If you look at a map of the county, you'll see why straightening out a line mattered to Mr. Lord. That forty-acre piece of pie lay between him and the only bridge across Sandy Creek within ten miles of his house. And not only did he have to cross the creek to get to town, but a part of his place was on the other side. This inconvenience had been brought about by the nineteen twenty-seven flood, when a crevasse in the nearby Mississippi River levee had washed out the old bridge and changed the course of the creek. After the flood, the new bridge and road (whose location were influenced by the superior power of other landowners in the area) were built to the north of Grandfather's farm instead of to the south.

Every time a mule or a man on a tractor crossed the creek from Mr. Lord's barns and sheds and his house on one side to his fields on the other, he had to go a mile out of the way, around that hardheaded old man—of whom Mr. Lord thought from winter to winter: Well, he won't last another year, and as soon as he's dead, the land should be up for grabs.

Land, incidentally, which would not only eliminate this intolerable inconvenience, but which was prime sandy loam, fine cotton land, worth, even in nineteen thirty-six or thirty-seven, when the Depression was just beginning to lift, as much as two hundred and fifty dollars an acre.

Consider that in Mr. Lord's view Grandfather would have been mismanaging his farm, wasting in garden and pasture and woodlot acreage that should be in cotton, nothing but cotton. Mr. Lord was the son of a thrifty Presbyterian Scots mother, and he knew his Bible. When he considered Grandfather's farming practices, he thought undoubtedly of the parable of the talents. *The* Lord, Mr. Lord's Lord, would not want land to continue in the possession of the kind of people who buried their talents as Grandfather had. And as for Julius—never! Everybody in the north end of the county knew Julius was a profligate who had gone off to Akron and abandoned his family, an irresponsible man—a bad nigger.

I don't think Mr. Lord wasted any time after the old man's death. To begin with, he would have assumed there was no will. Grandfather, after all, was illiterate and very likely no truster of lawyers. So Julius would be the heir. And he would undoubtedly be happy to sell, would perhaps have only a hazy idea of the land's value. Besides, Mr. Lord might say to himself, when you considered how many improvements would have to be made to get in shape for new tenants and spring planting, the land wasn't really as valuable as it might appear to be. And, another thing, a house would have to be built—although maybe he could move that abandoned shack over from the west sixty.

So he went looking for Tweet or Rosa (combination business and bereavement call) to get Julius's address; and he learned that there was a will and that Tweet, not Julius, was the heir.

I see Tweet standing in the front room of Nig's little house. Mr. Lord is facing her with his hat in his hand and Nig's two girls lean timidly against Tweet's flanks and peer out in curiosity at this unheard-of visit from the man.

Well, Tweet. He looks down at the children and around the crowded room. I started looking for you, I sure wasn't expecting to find you here, he says. You bit off a hunk, ain't you? You planning on raising up Nig's girls? Ain't nothing but a child yourself.

Yes, sir, Tweet says. I expect I'm up to it.

You don't want to be hasty, he says. After all, you're still grieving over your grandpa. Your judgment ain't so good.

Well. Tweet, too, is master of the noncommital *Well.*

I hope you won't get yourself married here in too much of a hurry, Mr. Lord says. You got to consider . . .

Nig and me already married, Mr. Lord, Tweet says. Got married Sunday a week ago.

Well, now, he says. Well, now, turning his hat around in his hands.

After that visit, Mr. Lord sat on his front porch and considered the matter. He liked the challenge of a puzzle, and he held the pieces of this one and examined them, looking for the places where they would lock into each other. There was the will. And there was Tweet—not a child subject to parents as he had expected her to be; rather a married woman with a new status and a new protector. But married to Nig, a quiet man, averse to trouble. And there was Julius—disinherited.

The next time he called on Tweet, he came just at dusk when he knew Nig was likely to be home and suggested to the two of them that Tweet might want to sell her land.

Tweet said, no, she and Nig meant to farm it.

Well, he said, but, Nig, you farming for me. You ain't got time to farm Tweet's land and mine, too.

Tweet, her and the girls'll do most of the work, Nig said. She's going to get James, lives down the road, to break it up for her. And I can give her a hand when I ain't too busy.

I got to have somebody on this land can farm full-time, Mr. Lord said. Maybe y'all ought to give this place up, just work Tweet's land. I got plenty would like to take your place.

There was, of course, no longer a house on Tweet's land.

No, sir, Mr. Lord, Nig said. I ain't going to neglect your crop.

Me and the girls can do it, Tweet said. Me and my grandpa was doing it before. And Rosa say she'll come help me some.

Y'all ought to consider selling, Mr. Lord said. Wouldn't be so bad to have a little cash money, would it? Think it over.

He left it at that for the moment. But after another visit to Tweet convinced him of her intransigence, he went in to the courthouse and took a look at the will. He came home delighted at an unforeseen stroke of luck. The old man had made the will only days before his death. Nobody nearly a hundred years old should be making a will to disinherit his only son. But, another consideration, the will had been made by Percy Quinn, who was a perfectly competent lawyer, and it looked OK.

He examined these new pieces in his puzzle and considered how to fit them neatly against the others. When the rates came on that night, he did something so extravagant it offended his deepest instincts. He called Julius on the long-distance telephone. Spendthrift nigger. Whoever heard of a nigger with a telephone? Never mind that it was in the name of his wife's beauty shop. It was just another indication of Julius's bad character.

But when he got Julius on the phone, he spoke with deep sympathy. He'd been shocked when he heard about the will, he said. It was a hard thing to have to say about a man's daughter, he went on, his voice fading and rising along the crackling long-distance telephone lines, but wasn't it likely that Nig and Tweet had influenced the old man to make the will? Why else in the world decide to make a will after a hundred years of not having one? Did Julius know about undue influence? About how to go about breaking an unfair will? I'm only saying this, he said, because I've always had an interest in your family, you know. Your family and my family been living side by side for many a year.

And Julius said, You so right, Mr. Lord. Ain't it a fact.

I can't think your daddy meant to do that to you. Always spoke well of you to me.

Yeah, Julius said. Me and Daddy was very close. I was just down there seeing after him.

Besides, Mr. Lord said, I worry about Nig taking advantage of Tweet. I hate to say it, but the truth is he's got a name around here for chasing the women.

Ain't it the truth, Julius said. And Tweet nothing but a child. Can't look out after herself.

Well, I don't want to interfere with your business, but there's a way you could look after Tweet, if you feel like it's the right thing to do. . . .

The static swelled to a crescendo of pops and crackles and Julius said, How's that Mr. Lord? I ain't hearing you so good.

I say, you can look out for her and yourself, too, if you feel like it's the right thing to do.

Yes, sir, that's exactly what I'd like to do—look out after us both, Julius said.

You could break the will, see, Mr. Lord said. It wouldn't be hard to do because of him being so old. You understand me? He probably wasn't right in his head. You see what I mean?

He couldn't see nothing at all, Julius said. Getting deaf, too. Acted like he was asleep most of the time.

Asleep, Mr. Lord said. Yeah, he was undoubtedly weakening. And died not a week after he made that will. Ain't that the way it went?

That's right. Sooner than that.

If you broke the will, you could sell the place, Mr. Lord said. Take care of the money for Tweet. Invest it for the both of you.

What's that?

You could put it in a savings account, Mr. Lord said.

I could do that, couldn't I? Julius said.

Well, if you want me to, I can look into it for you.

There was a long crackling silence on the line while Julius considered Mr. Lord's interest in his and Tweet's welfare.

I wouldn't mind taking the place off your hands, Mr. Lord said. I don't *need* it, far as that goes, but I wouldn't mind. Ain't nobody else going to be interested in it, is there? Since I own on three sides of it.

Yes, sir, Julius said. You look into it for me. I'd appreciate that.

What Mr. Lord looked into first was the office of Percy Quinn, attorney-at-law and vice president of the Farmers' Bank and Trust Company.

It was a matter of course in those days, when decisions were to be made about the affairs of black people, for the legal system to take into account the judgment of reliable white men. A word dropped at a dinner party, over cards at the Elysian Club, or over a game of golf at the country club made everyone's interest and the interest of justice clear. Mr. Lord did his banking at Farmers' Trust and he and Percy Quinn were old friends. And Percy, of course, had gone to the state university law school, had known the judge in whose court the estate would be probated since they'd been boys together.

Keep in mind that no great sum of money was involved. It was true, as Mr. Lord said, that people in that end of the county were not interested in Tweet's land, surrounded as it was by his. And such transactions, through which small farms owned by black people became part of larger farms owned by white people, were routine—to everyone's advantage. The land would be more economical to work and the Negroes could move to Chicago. That was what most of them wanted to do, anyhow, wasn't it?

The only delicate part of this negotiation involved the implicit attack on Percy Quinn's judgment of the old man's state of mind at the time he made the will.

Probity. The probity of a lawyer is a serious matter. The probity of a gentlemanly southern lawyer. I can't help thinking of it as a stiffish appendage (even the sound: probe-ity), a cherished appendage, sensitive to the touch, subject to shock, overheating, and the shriveling effects of chill; potent in the making and ruin of lives.

So Percy Quinn would guard his probity and Mr. Lord, to accomplish his ends, would have to consider it.

But then—is probity really involved when one is dealing with the affairs of nigras? Can't one lie to a nigra in the same way one lies to a woman or a child—because it's in his interest? Who would dream of telling a child the truth about Santa Claus, a wife the truth about one's necessary sexual arrangements, a nigra the truth about—anything? Nigras, like children and women, simply have to be managed for their own good.

So it may be that Mr. Lord could take Percy's complaisance for granted, could simply say the few words of reassurance that would make him comfortable: pass along his judgment on Nig, the fact of Tweet's youth and vulnerability, the assurance that money could be put aside by

Julius for Tweet—a measure that Mr. Lord might even intend to insist on.

Everything would be settled out of court.

So Mr. Lord hired a lawyer to contest the will for Julius. The probate was necessarily put off from one term of court to the next.

Did Tweet and Nig know what was going on in the courthouse? Not, one guesses, as much as would have been useful to them.

There it stood, the courthouse, an impenetrable keep, a crenelated monument to eighteen-nineties architecture, mustard-colored, rusticated limestone towers, echoing halls with sawdusty floors, walnut-paneled courtrooms and warrens of offices, rooms full of filing cabinets and shelves piled high with ledgers, records of ancient wills, licenses, and land transactions. Neither Tweet nor Nig had ever been inside that stronghold. They had not one tenuous connection with that legal system. No—that's not quite true. They had been born and they had gone to the circuit clerk's office and bought a marriage license. Records of their births and continuing existence had passed through the courthouse on the way to the state capital.

And in practical terms, with regard to Grandfather's will, it's a fact that such papers as might come along to Tweet from the courthouse would have come to a row of pigeonholes in Mr. Lord's commissary, for he was by default the Sandy Creek postmaster, and he could easily have filed away in his safe or destroyed what he didn't care to pass on to Tweet.

Are you aware that fortunes have been made everywhere in the United States (are still being made) simply by paying certain taxes which illiterate or careless landowners are unaware that they owe? That ownership of land is quietly transferred every year to people who pay the taxes on other people's land? And as for wills, they are not documents that very poor people either know or care much about. Wills and the processing of wills are for the purpose of safeguarding

113

wealth and making money for lawyers. The question of who gets the bedstead, the mule, and the middle buster is settled in other ways.

It was probably the case, though, that Mr. Lord dared not hold up the communication from Percy Quinn to Tweet, asking her to come in to his office. He may even have steamed the letter open and then passed it along, confident that Percy would look after things in a fair and equitable way.

And Percy did. He explained to Tweet that, given her grandfather's age and state of health, the will was indefensible.

I just didn't have any idea your father would contest, he said. After all, the two of you were sitting right here in the office with him when he made the will. I assumed your daddy thought it was OK.

No, Tweet said. He didn't think nothing of the kind. It was against him. My grandpa meant it to be against him.

And so the will was broken.

Tweet, after all, does tell this story of loss to Cornelia. She may not want to think about it, but at last she can't resist talking about it, can't resist giving the gift of Percy Quinn to Cornelia, can't resist watching Cornelia visualize that pleasant office in the secluded purlieus of the Farmers' Bank where all the decisions—all the important decisions—are made.

There he is, sitting behind the gigantic walnut desk left him by his grandfather, who was a United States senator. The letters S.O.B. are stamped into the brass fittings on the drawers and claw feet—*Senate Office Building*, those letters stand for. Few men outside the chambers of true power possess such a desk. Percy is dwarfed by his, seems to sit behind it as behind a barricade. His thin sandy hair stands up in cowlicks like Dagwood's, his long arms and his big-chinned face are gaunt.

Always did have poor digestion, Tweet said to Cornelia. I know the lady cooks for them and she says he don't eat enough to keep a bird alive.

I told him the whole thing, she said. About Julius and Claree coming and about the dancing and the fire and the washstand on the porch. He just looked at me.

She shrugged. I never thought it would make no difference, she said, and it didn't. He says Tweet, you got to have imagined that. You just a child. You dreamed it.

Then I say to myself: Mr. Lord, he's bound to be in on this. No way Julius is going to think about hiring a lawyer. He's like me, hasn't never heard of such a thing as breaking a will. And I know, of course, that he (Mr. Lord, I mean) has been after my grandpa ever since the flood to sell him the land. Not to mention, like I told you, he come by to see me right off and tried to get it from me. So he's got to've put Julius up to it.

But if Julius is going to sell the land, I say to myself, why shouldn't he sell it to me instead of Mr. Lord? Because I had the money. I had the bee tree.

I knew Julius was in the county. Hadn't seen him, but peoples carried word back from town one day they'd seen him on Blaze Street, and the next day James told Nig he seen him in the commissary. So I got two things to do. I got to get the money from the tree and I got to make him an offer before he settles his arrangement with Mr. Lord. Money first.

Yes, she said, Julius has come down to see about it. But Mr. Quinn hasn't told me he's here.

Maybe he didn't know, Cornelia said.

Come to find out, Tweet said, lawyers can settle all that kind of business without you or me ever going through the courthouse door. Did you know that? Only time you need to go through the door is when it's time to take em some money for one thing or another—taxes or a license.

You remember I told my grandpa that day when he was showing me the bee tree that I couldn't go down in the cypress brake without him? That I'd be too scared? But I went.

The day after I hear Julius is in town, when Nig gets ready to go to the field, chopping cotton, I tell him I ain't feeling so good, I'm going to stay home and lay down. He starts on out the door and before he's gone seems like my mind tells me, says: You got to trust Nig. You going through your life trusting nobody? What's the use in living thataway? And so I speak up and say, Nig, I'm lying. I ain't sick. He looks at me a while, doesn't say nothing. Well, I say, my grandpa left some money hid over on his place and I got to go get it. I'm telling you about it. Before Julius sell that land to Mr. Lord, I got to get my money.

I ain't stopping you, is I? he says. Go on and git it.

I'm taking the girls with me for company, I say. Scared to go by myself.

Them girls need to be helping me chop, he says.

Nig, where it is, I'm scared to go back there by myself.

Well, take Cynthia, he says. Leave Charlene with me.

Cynthia's ten years old, old enough to be company for me, and she and I already got to liking one another well enough during the months me and Nig been married—Charlene and I, too, for that matter, but she's younger. I reckon it was hard on the girls after their mama died, Nig bringing home one woman or another. They're glad he got married to me.

So, anyhow, we go, walking over to my grandpa's place, about a mile down the road. Stop in the turnrow a minute and I tell Cynthia this is the place my grandpa died. You don't need to be scared of him, I say. I wasn't never when he was alive.

But he don't speak to us. Silent.

We get the bee smoker out of the barn and hats and nets

and gloves like you got to have and while we're doing it, I tell her where we're going. Then we pick up a couple of poles and dig some baits, making like we might go fishing. Down by the slough, we turn over the dugout my grandpa chopped out of a cypress log a million years ago, and it takes all us strength to push it into the water.

It's June, water all backed up in the brake from Sandy Creek. Still and dark. Tree trunks standing up straight and black, quiet all around except for the birds, Tweet said. Redwing blackbirds everywhere, gurgling like they do in the fringe willows and sycamores along the bank, and you can hear the water thrush far down in the shadiest places, and the orioles. My grandpa name the birds for me and teach me to hear their calls and now seems like they're a comfort to me, and I point to them for Cynthia and tell her how to listen for this one and that one.

Lemme paddle, she says. I want to paddle. Cynthia's lively, always wants to be doing something. I give her the paddle, point the way.

She looks at me, looks at the water, the dark cypress, and then she says, I'm scared, Tweet.

Me, too, I say. We could sing. And we commence singing.

We're singing, I'm on my way to Zion and I feel like going on. . . Oh I love that song the way Mahalia sings it. Every time I hear her, reminds me of the bee tree.

So, anyhow, I bait a hook, drop it in the water for show, look to see if they's anybody around and there ain't. Cynthia paddles the boat up inside the tree like I show her and we put on the nets and tie our pants legs tight and our sleeves shut and we're still singing, looking at each other in them big hats and gloves, giggling. She braces the dugout against the inside of the tree as good as she can and I light the smoker and climb up them steps my grandpa had nail to the tree.

I'm dwelling in the mountains, I'm in sight of Canaan land, she's singing, and we commence giggling and forget all about the devil.

When the bees had settle down quiet, I pull the pipes out of the straps and come on down. We look out, don't see nobody, take off our bee outfits and paddle into the slough.

I told Cynthia this is a secret between her and Charlene and Nig and me and we mustn't let on about it to a living soul; and then we took the pipes and went on home. Pulled out all that sticky money and lick the honey off our fingers and then we dumped it in a washtub and washed it and counted it and it was four thousand and thirteen dollars.

More, Tweet said, a lot more than I dreamed it could be. And it's mine.

Sometimes, she said, it seems like money is more than money, and that's the way that sweet sticky money seem to me. I think about my grandpa, all the years he walks down the furrow behind one mule after another, throwing out his stiff leg to one side, snapping the reins with his little three-finger hand, got to be a claw time I first seen it to notice—singing, singing: Be so long till the sun go down—and the money now is all I got left of him. I'm going to take it and buy the land off Julius, never thought one minute about doing anything else. So I send Nig to find him—tell him I'll buy the land, I've got some money—and he finds him in town down on Blaze Street and tells him.

He's standing on the corner of Blaze and Quinn out in front of the cafe passing the time when Nig finds him, and Nig says he stares at him a minute, and then without blinking twice, he says, If Tweet's got money, it must be the old man's money and it belong to *me*.

No, Nig, says, right off. It's my money.

And Julius says, Yeah? Stands there in that Stetson hat and them viney boots, grins at Nig. Got that evil smile, could be Stagger Lee.

How you going to prove it ain't mine? Nig says.

Julius don't answer, but no doubt he's already thinking about how he's going to get his hands on it. All he says is, How much she's offering? and Nig tells him we'll give him seventy-five an acre. That seem like a lot to me, considering

118

ain't but thirty acres good cropland, the other ten in that slough alongside Sandy Creek. Well, he says, I'll think about it. So I reckon then he goes to find out what Mr. Lord is offering, see can he jack him up.

He comes up to the creek the next day, says Mr. Lord offered him ninety. I say, OK, I'll go a hundred.

Tweet, he says, you know the man's going to get this land if he wants it. No way you can outbid him. And the fact is, I don't believe ya'll got the money to buy it at a hundred. I ain't seen it.

I ain't got it where you can get at it, I say, but I got it. Nig's standing right there with me out in front of the house, the three of us. I will say, Nig backed me up the whole way.

Looka here, Julius says. We could do this. You could say you'll pay one twenty-five—whether you got it or not—and then he'll go to one thirty-five, and I could sell it to him and you and me split the difference. You got seven hundred dollars for yourself that way.

I looked at him a while. If I could've killed him then, I would. I'll give you a hundred an acre, I said again. You don't have to go back to him at all.

So he sold it to Mr. Lord, the land, the barn, the tools and all. We'd already took the mule and the chickens down to Nig's and he never got them. Nor the bee smoker either. Me and Cynthia had brought that home with us when we robbed the bee tree.

I heard the news at the commissary, Tweet said. It's Saturday. Nig and the girls gone to town and I'm down there buying meal, and Mr. Lord himself tells me. He's paying off choppers for the week and he stops counting money to tell me. Your daddy's done sold me his land and gone, Tweet, he says. It doesn't matter to him to talk about my business out in public like that.

I had in my mind, he says, to look after your interest in that sale. Maybe get Julius to put up some of his money for you. But you and Nig mess around here, run the price up, and that makes me feel bad. You ain't done right in this whole thing, Tweet, he says.

I say, He's gone?

Yeah, gone back to Akron. Told it around to everybody here how Nig wanted to buy that land, offered him a hundred an acre for it. How come Nig's got all that money? I never seen him when he had the price of a pint of corn liquor.

I got to go, Mr. Lord, I say, and I get my bag of meal and take off back to the house, fast as I can.

It wasn't Julius I was scared of. I reckon I figured he'd be so busy spending Mr. Lord's money, it would be a long time before he thought about me and mine again. I was just thinking how he had told it all around and how Mr. Lord announced it to the whole store that Nig and me had money. I knew I needed to get it to a safe place from anybody might come looking for it.

But that's not the way it went. Wasn't other people. It was him. He wanted it all. No doubt he said to himself over and over how the money belong to him. He broke the will, didn't he?

Yeah, Tweet said again, seems like that money wasn't money, it's something else: the power of my grandpa.

So I go straight home, thinking all the way. Well, I say to myself, bee tree ain't all that bad a place. Everybody's got bee trees—including Nig. I get the pipes and roll the money up and put it in, and then I head across the woodlot behind the house towards where I know there's a bee tree. I'm carrying the smoker and the nets and all, which me and Cynthia had brought back with us from my grandpa's barn. But when I get down to where I remember seeing bees coming in and out of a hole in a pecan tree, I see the hole is higher than I thought.

It's quiet everywhere, far as I can see in all directions, not a soul moving, Tweet said. That is, far as people are concerned, it's quiet. Saturday afternoon and I know just about everybody's in town. But the woodlot is buzzing, like

120

every place buzzes in June—horseflies and mosquitoes humming, bumbly bees and honeybees, dirt daubers, waspies, hornets everywhere tending to their business. Far off I hear James's jackass hee-hawing like he's announcing the end of the world; house wrens going tootle-a-tootle-a, gander down on the pond going Quawk, quawk. But all those noises make me feel easy. It's only people I'm concern about.

I set my smoker on a stump, push those pipes up under a log not far from the bee tree and head back to the barn to get the ladder.

Well, when I come out, start towards the woodlot, I see somebody moving down there. It's OK, I think, my pipes up under the log, couldn't be safer, all I'm doing is robbing the bee tree. But still, where did they come from? I walk along, quiet as I can, cautious, carrying the ladder, and in a minute I see it's him—Julius. He must've been waiting for me to come back, watching from behind one of the trees in the woodlot. Now his back is to me and he's bending over the log where I put the pipes. I lay the ladder down, run in the house, grab Nig's shotgun off the wall and I'm back in the woodlot almost before he's straightened up. I'm not thinking —just run, grab, run. I know it's loaded—always is. And when I get there, he's standing in the middle of the woodlot and he's pulled the money—mostly it's in hundred dollar bills, with some fifties and tens and twenties—out of the little pipe, and the long pipe is laying on the ground beside him.

Seem like, just like people tell you about a wreck or about drowning, everything happens very slow. I see everything like it's a picture, every leaf and blade of grass painted, still and green. There's the log on the ground, and he's got one foot on it, looking at the piece of pipe and the money in his hand. He can't believe his eyes. I see the curly gray hair springing up strong and the scar on his cheek and the muscles in his arms—he's got on a black tee shirt and jeans. I see his gold tooth shine. Bees coming in and out, in and out of the bee tree. A dragonfly lights on the pipe, like they do on the tip of your fishing pole sometimes—people say that means you ain't going to have any luck fishing that day. Behind him a low branchy young oak tree, and above his head, about twenty feet up, hanging from a limb of the oak tree, a hornets' nest, size of a basketball or bigger. Hornets drifting in and out.

I got a gun, Julius, I holler at him. I never called him daddy out loud or in my mind after I seen the washstand. Put that pipe down, I holler. Lay that money on the ground.

He looks up, sees me, busts out laughing. This mine, Tweet, he says. Mine. I ain't even stealing it.

I'm maybe fifty yards off and I keep my distance.

Put it down, I say again. You hear me? Get off me and Nig's place and don't come back.

He laughs again. He's not even scared. You ain't gonna shoot me, honey, he says. You know you wouldn't shoot nobody. He leans down and picks up the other pipe.

That's when I shot into the hornets' nest. It's an old double-barrel twelve-gauge shotgun I've got, loaded with number six shot and I line up the sights and aim at that big basketball and shoot and it kicks me in the shoulder, almost knocks me down. He's still laughing, but I see the nest jump and swing.

Haw! he hollers. You can't hit the side of a barn, honey.

And I shoot again and them hornets are boiling out of the nest and the first one stings him and then the next and he slaps his arm and his neck and then he yells and drops the pipes and the money flies everywhere and he takes off across the woodlot with the cloud of them all around him.

I went up to the house and got a pocketful of shells, Tweet said, and then I come on back to the woodlot and sat down and waited. I doubted he would be coming back. Heard a splashing noise—I reckon he's in the cow pond. Maybe he'll drown, I think. Would've been glad to see him die. And them hornets ain't fixing to give up on him just because he's in the water. Maybe they'll sting him to death. They been known to kill a man—my grandpa told me that. I think about him laying in the water dead with the hornets crawling over him, still stinging him. Yeah. Still stinging him.

So after a while, Tweet said, when things settle down in the hornets' nest, I pick up all the money and take it on back to the barn and find a place to hide it. I keep the gun by me and when Nig gets home, I set the girls to fixing supper and tell Nig what happened and me and him go down to see if Julius is still there.

We see where he drug hisself out of the pond and head for the road, she said, and we didn't look no further. Afterwards I heard he made it to the commissary, crawling. She laughed. Head swole up big as a pumpkin and knotty —you know them knotty gourds? Eyes swole shut. They took him to town to the Colored King's Daughters—only hospital colored could go to then. And you know what that was like. I wouldn't wish it on a dog.

Tweet's laughter is filled with pure delight. He never did get completely over it, she said.

FOUR

Do you remember when I wrote, early on, that Cornelia was like a dancer, a skier—skimming over the surface of her life as if it were a polished floor or a calm summer lake? For twenty-five years now she's managed to fly across the steely water under the bright sky—although sometimes, fleetingly, rising early from a forgotten nightmare, she may have thought (but only for a moment) that the flight was an escape.

When she first gets up into a silent world, when she leaves the bed where all night long she's lain against the throb of John's warm side, felt the rhythm of his breath against her cheek, his heart against her hand, she shudders. She is alone in a cocoon of dead silence. Outside her window, leaves move, but she cannot hear the wind. On the clock, the second hand clicks around the dial; in the next room, the children may be stirring, chattering. But she cannot hear the tick, cannot hear their voices. Like an LSD flash opening forward instead of backward, she sees for an instant a dead, a soundless future through which she drifts, alone. Where is John? She reaches back, touches him once more. Then she takes up her earpiece and fits it in her ear, snaps the switch, throws on her robe, begins to think of breakfast and tick off scheduled appointments at the bookstore—she begins to ski.

Oh, there have been tumbles, of course, over the years —crises in the lives of children and parents; wrecked cars and broken bones, an emergency appendectomy, the death of a mother whom, as she had told John uneasily, she'd never loved as she knew she should (I don't know why, she said. I just didn't. It's like I don't know how to love anybody but you and the children.) and at whose death she felt more guilt than grief. But, in a time when speed and reds and Quaaludes were already the stuff of parents' nightmares, the two children had managed to get through adolescence to the ages of twenty-four and twenty-two without burning up their brains or going to prison. There had not been a pregnant girlfriend for the boy or an unwanted pregnancy for the girl. No one had gone over to the Moonies or taken up Scientology. Vietnam? Not yet, anyhow.

They are lovely, *safe* young people—straight backs, straight teeth, straight A's.

Andrew has his mother's shining chestnut hair and his father's high wide Celtic cheekbones and marvelously joined and coordinated body, compact and muscular. At ten he was a sought-after first baseman, a switch-hitter with the highest average in the league. At fifteen a streak of his father's solitariness didn't keep him from being sought out by the girls his age. At seventeen John taught him to fly. (No need to learn, as John had, to fly too low to leave a contrail, no need to weave and watch for death in every quarter.)

Sarah, too, is handsome, and she did not, at least to Cornelia's knowledge, suffer the dreadful pangs of awkward adolescence, had a more-than-adequate number of suitors and friends. True, when she was called to supper she often looked up from her book with the drowned inward stare of absorption that Cornelia knew from her own childhood, but she always came to the table without a murmur. During her sophomore college year she dove into a marijuana fog from which she didn't surface for months, but then she decided that she wanted to live in another way. In any case, she had not told her mother the truth, had invented a plausible love affair and a broken heart to explain why all the A's dropped that year to D's and I's. And now she has moved safely on to graduate school.

But the marijuana fog was not the first thing Sarah concealed from her mother. She has, in fact (and this is true of Andrew, too), never told Cornelia much about her life—never.

Why is it that Tweet is the only one who raises her voice and tells Cornelia what is really going on? Tweet, to whom Cornelia listens so absently, her attention on folding in the whites, fluting the crust.

It's not just because Cornelia rules her household with consistent and, it appears, successful power; perhaps it's a quality in her love that keeps John and her children silent, a quality—is it expectation or fear?—as binding as blackmail or weakness or cruelty.

Cornelia is adept at creating imaginary people and imaginary lives. Her children, her husband, her closest friends, all are imaginary people. With her expectations she tempts them to be perfect (Yes, they will be perfect. She will brook no flaw in her kingdom.) and then, together, she and they create the characters she requires. How can anyone resist the temptation to perfection? So it is that everyone gives back her shining, soft-edged vision of him. Politicians may be venal, priests lecherous, other people's parents indifferent or sadistic, their lovers unfaithful, their children incorrigible, but these people live someplace else, beyond mountains and oceans, far from Cornelia's ordered world.

And John? What about John? What does he tell Cornelia?

Still, after twenty-five years, he holds her in his arms and tells her that he loves her. He has not tired of her long lovely body that responds so readily to his, that seems to him all the dearer for the stretch marks that record the travail of his children's births. He tells her how, when he was weaving through the skies over Europe, shifting, shifting, looking for death in every quarter of the sky, never sure

129

he'd live to land his plane, still, somewhere in the back of his mind, even though he didn't yet know her, she was there. He's an Irishman after all.

He speaks of his childhood, of his parents, receded now, as it seems, into what might almost be a dream. Occasionally they talk of his brothers and sisters, but they are scattered and he seldom sees them. They talk, of course, of Cornelia's brother, of their friends, of their business and of the children. But John is careful, too.

He knows, in fact, the true reason why Sarah's grades dropped that second year in college. He knows of certain adolescent episodes in Andrew's life of which Cornelia is unaware. One, for example, involves the theft and surreptitious return of a car and a narrow escape from . . .

But he doesn't tell Cornelia.

In some families these conspiracies grow up without the exchange of a word or a glance. The conspirators, although they may not ask what buried fears and hatreds must be whited over with such heavy paint, know well enough how complicated their lives would be made by confession. And besides, who in all the world will admire us, if this person who sees us as our best selves discovers our shortcomings?

But then, all at once, everything began to crumble.

There is an apocryphal tale of a water-skier that rolled like ball lightning through the Mississippi Delta during the late sixties. It is a summer day. A beautiful young girl is flying along the surface of one of the innumerable oxbow lakes that mark changes in the course of the Mississippi River. She swings back and forth over the cresting wake of the boat, and the driver (her lover or sometimes her brother) watches her maneuvers and admires her trim swimmer's body. Overhead the white August cumulus is piled in mountains across the western sky. A sickle of jet trail dissipates in the clear air. A green mist of willows fringes the shoreline.

Then something happens—the rope breaks or she loses

her balance and falls. No big deal. It's happened hundreds of times before. But this time is different: screams of agony —a thrashing and churning in the water. The lover spins the wheel, brings the boat about in less time than it takes to write this sentence. The young girl's lovely face is contorted with pain. Barbed wire, she gasps. I'm caught in barbed wire.

But there isn't any barbed wire. No. It's a writhing, tangled mass of water moccasins. She holds out a hand and he seizes it.

Wait. Wait! she says.

She's dead before he can drag her into the boat, snakes dropping away as she slips over the side.

This tragedy, they say, occurred on Lake Bolivar, Lake Washington, Lake Jackson, Lake St. John, Catahoula Lake, Lake Chicot, Moon Lake, Horn Lake, Eagle Lake, Lake Providence, Lake Concordia. Sometimes there is another boat nearby, a crowd of witnesses. Again, the two young people are alone on the lake. Or only the narrator of the tale witnessed the accident. Or he heard it from a cousin of the girl's.

But *you*—you're the one, I hear you say. You're the driver of this boat. You're pulling the skier. Is the story true?

It's always true. Always true that a tangle of water moccasins lies in wait for the skier. Always, always true.

Without warning, Andrew brought home a wife—a woman with whom, it transpires, he has been living for two years. Cornelia has not known she existed. She is five years older than Andrew and has two children (illegitimate) whom he intends to adopt. In fact, he explains to his mother, this is why they are marrying. The woman is exhausted by the threat, hanging over her now for several years, that the children's natural father may try to take them away from her.

Well, not exactly the father.

131

The father has not now and never has had the least interest in the children, and at the moment he is in the Buchanan County jail (the state penitentiary at Parchman is too overcrowded to welcome him) serving a sentence for possession of a controlled substance with intent to sell. But his parents are another matter. They have not only disowned their errant son, but believe that his ex-girlfriend, Willie Belle (yes, that's her name), is an unfit mother. She's living in sin *again*, isn't she? And she's a known user of marijuana. They have begun legal proceedings to take the children from her.

Andrew is twenty-four—only twenty-four—his life before him.

Here is how Cornelia heard this tale.

She was sitting in her kitchen one lovely June morning in nineteen sixty-nine—early in the morning, not much past six o'clock. On summer mornings she loves to get up early, to wander through her garden pulling an occasional weed, to snip a handful of fresh dill and basil for the day's salad, to stop by the kitchen door and break a sprig of rosemary from the bush by the doorstep. Today she has gathered her herbs and stuck them in a jelly glass on the windowsill. The first eggplant of the season gleams like a convex purple mirror on the scarlet countertop. Now, sitting at the table, drinking her coffee, she glances at the paper, turns the page—away from those always dreadful headlines—to the gardening section, glances out the open kitchen doorway, sees Andrew striding up the drive. She smiles and beckons him in, thinking how handsome he is, how marvelously lucky she is to have such a son to love, wondering how he happens to be out so early.

Andrew is a young man with a passion for precision. His walk and his body may be like his father's, but he has the gene that Cornelia puts to use arranging her household, tying narrow ribbons around stacks of linens, constructing a perfect Napoleon or a new catalogue for O'Kelly's Books. It has made of him a builder. He has always taken things apart and put them together in new and orderly ways—Tinkertoys, tree houses, watches, engines, guns. Until recently he has turned his face resolutely away from the chaos of his time. Of course he's tried drugs, but he scarcely ever uses them, and he feels uneasy about indiscriminate sex and religious fads, avoids demonstrations, whether for civil rights or for peace.

I won't go out there and fight that insane war, he said to his father three years ago. Not if I can help it. And he has arranged his life accordingly.

CO status? Canada? No. First he used his college deferment, and now he builds boats. He graduated from college a year ago with a degree in marine engineering and works for a firm in Baton Rouge designing and building towboats and barges. His work, in combination with a high draft number, has kept him out of the army.

Does all this make him sound like a cold-hearted, self-centered man? He is not. Rather, he is very young and he is caught like us all in the web of his time, struggling, acting according to his lights and the needs of the moment, not cold-hearted, no, and no more self-centered than the rest of us.

Now, in any case, he is in love and he is at home. Yesterday he drove up from Baton Rouge for a weekend visit to his parents, a confrontation with Cornelia. He comes into the room as Cornelia stands up and opens her mouth to say good morning and pour him a cup of coffee. He doesn't give her time to speak.

I've been out walking and thinking, Mama, he says. Sit down, please, and listen to me. I have a lot of things I need to talk to you about. She sits. Her heart begins to beat heavily. Has the army caught up with him?

Listen, Mama, he says and he sits down across the table from her, reaches out, takes her hand. I've made up my mind. From now on things are going to be different with us.

Different? she says.

Everything has to be out in the open, he says. Everything. Starting now. It'll be better for you, too, once you get used to it. I know it will. And for me . . . Well, I can't stand this way any longer, and besides, even if I could stand it, I can't get away with it anymore.

Cornelia has not the least idea what he is getting ready to say, but a huge NO floats up into her throat and bursts out before she can stop it. And she lays her hand gently on her breast, covering the receiver of the tiny hearing aid that is clipped to the brassiere strap under her loose shirt.

Things are a mess, Andrew says. Everywhere in the world things are a fucking mess. Did you hear me? Turn up your hearing aid. Move your hand, so you can hear.

Andrew! she says. What's got into you?

My God, you even got to fight in the right war, didn't you? Daddy got to be a hero. But look at *us. Look* at us.

We couldn't help that, she says. Andrew, what are we talking about?

So that's the way it is, he says when he has finished his story. And even though it's been the main thing in my life for two years, I haven't told you—because . . . I'm not sure why I haven't. Because it would be too hard on you, I suppose, because you wouldn't see it as something I would do. But I have to set things straight. I can't go on . . . concealing . . . dancing this minuet with you.

Minuet?

I can't behave anymore like a guilty fifteen-year-old, making myself into whatever I think is acceptable to you. Raising my voice so you'll be sure to hear and then saying—nothing.

I never asked you to, Cornelia says. Never. I've always wanted to hear whatever you wanted to tell me. Tears are rolling down her calm face, dropping on the gleaming walnut surface of the table, but her soft voice is under its usual control. Increasing deafness has not affected her as it does many deaf people. The memory of intonation and cadence keeps her voice flexible and expressive; it does not break unexpectedly, never gets too loud or too soft. Only, occasionally, she mispronounces a word, doesn't realize she's said Pospicle for Popsicle.

Have you? he says. Then, when she doesn't answer, It's been me, too, I know, I don't mean it's only you.

Andrew, you're only twenty-four, she says. Are you sure this is . . . is . . . Isn't there maybe some other way to . . . She can't, or doesn't, go on. Doesn't say either "some way to get out of it" or "some way to help her that doesn't involve marriage."

No, he says. We're going to be married.

She sits opposite him. Her hands now are resting in front of her on the table. She looks down, sees a tear on the tabletop, takes a handkerchief from her pocket, wipes it away. Of course you must bring her home, she says firmly, moving the handkerchief in a circle on the table. I know I'll like her. How could I not? I know if you want to marry her. . . . And the children, too. They must . . .

Andrew is shaking his head, frustration in the set of his shoulders and his grim mouth. The kids are as wild as stray cats, he says. They're going to be hard for you to take. Damn if either one of us knows what to do with them half the time.

Your father, she says. Have you told him? He'll be . . . Now she is folding the handkerchief, putting it back into her pocket.

He raises his voice: Mama, I said the kids are as wild as stray cats.

Oh, she says, children. Children will always . . . Then, Your father will be . . .

Daddy has known about us for a long time. Since the beginning. We've been together two years.

Two years! He's known? Cornelia's face quivers. She stands up. A light breeze through the open kitchen door lifts her chestnut hair and the morning sun picks out here and there a thread of silver. She has the absorbed and dreaming look of a sleepwalker. He's *known*? she says again.

135

Perhaps she's still skiing. She leans a tad forward and to the left, away from Andrew, as if gathering herself to ride a strong and sharply curving wake. She moves toward the refrigerator, takes out eggs and milk, sets them on the counter and stands with her back to him. Well, she says, I was getting ready to make pancakes. I thought you might . . . Would you like some breakfast?

Is that all you want to say to me, Mama?

Perhaps she doesn't hear him. She doesn't answer, breaks an egg into the bowl, then another, reaches up and gets flour from the cabinet and a measuring cup.

Finally she says, Have you set a date for the wedding?

Sometime next week. It's important to get respectable as soon as we can, because of this business of the custody hearing. We've done the blood tests. We'll go to a JP in Baton Rouge.

Cornelia's tears continue to fall. Without turning, she says, What about her family? I suppose they know all about it, too?

Andrew shrugs. She hasn't seen them in years. I doubt they even know where she is. He gets up, joins her at the counter. Don't cry, Mama, he says. It's not so bad. Willie Belle—when you get to know her . . . And then: Listen, she's here. In town. She and the children. They stayed last night at the Holiday Inn. I'm going down there shortly. I would like to bring them out here to meet you. OK?

I'll make pancakes for the crowd, Cornelia says.

Pancakes! Jesus Christ, Mama! Who gives a fuck about pancakes!

Andrew! Cornelia says. Andrew!

You don't want to look at anything, Mama, Andrew says. Not anything. Not me. Not Sarah. Not the war . . . the world . . .

Sarah?

Oh, God, Sarah's all right. I didn't mean that. Shit!

He reaches into his shirt pocket and throws a postcard on the counter in front of her. I got this in the mail yesterday, he says. Ordinarily it would never have crossed my mind to show it to you. But what did I say to begin with—that things would be different between us? Look at it for me. Please?

Cornelia stares down. The postcard is a color photograph of a woman holding a dead child in her arms, mutilated leg dangling, face bloody. The woman's mouth is open in a scream of anguish, her cheek smeared with blood. In the blank space below the picture a heavy black scrawl reads: Greetings to you, Andrew, from Vietnam. Your pal, Winston. She turns it over. The message side is empty except for the address.

My God, Andrew! Cornelia covers the card with her hand.

What does he mean? Andrew says. Does he want me to come help him kill slopes? Or is he telling me to take off for Canada? He sits down, buries his head in his hands. Then, Oh, God, Mama, he says, this doesn't have anything to do with me and Willie Belle. What the hell am I talking about?

Andrew, my dear, I'm sorry, Cornelia says.

Where do you *live*? Andrew says. Where *are* you?

Cornelia feels a pain in her left breast, a burning pain that trickles down into her belly.

I don't know what to do except tell you to bring them out for breakfast, she says.

All right, Mama. I'll bring them out for breakfast.

Her name is Willie Belle? Cornelia says. This woman you're planning to marry. And she is threatened with the loss of her children?

Yes. Willie Belle. And *she's* OK. It's these born-again maniacs who are causing the trouble. It's not her fault.

Naturally not.

That's the ticket, Andrew said. Get mad for a change. I deserve it.

I'm not angry, my dear. What would be the point in . . . ? Willie Belle what?

Gorton.

137

Ahh, Cornelia says.

Can this be the Cornelia who danced with John to the Beer Barrel Polka; who escaped from her tower dangling thirty feet above the ground on John's makeshift pulley while the ginkgo tree shed its golden hair around her and her mother called piteously from below: *Oh, wait, wait. Go back. I'm sorry. It was an error in judgment?*

It appears that one escape from a tower, one awakening from enchanted sleep, may not be all that is required of an imprisoned princess. Other towers, other thickets of thorns may await her.

Shortly Andrew returned with Willie Belle and the two children—Louise, large for her age at five and dark like her mother, and nine-year-old Purvis, who looks furiously at Cornelia from beneath straight white bangs and says not a word. In the course of an hour or so, while Cornelia (and John, who has joined the family for breakfast) make conversation with soft-voiced Willie Belle, the children, who have already eaten Sugar Pops and Cokes, ignored by their mother, range over the house and yard. Purvis tilts back in one of those ancient Empire chairs and the back legs snap off.

Don't worry a minute about that old chair, Cornelia says. It was on its last legs.

I'm the one who weakened it, John says. I never can remember not to tilt back.

Louise turns over a pitcher of syrup on the dining-room table and before Cornelia can sop it up, it drips down on the flame-stitch upholstered chair and the worn old Karistan rug. Later, outside, the two children chase a neighbor's cat into the vegetable garden and trample the fruiting bush beans. Louise gets herself scratched and, shrieking with rage and pain, tracks mud from the just-watered garden into the kitchen.

Inside, Willie Belle speaks softly of her life, of how Andrew came to her rescue when she'd been abandoned by a

treacherous lover, evicted by her landlord. I've had bad luck
with men until Andrew came along, she says. Purvis's
daddy—I've never gotten a nickel of support from him, and
Louise's—well, of course he was killed in Nam. Worse luck
for him than for us. But no way I could prove . . .

I thought the children had the same father, Cornelia says.

Well, supposedly. But . . .

John lays his hand over Cornelia's clenched fist. Difficult
times, he says. Difficult times for everyone.

For once in her life Cornelia can say to herself without
a twinge of guilt, It's a blessing Mother isn't here.

What about Willie Belle? Who is she and where did she
spring from? How did she get into Andrew's orderly life?

One thing—she's large. Once she loomed above his ho-
rizon, he had to notice her. Large and soft and dark, with
resilient olive skin and eyes the color of Cornelia's eggplants.

It began one winter afternoon in Andrew's final year of
engineering school. He'd come to New Orleans for a job in-
terview and a long weekend before beginning his last semester, and he dropped into a French Quarter bar for a drink.
She was crying quietly and politely over a draft beer, her face
shielded by a protective hand and a cloud of fine dark hair,
and when he sat down beside her, she turned away.

But Andrew is an observant and sympathetic young man,
and it wasn't long before she was telling him her predica-
ment. She'd lost her job—been out of work for a month.
Today she'd been out interviewing, had picked up her kids
at school (one in nursery school, the other in second grade),
and had gone home to her apartment to find a note from her
current lover announcing that he was leaving. Last week
he'd borrowed two hundred dollars from her—all her savings. He had some terrible problems, Willie Belle says, and
I felt like I couldn't let him down. But the rent was already

past due then, and today, while she was sitting at the kitchen table reading the note, the landlord had come by again, and they'd had a terrible row, and he'd locked her out of the apartment. Now the two kids are outside in her locked car.

Something in Andrew's face stops her here. They're OK. I'm keeping an eye on them, she says. See?

Through the etched glass pane of the doorway Andrew sees, parked on the street directly in front of the bar, an old blue Buick. A small, dim face crowned with a thatch of white hair is pressed against the back window.

He turns back to Willie Belle. Where has she been working? he asks.

In an antique shop on Royal Street. But it's gone bankrupt, she says. She's sure she can get another job, maybe even a better one. But what about today? Tomorrow?

What am I going to do? she says in a soft southern voice that raises the hair on Andrew's susceptible forearms. I just came in here for a few minutes to try to think what I'm going to do. The dark hair moves softly on her shoulders.

Andrew, who spent his boyhood in his parents' bookstore gazing at many things besides da Vinci's marvelous machines, thinks of Saskia in her bath. He thinks of Rubens's young wife with the fur draped around her naked body. We'll figure out something, he says.

And when she looks at him with the detachment and skepticism of experience, he says, I'm harmless, really. Then, with a wry smile, I'm only twenty-two years old. A mere child. Finally, You don't need to be scared of me. You're big enough to tie me in a knot, you know it?

She smiles. For goodness sakes, I'm not *afraid* of you, she says. That's probably one of my problems. I don't have sense enough to be afraid.

For tonight, you can bring the kids and stay in my motel room, he says. Then tomorrow you can start figuring what to do next.

Thanks, she says.

* * *

Where did she spring from? Well, she sprang from the same
place Tennessee Williams and many another bewildered and
fearless southern soul sprang from—the rectory. Only in
her case, it's a Methodist parsonage. She is the child and
grandchild and great-great-grandchild of Methodist preachers. Later she'll tell Andrew stories of the circuit rider great-
(or was it great-great-) grandfather in east Tennessee who,
family legend had it, whipped his congregations to such a
frenzy of religious passion that they held him captive in the
meetinghouse, shouting, More, preacher, More! until the
deacons finally had to pass him hand to hand above the
heads of the congregation and through a window to his waiting horse, so that he could ride on to the next meeting. Oh,
he saved souls, her mother said. The harvest was bountiful.
My grandmother told me . . .

And then there was the great-grandfather on the other
side of the family who was shot—murdered—by bush-
whackers in the late bitter days of border state abolitionism.

The two grandfathers had been, it seemed, equally zeal-
ous, but less picturesque. Methodism had changed, gotten
less passionate, less joyful, less hazardous, and more respectable.

As for her own father, he'd been a bitter, silent man
whose churches never appreciated him. He always did the
right thing, never hesitated to anatomize the sins of his
parishioners, set the example of tithing for his congregation,
didn't allow cards or spirits in his house or croquet on
Sunday, and sank from middle-sized church to smaller church,
to churches that couldn't pay a full-time preacher and used
him only once or twice a month. He died young of rectal
cancer and Willie Belle's mother promptly married another
preacher. He was a great saver of souls. No doubt if that
couple had known where Willie Belle was, they, too, would
have been battling for the custody of Purvis and Louise.

141

All those preachers, Willie Belle told Andrew later. All that soul-saving. She shook her head. Like you might have all your ancestors back to . . . back to Wesley himself looking over your shoulder, hiding under your bed, telling you to do right. What can you do but run?

Like Tennessee Williams's Alma, Willie Belle had got to smoking at an early age and slipped precipitately down the broad path to perdition, leaving her family behind, taking along only her good table manners and soft, cultivated southern voice to confuse the bystanders.

Once, in an idle moment between fucks, Andrew asked Willie Belle what the happiest day of her childhood had been. Lying naked in his arms under the tropical whiffle of the ceiling fan (by that time she had moved to Baton Rouge and they'd found her a job and an apartment in the same building as his, although they had not yet moved in together), she stretched out her long soft body with a sigh of contentment, twined her fingers in a dark curl of his pubic hair and answered without hesitation. It was when I was nine. The day Mama married Mr. Pirkle. Never mind that he was another preacher—his daughter Adeline smoked. I caught her flapping a towel to blow the cigarette smell out the bathroom window. Of course, she couldn't tell on me if I stole her cigarettes. So that was my happiest day. I could stop smoking the wicker porch furniture.

She stretched her brown body like a big cat, rolled over on top of Andrew, propped herself on her elbows, and let her hair fall around his face.

My God, you're heavy, he said.

Heavy, Willie Belle said, pressing her pelvis against his and gazing into his eyes. Oh, I am. I'm heavy. She moved gently against him. It's love, love, love, she said, bearing down. And then: Of course I quit when I was fourteen, she said. It's a terrible habit. Besides, as soon as I left home and didn't have to sneak, it lost its appeal.

Shh, Andrew said. Let's don't talk anymore.

Outside the bedroom door they heard the clatter of blocks

falling (This was when the children were four and eight.) and then shrieks of outrage from Louise: Mama! He knocked my house down.

Well, she's been messing with my bug collection, Purvis said. My stag beetle's leg is broken.

Shit, Willie Belle said, and got out of bed. I knew they wouldn't give us time for another fuck.

Andrew took her hand, pulled her back, put his arm around her waist. Calm down, children, he said in his deepest, most reassuring voice. Play nicely together for a little while, OK? And then your mother and I will take you to the zoo.

I think Willie Belle is exactly the woman for Andrew. With her around, it's as if he has permission to be his own passionate and orderly self.

What else in their lives is hidden from me? And why? What else do they not say, or say only in whispers? Cornelia doesn't ask these questions—not of John or of her children. But it is as if the slowly deepening silence of the world beyond her frayed and crumbling auditory nerve had always been calling out its voiceless warning to her. She'd been right those evenings at the supper table when she'd watched her husband and children, seen their lips move, their heads nod, hands signal. They had been excluding, deceiving, betraying her, had constructed their life together as if her presence were a hole in its center.

Well then, let them! She would never never reproach them. She turns off her hearing aid and deliberately closes them out.

The weeks and months pass and still she says nothing. Andrew and Willie Belle are married. They have bought a small house in the country across the river from Baton Rouge. They bring the children occasionally and blow like a tornado through a weekend at home. Sometimes Sarah comes with them. She's in Baton Rouge, too—at LSU, where she's begun work toward a graduate degree in English literature which she has no intention of using—I just enjoy school, she says. She likes the children—regards them with wry amusement—and has easily made a connection with her new sister-in-law. This is an in-between time for Sarah, a time to be carefree and tolerant. Like her mother, she brushes out her long chestnut hair and reads and reads. It's Henry James now, I think. She considers taking a new lover, rejects the notion for the moment, absentmindedly comes and goes away, unaware of the subtle change in her mother's voice, the cheek turned coolly to her kiss. And Tweet? Well, Tweet would say she feels the same about babies as she does about little bitty chickens—they're too soft, feel like they hadn't got no bones. But Purvis and Louise are not babies, they're tough kids. She brings out new tales to amuse them, listens intently to theirs.

And John? All these twenty-five years John has been a faithful husband to Cornelia. When at twenty-seven he married her, he was ready to settle down. At that age he'd already spent more time arranging one-night stands than he had ever had a stomach for. (Not so many, at that: There had been a couple of long-term affairs.) He wanted never again to go out looking for sex. Bachelor life was over and done with. Now he would be lover, householder, settled family man. This passion to be grounded at last was, of course, a commonplace among the young men of his generation. They'd all had, perforce, to wander too long, risk more than they'd meant to risk. There were some who had so fallen into the habit that they could not stop. But there were others who never wanted to be moved again.

For John, by the time he left the Army Air Corps in nineteen forty-six, the war had been seven years of terrible life-and-death uncertainty. He'd crash-landed his plane in the fields of Sussex and walked away from it, had seen his friends killed by ones and twos—dropping into the icy waters of the

English Channel, spiraling down in flames over the cities of Europe, swinging like seedpods under the white blooms of their parachutes until the blooms collapsed, shot through from below with machine-gun fire. In the North African desert he had lain with a broken arm and ankle for two days before he'd been picked up (buried himself in sand under the shadow of his crumpled fighter, sipped at his canteen, gnawed C rations, and tried to keep himself damp with urine).

Later, before he was sent back to the United States as an instructor, he'd done a brief stint as pilot of an unarmed reconnaissance plane, solitary, weaving through the empty skies with the trip wire of a camera under his hand. I killed more people that way than I ever did in a fighter, he told Cornelia. Hundreds of people. Thousands. Trip the wire. Record the location of ammunition dumps, ships in port, staging areas—and take it back so somebody else can blow them up. But I loved it, he said. To be up there, alone, the whole sky belonging only to me. . . . I'd climb until I could see my contrail and then drop down a couple of thousand feet, so I could see the trail of anything above me and not show to anything below. Blue. . . . Our planes were blue against a blue sky. We'd ease along. . . .

But weren't you too afraid to love it?

Scared—yes. But even so . . .

It was on those solitary flights, he told her, that he'd known he would marry her even before he ever saw her.

He's saved enough money during the years of high pay and low expenses to be able to afford to look around for what he wanted to do, and it was he who had said to Cornelia at the beginning, How would you feel about a bookstore? I wouldn't mind running a bookstore. Would you? She'd been delighted. Father had been interested in adding to the investment and that was the life they'd made.

In the fifties they had moved out, first buying and selling rare books, then with an occasional publishing venture—a regional book that interested them, a collection of stories from an unknown but promising young writer in the area.

145

Now their shop and press were known all through the South, their catalogs went out to every state and even to European customers. All had gone extraordinarily well in that hazardous business.

But it's true that John was sometimes restless. He bought a sailboat, taught himself to sail. Later (He still loved the solitude of flight.) he bought a plane which he kept at the local airfield. Sometimes in the afternoons or the early mornings he takes off, flies along the meandering course of the river, lands on a deserted sandbar, crosses a levee to fish for a while in an oxbow lake. He has rigged a camera with a trip wire in the plane and has taken marvelous pictures: ducks lifting from the ruffled water of Old River Cutoff, leaving a pattern of wake athwart the rows of wind-driven ripples; startled deer dashing across the white sand of a towhead. Pictures that lie like obliterating palimpsests over old shots of staging areas, oil fields, solitary troop carriers.

And he is always home in time for supper.

Now, in this crisis in her life, Cornelia goes every afternoon as she has for years to work in the bookstore. There, as in her kitchen, she can be sure that order prevails. Customers make themselves heard. Three-by-five file cards hold the secrets of all their needs and preferences. Regularly as the sun, on Tuesday morning, the *Sunday New York Times* arrives, and on Wednesday, the *Publishers Weekly*. Catalogs come in from Bookman's and the American Book Collector and the Gotham Book Mart, fall and spring lists from the trade publishers. Field reps drop in and linger after orders are complete to talk shop in the comfortable atmosphere of O'Kelly's Books. There are easy chairs to loaf in, coffee is in the pot, and in the back room, always, a few new treasures to look at: a marvelous Rembrandt from Abrams or Skira, the Baskin illustrated *Iliad*, a limited edition of *Go Down, Moses*, a book from their own press, bound in

French marbled paper over boards, quarter-leather spine, gold stamped. . . .

Here, it is easy to avoid unnatural silences with John. Business demands consultation, and besides, there's always someone dropping in, looking for the odd Faulkner item, the out-of-print Rhys—someone interesting who lingers to talk politics, local gossip, books, and the latest controversy in the Letters section of the *New York Times Book Review*.

Or it may be that she goes up into her office off the balcony overlooking the shop, clicks off her hearing aid, and goes over bills and orders. She wanders out onto the balcony and, alone in the cottony silence, watches as below her on the shop floor John greets an old friend, gestures, nods, moves his lips, takes down a book from a high shelf, answers the telephone.

But driving home in the late afternoon, shoulder to shoulder with John, Cornelia sometimes thinks that she has become two people, that under the skin of her cool, still-slender and smiling self, inside the efficient lady with the almost invisible hearing aid, the competent partner, the reader who always knows what she thinks of the latest book, a monster may live. She has not yet met the monster, who seems in her fancy to be hiding behind dust-heavy curtains, spinning there a web—is the creature a spider? Absurd! It's a waking dream. She shakes off the uncanny conviction that there is someone—something—back there, something in the dark; speaks instead to John of advertising for a set of the Scribner's James, of a new Faulkner collector on their mailing list, falls silent again.

I will *not*, she says to herself, I will not question him. Will not insult him with my . . . The curtain moves and subsides, shakes dust into her mind.

I think I'll get Julia to ask Mr. Carrier if he'll help us with fall cleaning on his off days, she says to John.

Fine, John says. Fine.

Julia. . . . Lately she's seemed—I don't know—ailing.

I found her in the kitchen the other day, just standing at the sink, don't know why I noticed it, but she just stood there and kept washing the same fork over and over again for the longest time. And when I spoke, she didn't answer.

Daydreaming? John says.

Maybe. More like she was in a trance—or, I don't know. It was more—physical.

Checkup? John says, his mind clearly on other things.

Yes, I think she should have one.

At home she puts supper on the table, afterwards leaves John to wash up, goes to bed early, lies staring at whatever happens to be on the television screen, never bothering to change the channel.

He sits in the living room, has a brandy or two, perhaps goes out to play poker for a couple of hours at his club, comes home to find her asleep.

These nights she's always lying still, unrouseable, when he comes to bed. He draws her to him sometimes, or, in the early mornings, senses that she is stirring, wakes and touches her tentatively. But she turns away. He has asked her what the matter is, and she has said that she doesn't know. I must need a little time to myself, she says. I don't know why I don't feel like sex these days. She pats his shoulder reassuringly.

He has taken to getting up early, driving to the airfield, taking off in his Beechcraft, flying out over the river, landing perhaps on a sandbar and sitting there watching the water for an hour or so. Once or twice, he rouses her and asks her to go with him, as she used often to do, but she shakes her head, mutters in her sleep, pulls the covers closer around her, falls into dreams of a bile green taffeta dress, an endless silent dance where no one breaks in. Her partner's lips move, he speaks and laughs and she hears nothing. Hour after hour she circles the floor under the pitying eyes of the chaperons.

At work, on the days John flies, she does not ask where he has been.

148

At night now, although he's never been a heavy drinker, he may, if he stays at home, have two, or even three or four brandies before he comes to bed. Two or three nights he doesn't come home, or comes so late the sun is rising when he slips into the house. Cornelia is sure that on these nights he has found a woman to comfort him. The curtain in her mind shakes and wavers in the wind. Maybe it's always been like this. Maybe in her fond ignorance, her foolish trust, she has lived her whole life in a false, an imaginary world.

A ferocious passion takes possession of her. No matter that her body is like a frozen board, a corpse buried for thousands of years in the permafrost, still she feels burning outward from her heart a lava of hatefulness. Somehow she will punish them all.

Does all this seem absurd beyond belief? And even more absurd that she keeps silent? What is she planning? I don't think she is planning anything. She is too busy keeping silent—and burning.

Late in the summer John and Cornelia went to a southern booksellers' meeting in Atlanta. Again, as in the bookshop at home, there was more than enough to occupy them (writers to meet, promotional materials to display and look at, old friends to have lunch and dinner with, sales to conclude) to ward off again and again the silence that falls between estranged couples—forces them finally to confront each other.

But John is a photographer, remember, an ex-reconnaissance officer, trained to look with alert and clear-eyed concentration at the terrain over which he is flying, to snap his pictures at exactly the moment when they will be most revealing, when a particular slant of sunlight exposes the staging area under the camouflage nets. Over the years, observing the terrain of their marriage, he must have occasionally glimpsed some shadow across the ground Cornelia has so lovingly, so carefully cultivated—but if he has, he's kept his own counsel.

It may be that he had enough in his youth of reporting ships leaving harbor, convoys on narrow back roads. Now, he wants only to let everyone come and go in peace.

In any case, the meeting is over and they are booked on a late-afternoon flight home. John has gone down to the lobby of their hotel to check out and Cornelia is finishing her packing. She gathers her possessions, takes the usual last look around the room, goes to meet him, finds him in the hotel bar. On the way to the airport they are quiet. She manages to bring out an occasional distracted observation on the books they've seen, on the difficulties of the Atlanta airport. He responds with monosyllables.

I'll be glad to get home, she says. It's been so dry. . . .

He is silent. The static of the city mutters in her hearing aid.

It's been so dry. . . .

Still he is silent.

I wonder if we've had a rain. I hope Julia remembered to water those tomato suckers I put out a couple of weeks ago. I never should have . . . This late in the . . .

He turns a strange look on her. Home? he says, as if he's never heard the word. Home?

She had reached out her hand to pat his—a perfunctory wifely gesture—and at this she snatches it back as if she's touched an unlit burner on her stove and found it hot.

The rest of the way to the airport she looked straight ahead and said nothing.

At the airport, getting out of the taxi first, she said in her ordinary soft voice, I'll pay, John. OK? You see about the bags. But then she watched him fumble with the door, groping for the handle, and climb clumsily out, and realized that he was drunk. He stood staring, not at her but at the sidewalk, as if there might be something—an answer to a question—written in the concrete at his feet. She paid the taxi driver, took charge of their two suitcases, carrying first one and then the other into the airport lobby, put the strap of their carry-on bag over her shoulder, while he continued to stand and stare. She took his arm, led him inside, and took him over to the nearest row of seats. Sit down, she said. You're in no shape to check us in.

C'nelia . . . he said. He touched his own cheek and then looked at his hand wonderingly, as if he were a baby just discovering his body. I jus . . jus . . . But she turned away and took her place in the line at the ticket counter.

In a moment she felt a tugging at her sleeve and there he was standing beside her. I want . . . he said. C'nelia, I . . . He cupped his two hands, made rings of his thumbs and forefingers, held them up to his eyes like binoculars, stared at her or perhaps beyond her, as if he might be scanning the heavens. You so far away, he said. Far away. You ever coming back? Laughed what sounded to her a loose mindless laugh. She stared at him and for a moment his face seemed to loom and retreat like the face in a funhouse mirror. The curtain shook in her head, scattered its dust. Who *is* that man? someone asked.

Go sit down, John, she said sternly. Sit down. I'm right here. We'll be on the plane in just a minute. She spoke quietly: They were surrounded by people who had begun now to glance curiously at them. She watched him shamble across the lobby. He did not sit down, but stood looking at the row of chairs, as if wondering what their function might be. She observed that his buttocks were beginning to sag like an old man's. His head was bent and under his lank black hair, thinning now and streaked with gray, the pale scalp gleamed. She remembered that lately when he'd undressed and exposed the roll of aging flesh around his middle, she'd felt a flood of revulsion. Now he seemed to her to be slumping earthward, as if gravity were too much for him. A needle of rage probed at her heart, dripped in its burning poison. She crossed the room, guided him to a chair. Sit down, she said again calmly.

Back in line at the counter, We've got to get on this plane, that's all, she said to herself. Once he's in his seat, we'll be OK. Nearly two hours to sleep it off. She put her mind to planning the next fifteen minutes. First, turn up the volume on her hearing aid. She must hear the ticket agent and answer him intelligently in all this confusion. She would check the carry-on bag as well as the two suitcases, so as to be free to guide John. This damn airport is so big, she said to herself. How far will we have to walk? What gate . . . ? She glanced surreptitiously at him, not wanting him to see her look. There he stood, swaying. He might pass out, she thought. She felt the fiery poison in her breasts, her nipples shrank and burned. Bastard, somebody said. Fucking bastard. Cornelia never uses such words even to herself. Fucking bastard.

In silence they made their way through the endless corridors of the airport, in silence she managed to get him past the stewardess, present their boarding passes, settle him in his place, fasten his seat belt for him, for by now he was clearly incapable of fastening it himself.

When did he have a chance to . . . ? And why had he . . . ? She went over their last hour or so in the hotel. He'd complained of a headache, had left her to finish her packing, taken his bag and gone down, to buy a paper, he had said, had been gone—how long? before she joined him in the bar. An hour? An hour and a half? But he had checked them out of the hotel without difficulty, hadn't seemed drunk at first when they got in the cab. He must, she thought, have had three or four quick drinks—doubles—in the bar, as fast as he could gulp them down. And they hadn't hit him until after he'd left the hotel.

Cornelia, of course, has smelled the brandy on his breath these past few months, has known that he's been sitting alone in the study with a glass in his hand while she has been lying as still and alert as a cat at a mousehole, waiting to feign sleep when he finally lies heavily down beside her. (And what kind of child's game was that? What could he have said to appease her?) But she hasn't thought of two or even three or four brandies in an evening as—*drinking*. He's always gotten up in the morning without a sign of a hangover and gone about his business.

She leans toward him now. (They are taxiing down the runway, taxiing and pausing, taxiing and pausing, as they wait their turn in a line of planes ready to take off.) She is entirely in control of herself, generous-hearted, understanding. What possessed you, John? she says. You're just as drunk as you can be. Why in the *world* . . . ? She laughs lightly, with the laugh assigning this behavior to its unimportant place in their lives. But in her breasts the fiery poison burns. Who were you drinking with? she says. She had not known she would say it.

He looks at her strangely and for an instant, before she wipes it out of her consciousness, it seems as if one eye bulges unnaturally at her. Not . . . he says in a guttural voice. Not . . .

Not, my foot. You're getting ready to pass out.

He opens his mouth, makes a grotesque face, becomes for a moment a gargoyle. Then, astonishingly, he sticks out his tongue at her.

They are in their place at the head of the runway now and the pilot's voice comes over the intercom: . . . ready for takeoff now, ladies and gentlemen. Thank you for your patience. The plane shudders against the brakes, as the pilot revs the engines.

And now she is turning toward him, gripping his shoulder, feeling the shuddering of the plane all through her body. You fucking bastard, she whispers in his ear. You bastard. I know. I know. All these years. You . . . You . . . To have secrets with them . . . To conspire with them against me. How could you do it? And what else? Why? Am I not . . . Is my judgment so bad, am I so mean-hearted that . . . ? Am I so ugly, so awkward, so stupid . . . ? She broke off. Ugly? Awkward? What was she talking about. Find somebody else then, she said. I'd be glad. I hate you. I hate all of you. Every one of you. They're in the air now, climbing steeply. In her ears she feels the cabin pressure changing. John is staring sideways at her hand on his shoulder. Then he raises his own hands to his head, presses his palms against his temples, moans, bucks forward once against the restraining seat belt, gives a low, hoarse, agonized groan, and slumps sideways in his seat, his head falling heavily against her as she leans over him.

She felt his body slump against her, the weight of his head on her arm, passive beyond sleep or coma. She buzzed for the stewardess, knowing already, already refusing to know that he was dead.

He's ill, she said. My husband is . . . He needs a doctor. The stewardess looked once, raised his warm limp hand, felt for the pulse.

Cornelia cradled his head against her. Get a doctor, she said again.

The stewardess hurried forward and in a moment the request for a doctor came over the intercom. But there was no doctor on the plane and no doctor could have brought him back. The stewardess came, the copilot joined her, there was a flurry of activity. They laid him out in the aisle and the two worked over him: mouth-to-mouth resuscitation, the routine CPR procedures.

Cornelia reached down and took his hand in hers. Put a pillow under his head, she said. They paid no attention to her, kept on working.

Everything went forward in an orderly way. The passengers on either side of the aisle, reticent, as one should be in the presence of a dead stranger, took up their magazines or gazed out their windows at the snowy banks of cumulus, brilliant and solid as clouds in a picture. At last the stewardess rose, took down a couple of blankets from the overhead bin, and laid them over his body covering his face.

Cornelia was holding his hand in both of hers now, turned toward him, looking down at the still mound of his body. Put a pillow under his head, she said again, and the stewardess did.

Cornelia did not speak again. She did not weep. She did not answer the questions or respond to the comforting noises of the stewardess, who continued to stand in the aisle, leaning solicitously over her, did not say *yes* or *no* to: Whom shall we call so that . . . ? Children? A friend to meet you at the airport? We've radioed ahead to . . . She held John's hand and did not speak as they flew through the deepening twilight.

At last the stewardess took her purse from the seat beside her, found in her wallet a card that read, *In an emergency call* . . . But of course John was listed as next of kin. In an emergency call John O'Kelly.

Mrs. O'Kelly? Is there anyone at your home? Can you hear me? Then: Mrs. O'Kelly, we have had to radio ahead for the coroner. Do you understand what I am saying?

A doctor, Cornelia said.

It's the law, the stewardess said gently. The law says you have to call a coroner. They'll . . . You understand? They'll have to establish the cause of death. It's a formality.

By now a second stewardess had joined the first. She tried without success to withdraw John's hand from Cornelia's. She's in shock, she said, and tried again. Then, Someone needs to meet you at the airport, she said.

Our car is at the airport, Cornelia said. No one needs to meet me.

We'll have someone available to drive you home, Mrs. O'Kelly, the stewardess said. You shouldn't drive yourself.

Cornelia did not look up. Call Julia Carrier, she said. Her telephone number is 638–3873. Then, No, she said. That's my number. Her number is 670–1283.

Cornelia sat silent in her bedroom. Voices washed over her as if she were immersed in water—clicks of dolphins, whale song, waves on sand.

The funeral would be private, Andrew and Sarah said. It would be tomorrow—as soon as the coroner released their father's body. The coffin would be closed. The service would be at home. Except for an occasional wedding or funeral, their father had not been inside a church in all the years since they were born, had shed his Catholicism (in any case the outward trappings) without apparent pang.

Sometimes, as they talked, Cornelia turned off her hearing aid. Even when she kept it on, voices sounded and subsided, waves on shingle, grating, then whispering.

Mother, who will . . . ? Somebody has to . . .

A friend who had served with John in the Air Corps would say something at the graveside. Somebody has to say something, Sarah said.

The hearse arrived with its load, the coffin reposed on its velvet-draped stand in the middle of the living room.

Take away the pink lamps, Andrew said, the sprays of peach-colored gladioli. Take away the register, the black ribbon for the door. Mother? You want the coffin closed . . . closed . . . ?

Close the coffin, Sarah said. We will not have it open.

The hinges moved noiselessly, the lid closed with the thunk of an expensive car door.

Andrew paced the yard, stared at the ground.

In her bedroom Cornelia walked to the closet, opened the door. John's seersucker robe hung there, the belt dragging the floor. The shoulders seemed still to hold the shape of his shoulders—he had taken a newer one to Atlanta. His suitcase, still unopened, filled with his clothes, sat on the closet floor. Cornelia stared into the closet until Sarah came and led her to a chair by the window.

The two children chose pallbearers, their own friends, John's poker and sailing companions.

Neighbors gathered—townspeople. The kitchen table and counters were spread with funeral meats. In the living room the women arranged flowers and in the dining room platters and casseroles.

156

Eat, they said. Eat.

In the kitchen the men set bottles of whiskey on the counters. Where are the glasses? they asked Tweet. Where shall we put this case of Cokes . . . ? What shall we do with this ice? Can you make room in the refrigerator for . . . ?

Eat, the women said. Drink.

Cornelia's father arrived from Mobile. Her brother and his wife were in Europe and could not be reached. John's eldest sister and a niece flew in from Dallas, two elderly aunts and an uncle from New Orleans, small, round-faced Irish people with gray hair and blue eyes and prominent chins, they flew in and settled like birds, perched on the chairs around the coffin.

Attention would be paid. Everything was as it should be.

No, it was not.

Where was the priest? the sister asked. Surely the service would be Catholic. And, for her peace of mind, even knowing how hard this was for Cornelia, she must ask: Had Cornelia tried to hear his confession as he lay in the aisle of the plane in the air over Georgia? She could have, of course. Under such circumstances anyone can hear a confession.

Cornelia got up, opened the closet door, stood staring in again at his robe, sash dragging, shoulders sagging.

He was dead, Sarah said bluntly. He had a stroke.

What kind of funeral—what kind of shameful funeral was this to be—without God, without the Church? the sister said.

But Daddy . . . the children said. Daddy . . . He didn't . . . Not for years.

The sister wept and with the aunts and uncle returned to the Holiday Inn where they prayed and consulted with a priest.

Outdoors Purvis and Louise sat on the swing set Cornelia had bought to amuse them and watched the cars pull in and out of the driveway.

What's it like to be dead? Louise said.

You know what dead is, stupid. *That's* dead. See that roly-poly? Purvis crushed the sow bug with his foot.

But that's a bug, Louise said.

When you're dead, they put you in a box and dig a hole and put you in and cover you up with dirt.

But how do you get out? Louise said.

You're stupid, Purvis said kindly. Nobody gets out.

In the kitchen amid the comings and goings, Tweet crashed dishes together, muttered her disapproval to Willie Belle. Well, they're as crazy as any other white people, she said. You, too, Willie Belle. Y'all all crazy except maybe some Italians. At least them Catholics have rosaries, light candles. I worked for an Italian lady one time wasn't as crazy as most white people. (Yes, ma'am, put that casserole in the oven please, Mrs. Carpenter. I got it on warm. Thank you, ma'am.) I think y'all must be so scared of dying, you got to hurry somebody under quick, get a ton of dirt on top of em. That's what it is? Keep em down? Or maybe you don't believe they was ever real. Had nothing to say for themselves living, got nothing more to say after they dead. But dirt ain't going to shut anybody up, keep anybody down.

Purvis is standing in the kitchen doorway. I want a Popsicle, Mama. Louise wants a Popsicle. In the yard Louise is crying. The abandoned swing creaks.

What's the matter with her? Willie Belle says. Here, give her a Popsicle, darling, and try to get her to hush, will you? Come in, Mrs. . . ? I'm Andrew's wife, Willie Belle. . . .

Poor babies. Mrs. Carpenter is speaking. Or is it Mrs. McCloud? Willie Belle, would you like for me to take them home and . . . ?

You suppose to give somebody a decent burial, Tweet said. You *wake* somebody. Waked my grandpa three nights before they buried him, and had three preachers for the funeral.

Purvis again, purple Popsicle juice dripping down his

arm: But he was a hundred years old. You said he was a hundred years old.

Here, Louise. Here. Don't cry, baby. Look, Purvis has a Popsicle for you.

Thank you, Mr. Weiss. Yes, sir, we got plenty of ice. More ice than iceboxes. Got a sack melting outside.

In her bedroom, Cornelia took the sleeve of the robe in her hand, smoothed the soft threadbare cloth, picked up the sash end and looped it over the hanger.

But your grandpa was a hundred years old and little bitty, Tweet. You wouldn't need a ton of dirt to keep him down.

What are you talking about, Purvis? Willie Belle said. Wipe that juice off your arm and go see about Louise, honey.

If you would like me to, I could take the children and . . . (Mrs. Carpenter)

You're scared, too, Tweet, Purvis said. You told me everybody is scared of dead people.

Hush, Purvis, hush. Listen to Mama. You know Andrew's daddy—your grandaddy—is . . .

He's not my grandaddy, Purvis said. I didn't even know him until last year and he's not my grandaddy. We haven't got a grandaddy. All we've got is you and Andrew.

Shhh!

Well, if there's anything at all I can do. . . .

Come in, Mrs. Grant. Yes, ma'am, she's in her room right now—says she ain't up to seeing nobody yet. Yes, ma'am. Won't you . . . ?

Now Purvis and Louise have vanished and Tweet is back at the sink washing glasses. God don't care about funerals, she says. God do the best he can with what he gets. But *we* suppose to care. It's a disgrace. See if you can make some room in the icebox, Willie Belle, and put that ham in, please. And then—look at this dishwasher—we got to unload it before we can get anything else in. A disgrace. Hurry up and get him under—like he's a murderer or something.

Well, Tweet, they have to bury him before tomorrow, you

159

know, because, if you don't, you know, if you don't get somebody embalmed, you can't keep them out of the ground more than twenty-four hours and . . . That's the law.

That ain't it. The law don't have a thing to do with it. I know em. They'd do exactly the same if there wasn't no law.

Cornelia's bedroom window is open. Dolphins whistle and click, whales sing in her earpiece. Tires on gravel like waves on shingle. Voices. Has she turned up the volume to drown her own thoughts? Andrew's voice outside the window talking with his father's friends roars in her head. Do you remember when he . . . ? That was the year . . . Someone is laughing now, *laughing*. Laughter screeches in her ear, sets the auditory nerve to jumping, wincing. She sees him again in the plane, his face close to hers, grotesquely twisted. He is sticking out his tongue at her.

Now she has thrown her hearing aid on the floor and the battery box and earpiece lie next to each other. The box gives off a high-pitched shriek, but Cornelia cannot hear it. She is in the bathroom vomiting.

That ain't it, Tweet says again. Her nose is running and her eyes, too. I want to see him, she says. Shut him up in there, won't let nobody look at him. Act like ain't nothing in the coffin. And a little two-bit social security coffin. No flowers. I wouldn't bury a dog like that. She grabs a towel, dries her face and hands. I'm going to see him, she says. You going to let them bury him without them children seeing him? Like he ain't in there? I'm going to see him.

Wait, Tweet, Willie Belle says. Wait. They've got to do it their own way.

What are you going to wear to the funeral? Tweet says. I got to go downtown, get me a decent dress, if it takes all next month's wages.

At the graveside, the priest stood with the drab old aunts and comforted them. Cornelia walked with Andrew and Sarah, unstumbling, across the cracked dry earth, the yellowing

August grass, and stood without support, gently pushing their hands from her arms, stood straight-backed, sway-backed, staring across the grave into the shadowy laurel trees that lined the curving roadway. John's face peered out at her from among the dark green laurel leaves, grotesque and dappled in the dappling shadows.

And Tweet lit among them all like a painted bunting, a peacock among sparrows, crows, cowbirds, starlings; iridescent in a dress of teal blue, shot, like a peacock's tail, like a grackle's neck feathers, with shining green and purple threads, the skirt full and rustling. Rustling and resplendent, she settled among all those drab birds and mourned John for Cornelia with peacock cries, while all around her the sparrows turned away, hopped to another twig, shielding themselves from her brilliance, and twittered their sad farewells. And Cornelia turned off her hearing aid and gazed at John's face staring out at her from among the laurel leaves.

Six months after John's death, Cornelia is living in Andrew's house. She is not sure, doesn't care, how she got here, what will happen next. She does not intend to stay. Willie Belle's and Andrew's lives wash around her, the children . . .

Tweet has used her absence to make long visits, first to Cynthia in New York, then to Charlene in California. Now she's at home, but in no hurry, she says, to go to work. I been having these dizzy spells, she tells Cornelia on the phone. The doctor's got me on some medicine for high blood. But you come on home. I'll come back to work when you get here.

I'll be back soon, Cornelia says absently. I can't decide whether . . .

She cannot bear to say more, to think whether she should sell her own house, abandon the bedroom closet in which John's robe still hangs, shut away, the belt looped over the hanger, the closed suitcase still on the floor beside it; but she is almost always successful now in not seeing his twisted face, his bulging eye, his extruded tongue.

When she has hung up, Willie Belle says, No hurry, Cornelia. Don't do anything hasty. Stay on awhile longer with us. Neither she nor Andrew know what to make of Cornelia's paralysis. Surely all people grieving for a mate, even a mate beloved as John was, are not so paralyzed as Cornelia. But Willie Belle is practiced at living in communes, living with weirdos, living with crazy boyfriends, drugged girlfriends. Let her alone, she says. Give her time, Andrew. It's as if she tries to interpose her warm dark peaceful bulk between Cornelia and whatever nightmare gallops with wild eyes, dark mane, and bared teeth across her sky, as if she knows it's not time yet. . . . not yet time. . . .

Sarah has left graduate school and is living at home, making a stab at keeping the book business and the press going, struggling through long, frustrating telephone conversations with her mother, conversations which Cornelia usually cuts short: Do whatever you think best, darling. Whatever you do is fine with me. . . . And from Sarah, *Mama*, listen . . . Do you . . . ?

But Cornelia has already gently laid the telephone in its cradle.

Evening after evening, morning after morning she sits, incapable of any action except walking between table and bathroom and bed, lets the waves, the children's muffled voices, the distant ringing of the telephone, wash over her. She leaves off her hearing aid unless Andrew or Willie Belle or Purvis or Louise picks it up and hands it to her. She drinks too much whiskey, eats whatever is on the plate Willie Belle sets before her. If Louise brings a book and thrusts it into her hands, she reads aloud. She goes to bed early, sleeps a heavy, alcohol-induced sleep for three or four hours, wakens to darkness. Occasionally, drifting to sleep, she seems to hear someone saying again and again, *I didn't*; and an answer: *Yes. You did.* In the mornings, sometimes, she holds a book or a magazine on her lap and if someone comes into the room, she picks it up, pretends to read. Time passes. A week, two weeks, a month, two, three, now almost six months he's been dead.

After the first month or so, Willie Belle had begun to invent tasks for her, or to insist that she assume necessary ones: Will you brush Louise's hair, please, Cornelia? It's a rat's nest and she's running late for the bus. Can you do a couple of loads of wash for me this morning? Her fingers felt swollen, fat and tight as sausages, clumsy with the pins on the clothesline. (Willie Belle likes the smell of sun-dried clothes, hates using the dryer.) Help me this afternoon with gumbo? Peeling onions, she cut herself. She had difficulty fitting the lid on the food processor to chop the vegetables.

Willie Belle seemed to pay no attention. She began to assign more responsible tasks. Purvis and James want to go to the movies this afternoon. Would you mind taking them? Would it be OK for me to leave Louise with you this morning? She has a little fever. (Willie Belle works half-time in the mornings.)

It was when she began to drive the children here and there that it occurred to her something had happened in her head. Synapses were not working. She visualized her brain —stacks of grayish worms doubling over and under, netted as if in a shopping bag with throbbing veins and arteries. When John died, she decided, it was as if God had taken a needle and slipped it carefully into her brain—perhaps through that soft spot below her ear at the hinge of the jaw; and when he had it in place, he had connected it to a thunderbolt and zapped a minute segment of the bland gray custard of thought with a billion volts of lightning. The area he had struck stored recall of new faces.

She could recall the faces of the absent, saw old friends' faces when they called. At night she saw the dead, heard their voices in her dreams, saw her mother, double chins quivering, filled with the fury of victory, slapping down the last king in a game of double solitaire. Saw John, bent eagerly over a new book, turning the pages, his tongue caught between his teeth in concentration, or looking up at her from beneath the branches of the ginkgo tree, saying: It shouldn't be too much of a problem. He spoke in her dreams with his own authentic voice, youthful, hurried, that trace of Brooklyn, of the Irish Channel under its supple articulateness—the voice of a thirty-year-old tenor, apologetic, ironic. Let's dance, he said. It was a mistake, he said. I'm not dead after all. He came home from a trip, walked in with his own balanced light walk. You didn't say that, he said. Never. His face was clearly his own, dark blue eyes full of the joy of seeing her. He put his suitcase down and opened it, drew out a shimmering robe, striped with bronze and gold, that he'd bought for her in some foreign city. It goes with your hair, he said.

But Purvis's friends? Andrew and Willie Belle's friends, the neighbors? Every afternoon for a week, when Willie Belle was working overtime, she picked the children up at school, took Purvis and his friend James to the neighborhood where the boys played touch football. But then, the following week, when she saw him on the school yard and he spoke, she did not know him. Who was that? Purvis gave her a look. That's James, he said. James Lake. You took us to his house every day last week.

Of course. James. Deliberately she associated his name with the James River and the river with his wavy hair. She closed her eyes and visualized water—brown wavy water. But he's not a river, he's a lake. The next week when he came home with Purvis, she did not know him.

Can the capacity to recognize new faces, to store and recall them, be destroyed by grief? Ridiculous.

Now, this night, they are sitting at the supper table. Cornelia has had three drinks before supper. Purvis and Louise sit across from her. Over the past three years order and security have come into their lives. They are calmer and their manners have improved since they first ate pan-cakes at Cornelia's house, but Cornelia is not aware of it. I think she has forgotten that they broke her chair, trampled her garden. She may even have forgotten why it was Willie Belle and Andrew married.

The children tend now to watch with awe, perhaps even fear, this strange silent lady whose husband is in a box in another town, weighed down with a ton of dirt. Who knows what she may do? Is she sad? She never cries. Once or twice they have come in the early morning into the room where their mother and Andrew sleep and seen Andrew—a grown man—sitting naked by the window, weeping. Their mother has explained that he is grieving for his father, but I am not sure how they understand this. They have no father. Or their father might as well be in a box under a ton of dirt for all they know about him.

Cornelia picks up a boiled shrimp from her plate, peels it, dips it in mayonnaise, eats it. Everything smells like roasted peanuts, she says in a meditative voice. You know those sweetish peanuts with a honey coating on them? She shudders. Curious. Even shrimp. I think I've lost my sense of smell, too.

Peanuts? Andrew says. Those peanuts they give you on airplanes?

She flinches. No, not those, but . . .

Too? he says. What do you mean, *too*?

Even peaches. Honeydew melons. Remember how flowery they used to smell? Rosemary. Mint.

Too? he says again sternly. Too, besides what?

She looks at him, sees John's squarish high-cheekboned peasant face; and about his eyes a curious, almost oriental, slant and flatness that comes neither from her nor from John. His eyes are cruel, she thinks. She cannot bear to look at him for more than a moment, looks down at her plate, thinks indifferently, Maybe I have a brain tumor.

Too? he says again.

I mean, she says, concentrating all her attention, I mean, besides not remembering what the children's names are. Purvis, you know what I mean. Like James last week.

My name is Louise, Louise says. Purvis looks at his plate, says nothing.

Not the names, she says. The faces. Sometimes I remember their names, but I can't put them with the faces.

You don't pay attention, Mama, Andrew says clearly, emphatically. You need to try to pay attention.

Maybe people lose nerve cells in their noses, Cornelia says. Like color cones. Mama got to be color-blind in her old age. Remember, Andrew, she bought that rug she thought was mainly shades of blue and gold? Fuchsia! Cerise! She smiles faintly.

What are colored cones? Louise says.

Your mother was seventy when she bought that rug, Andrew says. You are forty-five.

Everybody knows the difference between gold and fuchsia, Purvis says.

Where did you ever hear of fuchsia? (Willie Belle) Are you studying . . . ?

What are colored cones? Louise asks again. Like vanilla, chocolate, and strawberry?

Tiny little cones in your eyes that tell you the difference between colors—like red and green, Andrew says.

That's silly, Louise says. Everybody knows . . . She crossed her eyes. I'm looking at my own eyes, she says, and I don't see any.

To some people everything looks like different shades of gray and black and white, Willie Belle says. Like an old movie on TV. That's called color-blind.

Did you know that dogs . . . ? Andrew began. He got up and with an impulse, a grace of gesture so like his father's that it broke Cornelia's heart in two, pulled down a volume of the encyclopedia. Let's read about animals' eyes, he said.

She excused herself and made her way blindly to the kitchen where she began to clear the counters.

She has no trouble remembering the smell of John's hair, the way a straight lock dropped across his cheek, his characteristic reach when he pulled a book from a high shelf, the touch of her fingers on the velvety tip of his naked sex. Where in the stacked coils of gray custard are those memories stored?

Now Willie Belle is in the bedroom with the children and Andrew is sitting in the living room working a crossword puzzle, while Cornelia still putters around the kitchen. She has found an old knife and is methodically cleaning a minute line of embedded dirt from between the countertop and its chromium edging. He calls to her from the living room: What's a seven-letter word for composed of crossing lines and interstices? His voice echoes inside her head as if from mountain slope to mountain slope. It's a word she's sure he knows. He's just asking her to be asking. Mama? he calls.
Reticular.
An eight-letter word for . . .
Littoral.
Aromatic bark used in . . .
For a long time she does not answer, continuing to scrape the thread of dirt from the edge of the counter, to watch in careful concentration as it humps like a skinny worm ahead of her knife blade. Finally, she says, Cinnamon, Andrew.
Yes, he says. I already had it.

Some days, here on the land across the river from Baton Rouge that Andrew has bought with his inheritance from his grandmother, Cornelia sets out walking. She rises in the early morning from one of those vivid dreams (I'm not dead after all. It was a mistake. . . .), stumbles out of the house, leaves her son's few acres and walks mile after mile, circling through the willow flats along the edge of the oxbow lake that Andrew's land borders, finds herself climbing a spur of abandoned levee grown up with cottonwood trees, persimmons, bois d'arcs, sycamores, hedged in on either side with cane brake, blackberry briars, and palmetto and willow flats. She stumbles, drags a fallen limb out of her way, looks down at the back of her hand, sees a ragged tear in the skin, drops of blood. She must have snagged it on the barbed wire of some fence she scarcely remembers climbing.

Two hundred miles to the north—and how long ago? how many years? although still, today, she sees them walking ahead of her, hears their voices—she and John and the children used to walk together along the levee on June afternoons, the children carrying coils of rope over their shoulders, yodeling to each other, pretending to be Tarzan and Jane. By a blue hole scoured out in some old flood or channel shift John finds a tree with a long branch reaching out over the water, secures a rope for them to swing on, out and back and out again, dropping into the water, silent, ecstatic, stones of delight, and then popping up, buoyant as wood chips.

On those walks they would look in the deep shade for trillium or the rare wild maidenhair fern or, on the open levee, for blooming ironweed, French mulberry, strung with clusters of purple berries like drops of blood or white ones, gleaming like knotted ropes of pearls. Look, she heard him say, and he would have found a piece of driftwood, a central body with eight roots twisting out like a deformed spider's legs; or, half-buried, a bent and fish-shaped limb, looking ready to leap out of the sand, the crack there at the end and the sunken knothole like the mouth slit and eye of a shark. Or he would say, Here's where we found morels last year. Remember? Or boletes or chanterelles. He was a namer of birds and plants and stars, a gatherer of field plums, dewberries, persimmons, remembered where the flush of inky caps came each year on a particularly heavy mat of decaying willow leaves, the dissolving log that after every

168

rain continued to thrust up its harvest of puffballs, round and light as fresh loaves of bread. He would lay back a crust of bark and point out the thready white network underneath: See? The mycelium is always under there, working away.

And the inky caps, those curious fungi that eat themselves like ouroboros, dissolving inward from black ragged edges toward their own stems.

Now he gives her a double handful, gathered from the spongy ground under the willow trees. She is standing at the edge of a steep drop where the levee must have washed away in some old crevasse, and she sees him reaching up with a machete in his hand. What is he doing? He hacks at a vine, cutting one end loose so the children can swing across to the stretch of levee beyond this gap.

Even in winter you can tell if it's poison ivy, he says. See there, that's poison ivy, see how it puts out suckers, grows flat against the trunk? This is probably possum grape or muscadine.

Now they are swinging across the gap, first the children, then John, whose weight must surely bring down the vine from the cottonwood tree.

Wait, she calls, wait for me, looking down at her hands, filled with the inky caps he's given her, neat rigid stems and swelling not-yet-opened heads. She must find a safe place to put them. Now she stumbles down the slope out onto the willow flat below, sinks to her knees. She feels a cold liquid running down her legs, looks down. The mushrooms are dissolving, turning to slime, black blood dripping from her hands to her thighs, trickling like menstrual blood down the insides of her thighs. John and the children are gone. She hears their voices fading, far off along the levee.

She lay down on the mat of willow leaves, twisted and black, still damp from the last rain, cold under her empty hands, under her cheek, closed her eyes, felt herself sinking, as if into quicksand, the weight of her body seeming too great for the earth's surface. She would sink downward toward the earth's center, toward John, where he lay—like in the poem, she thought—rolled round, rolled round—the words rolled in her head—rolled round with rocks and stones and trees. . . .

Purvis is ten. Nearly three years it's been now since that night in New Orleans when he and his mother and Louise were joined, at the nadir of their lives, by Andrew. Purvis remembers (although Louise says, when he asks her, that she does not) the day they were locked out of their apartment, remembers the angry shouts, sees the landlord with a sweeping gesture throw open a closet door, gather everything hanging there, and thrust it into his mother's arms, shouting, Out! Out! Remembers sitting with Louise in the locked car that cold winter evening as the sky darkened over the French Quarter and night people began to emerge from shadowy doorways, while his mother was—where? He didn't know, knew only that she had gone away, saying, Take care of Louise for a little while, darling—I'll be right back.

And that she had come back later with Andrew behind her. How much later? A long time. Hours? Days?

Darkness was all around them. Once a man had stopped and gesticulated strangely at them, signaling with mysterious hand movements to Purvis to do something—open the car door and come away with him? Purvis is sure he did not cry. He turned away, pretended to be talking to Louise, blocking with his body her view of that stooping, threatening presence. Once a couple had slowed down, pointed out the two children to each other, shaking their heads. But then it was dark and Louise was asleep, and perhaps he had fallen asleep, too.

Purvis knew well enough that afterwards—after Andrew bent down toward them out of the darkness, greeting him soberly, after his mother got in the car and followed Andrew to his motel on the outskirts of the city—that afterwards their lives had changed. Never since that day had his mother had to leave them alone in darkness.

Now Purvis is ten. He stands at the peak of childhood's maturity: between those years of terrified self-absorption when he competed with Louise for his mother's distracted attention —years of alternating savagery and generosity toward his sister, of terror and courage in the face of his life—and the years ahead when he will be struggling to become himself. Now he is a grown child, ready to be a hero.

There is a grace at ten, a gatheredness. Hansel was ten when he scattered the pebbles and then the crumbs to guide him and his sister home. They must have been twins—or else Gretel grew up fast—because I think she, too, was ten, when she pushed the witch into the oven and slammed the door. Jack was ten when he climbed the beanstalk, captured the golden goose from under the ogre's very nose, climbed down, and chopped off the stalk at its root. Sister was ten when she cared for little Brother transformed into a fawn.

In any case, today, on this particular morning, Purvis has followed Cornelia deep into the woods.

Unlike Cornelia's children, Purvis had little practice— until Andrew came along—with ropes and swimming holes and adventures. He's a city child, just beginning, with Andrew's help, to wander through these woods, and he does not feel at home. He is afraid, not just of unknown grandparents who may take him from his mother, but of snakes and bears and panthers and hulking men who carry off little boys and do unspeakable things to them. Sometimes the piercing cry of a screech owl wakes him at night and he lies for a long time rigid in his bed. The man is creeping through the woods. Now he is outside a bedroom window. The screech is the cry of a child he is murdering.

Nevertheless, today, under the low-sweeping branches of the live oak trees, around the thickets of cane and briars, the palmetto and willow flats, hearing the inexplicable snap of a stick, the rustle of invisible animals, he follows Cornelia. He wishes he had a rope, a compass, a bowie knife, a gun, but he has followed her on impulse and he has nothing. He brushes his white hair, still tousled from last night's sleep, out of his eyes. Lying in his bed this morning, still drowsing, he heard the door close behind her, through his window saw her walking away, and he dressed so hastily he is wearing tennis shoes without socks. His ankles are cold.

Sometimes he puts his hands in his pockets and whistles softly so that anyone watching will know how poised he is, how unafraid.

He follows her.

Why? Perhaps she is a threat to him and his mother and sister and he feels that he must watch her, learn more about her. She is Andrew's mother and she may steal Andrew away from them—Andrew may choose to take care of her instead of them. Any ten-year-old child can see that she needs someone to take care of her.

He has been walking quietly behind her for a long time, for miles, keeping out of sight in the fringes of the woods, cutting across here and there, where he knows there is a bend in the levee, to intercept her farther along. He is ahead of her now, and tired, fears he may be lost. He thinks about scouts, explorers, remembers that Andrew has told him how they locate themselves in the wilderness: They look for moss on the north side of the trees, they have compasses, or if they don't, they calculate the time of day and the direction they are going by the sun. They climb up into a tree and spy out the countryside.

He climbs up into a cottonwood tree with branches low enough for him to shinny up and swing onto, hitches himself into the lowest crotch, and scrambles upward. He sees her far off, walking toward him along the top of the levee.

Lost echoes somewhere under his whispering consciousness. Now she is passing below the tree where the scout has

172

concealed himself. The scout lies motionless on the limb above her, knowing one false move may bring hostile warriors out of the surrounding woods. She is a decoy, a trap to draw him from his hiding place.

She passes under Purvis's tree, and, a little farther along, stops at the edge of a break in the levee. It's February now, almost spring in this southern wood, buds swelling on the cottonwood trees, a few leaves unfurling. Andrew has pointed out to Purvis how cottonwood leaves are hinged to their twigs so that they shimmer and twist in the least breeze and sound like a continual shower of rain. He listens to the leaves whisper.

The scout lies perfectly still along a branch, balancing effortlessly. No one will see him here high above the trail, and when the moment comes, when they reveal themselves . . .

He waits to see what she will do, but she does nothing. Once he hears her call out, but who is she calling?

Nothing escapes him. He hears a branch crack. They've given away their position. Yes. They . . .

Then she stumbles down the slope of the levee, drops to the ground, and sprawls under the willow tree at its base, as if someone has struck her. Again, for a long time she does not move.

How long has she been lying there? Fifteen minutes? An hour? He looks for the sun, but the sun, after all, doesn't tell him where he is because he is not sure where he came from or what direction they have been walking. Is she asleep? Dead, maybe?

Yes, she's dead. She's taken poison and killed herself and now the scout must go down, must brave the possibility of an arrow from the cane thicket, go down, climb down this cliff and . . .

She's Andrew's mother. Yes, he has to touch her and find out if she's dead. And then? Should he go for help, leave her here where a panther or a bear may come and gnaw off an arm and drag it away to feed her cubs?

173

Was that a growl? There's something hiding . . . Well, he has to.

He clamps his teeth together, climbs down from the cottonwood tree, scrambles down the levee, walks out onto the willow flat, feeling the line of nerves on either side of his backbone prickle and shrink, sits on a fallen log washed up and half buried under a sycamore tree a little way off from her motionless body.

There is nothing behind him, nothing.

He picks up a curl of sycamore bark, examines it, rubs his thumb along the enclosing, conelike curl, a tiny scabbard for an elf's dagger, begins to break fragments from the edges and throw them toward the trunk of a willow tree a few feet beyond her. In a few moments she sits up, looks around, and sees him sitting there. He says hello.

She brushes vaguely at the shirt pocket above her breast. I don't have my hearing aid with me, she says.

He shouts hello.

She nods.

Then he sees, hanging from her jacket pocket, a loop of cord. He points to it.

Ah, she says. Yes. You're right. I do. She pulls it out, the earpiece dangling at the end, holds the earpiece in her hand and stares at it, a tiny translucent pinkish shell through which one might hear the ocean breathing. She turns it over, drops it back into her pocket.

I followed you, he shouts.

Yes.

He says no more for a few minutes, then looks at her with a curiously assessing stare, the vulnerable look of a child about to reveal a secret which an adult may use against him. He opens his mouth, starts to speak, closes it, gets up and turns toward the foot of the levee as if he might climb back up its slope and go away. But he turns to her again. He moves closer, gestures to her pocket. I need to tell you, he shouts. Then, Please.

174

She takes up the cord again, earpiece dangling at one end, battery case at the other, stares at it, puts the earpiece in her ear, then finally drops the battery case in her shirt pocket.

He stands in front of her, thin childish arms crossed on his chest. But then he shakes his head as if to brush the hair from his eyes, steps forward, stands with his legs apart, puts his hands on his hips. Maybe I'm lost, he says sternly. She will think he's silly if he tells her what he really thought—that she was dead, that he alone was responsible for taking the news to Andrew.

She appears not to hear him.

For a while you were talking, he says.

Was I? I didn't hear myself.

You were calling somebody.

Ah.

We'd better go home, he says.

Home?

Yes. He reaches out a hand to her. Come on.

She shudders, looks, finally, at him instead of into some terrible place he can't see. Purvis, she says, why aren't you in school?

It's Saturday, Purvis says. We need to hurry. I'm supposed to go over to James's house to play this afternoon.

HRV is going to sell itself, she heard him say. Did you get your letters?

. . . .

Well, we were right to hold on to it. Fifty-five bucks a share—that's nearly twenty thousand for each of us—Mama, too. Nice little windfall.

. . . .

Not good. The truth is, Sarah, she's about to drive me

out of my box. Willie Belle, too, I'm sure, although Willie Belle just accepts, you know, whatever comes along, never gets . . .

. . . .

No, no, she's not here. Gone for a walk. Wanders around the yard, walks on the levee, but except for that . . .

. . . .

No, she won't. Just sits there. Just sits. Won't make an effort to do anything. And the children . . . She hardly speaks to them. It's like they don't exist. Or else . . . I don't know—she's short, irritable. And another thing. She repeats herself. Forgets what . . . It's a mess.

. . . .

God knows, yes, I do. But you can't help much when . . . when she won't make the least effort to . . .

Cornelia is sitting by the window in the small bedroom they have turned over to her. She has not moved for an hour. The door into the living room is half open, but she did not answer when she heard Andrew call to her a little while ago. I'm not dishonorable, she thinks. I just don't care at all what he says or thinks. What anybody says or what anybody thinks. I don't even care what I think. Do I? Think? She holds her left hand up, sees its outline against the square of light from the window, and it seems to move with a will that is not hers. The little finger moves with a scissors motion and she feels the muscle that controls it pull inside an arm that is clearly attached at her shoulder.

Well, maybe if you try again, Sarah. She needs to, God knows, and if she will, I could drive her up. I'd hate to see her get in a car and drive off to anywhere farther than down the street. God knows where she might end up.

. . . .

She reaches across with her right hand and pinches her left arm just above the elbow. Hard. Harder. Harder. With interested detachment she notices that the arm feels pain. She digs in her fingernails. Yes. Considerable pain. She

176

thinks briefly about someone of whom she's heard—a schizo-phrenic—who persisted, when left alone, in grinding out cigarettes on her own flesh.

After a while she gets up from the bed and walks out into the living room, where Andrew sits reading. He looks up, guilty. I thought you were taking a walk, he says. I was beginning to worry. It's getting dark.

Yes, she says, walks over to the window, looks out into dusky late afternoon sky. I was asleep, she says. I took a walk and then I went to sleep.

You sleep a lot, Mama.

Yes. She sits down, picks up a magazine, opens it, and lays it in her lap.

He puts down the book he's been reading. Sarah called a little while ago, he says abruptly. She wants you to come home. She needs you to begin to see about the business.

Cornelia says nothing.

She *needs* you.

Yes, she says. I should go.

Maybe Sarah is going to want you to take over again, he says. Or . . . You need to talk about the alternatives.

Yes.

He crosses the room, pulls a chair close to where she's sitting. (She's chosen a chair isolated from the rest of the furniture in the room.) Mama . . . he says. Breaks off. Then, What happened to your arm?

I . . . I . . . must have bruised it somehow when . . . I'm thin-skinned, she says. . . .when I was out walking . . . It doesn't hurt. I didn't even know I'd done it.

Think about it, he says. Think about going home. OK?

Yes, she says. I have to think about it. Then she said, I'll go, Andrew. In a few days I'll go.

Someone . . . (Who? Whoever it was raised her arm, waggled her finger, pinched the muscle above her elbow so viciously a little while ago. Not a stranger, no. The voice —insistent, plucking at her brain—is a voice she thinks

177

she must know intimately. *Familiar*, then? But that word calls up images of cats and broomsticks.) anyhow, somebody spoke now: You need to write to Evelyn.

She got up and returned to her room where she sat down at the desk and taking pen and stationery began a letter to an old friend. Dear Evelyn, she wrote, I think it would do me good to get away by myself for a while. You've written twice to ask if you can do anything for me. I'm sorry I haven't answered your letters, my dear. I just haven't.

She stopped writing and sat for a few minutes staring at the wall.

Go on, her companion said.

She began again. You must be heading back to San Francisco, she wrote, as you said in your last letter you soon would. There is something you could do for me. Would you mind if I used your little apartment for a few days—maybe even a couple of weeks? The children couldn't be kinder and more thoughtful, but . . .

She stopped again, stared out into the gathering darkness for a long time. Then she picked up her pen and wrote slowly, I can't bring myself to go back to my empty house . . . She stopped again, then wrote: quite yet. She began a new paragraph. Since you keep that little roosting place in New York, I wondered if you would mind if I used it for a few days. Don't hesitate to say if it's not convenient, my dear. I can always stay at a hotel. It's just that I thought I might . . . She had reached the bottom of the page. She stopped again.

Why can't I stay at a hotel? she asked.

One excellent reason is that the children would never consent to your going off to New York alone. You know you're not going to argue with them. It's simpler for you to lie and say Evelyn has invited you to come and stay with her, that she's in New York for a couple of months.

Why am I going? she said.

I'm not sure. Probably because you're angry.

No, she said. I don't care. I simply don't care.

After a while she said, I *will* be alone. That's it. I will learn to be alone.

Or something.

She picked up a second sheet of paper. Listen, my dear, she wrote, if you love me, write me a letter inviting me to come to see you—I mean in New York. I do need to be by myself for a little while and . . .

Write something that will reassure Evelyn and that she can write to reassure the children.

. . . and, well, you know how oversolicitous the people who love you can be, Cornelia wrote. I simply need to be by myself and they are likely to refuse to understand that. And New York has so many distractions—there is so much I'd like to begin to see and do again. Remember, now, don't hesitate to say if it doesn't suit. Affectionately, Cornelia.

She made her arrangements, reassured her children, paying no attention to Andrew's anxious questions, Sarah's cautionary calls. She would go.

And so, on the appointed day, Andrew and the children take her to the airport. Standing in the waiting area, they look unhappily at each other. Andrew lays a hand on Purvis's shoulder, stoops, picks up Louise (too big now, of course, to be picked up and carried, her legs dangling to his knees), as if to shelter her from some genuine but not yet identified threat. Cornelia sees in his eyes a kind of baffled pity—not for the children, for her.

Mama . . .

She kisses Purvis and Louise, touches Purvis's head. I'll be back soon. I'll . . . I'll bring you . . .

Will you? It seemed to Cornelia that the weight of the strap on her carry-on bag was the weight of someone clinging there, a creature heavy with messages: Will you? What will you bring?

She turns away, walks toward the boarding gate.

This is the first time she has been on a plane since John's death. She will fly. She will not see his face when the pilot revs the engines and the plane shudders against its brakes at takeoff. Now, sitting in her place, fastening her seat belt, she hears Tweet's voice. Well, I reckon I'll go, too, Tweet says and Cornelia almost speaks aloud: Hush, Julia, Hush.

The dead live, Tweet says. The dead stay in the place where they die and their power is in that place.

All very well if you die in the furrow by the turnrow on your own land. But on the floor in the aisle of a DC-3? Flying over Birmingham? Has John, then, been flying back and forth above her head all these past six months? She smiles. Well, at least he's flying. But . . . But not under his own power.

She will not think about him.

FIVE

Everyone knows how threatening the city is these days. Her friends who go every year to shop and for the theater and museums, or on their own or their husbands' business, go everywhere in taxis. They never used to ride the subways, even when the subways were safe. Now the mere suggestion fills them with horror. Never mind that three or four million people ride subways unharmed every day of every year.

As for going out at night alone to a movie or the theater —Never!

But Cornelia and John always prided themselves on being almost like city people. They did ride the subways, went everywhere in the city whenever they wanted to, and of course they've always gone to the theater and . . .

They. They've gone. But Cornelia? Cornelia has never walked any city street alone, day or night, because she has always been with John. Since she was nineteen years old and flew from her tower bedroom to John's loving arms, she's never done anything alone. She's like a queen borne up from dawn to dusk by attendants who never allow her foot to touch the earth.

Now, she says, she will learn to be alone, and the city is where she will start.

But I can't help wondering if that's the real reason why

Cornelia is coming to New York. To be alone? Why should she choose so distant and threatening a place to learn what she could learn in her own house? What every widow or widower, every broken couple, torn from no matter how loving or how hateful a marriage or love affair, has either to learn or to avoid learning.

Does it seem almost beyond belief that at forty-five, having been to New York a dozen times in the past seven or eight years, she sits rigid and fearful in the taxi from the airport to Evelyn's apartment in the Eighties, east of York, wondering if the driver is taking her to some deserted street or alley behind an empty warehouse where he intends to rape and murder her?

She looks at the back of his head, studies his photograph —a swarthy, bearded (sullen?) face—and memorizes his license number. But what good will his number do her, or her capacity (not to be depended on) to remember his face, to recognize him, if he murders her? A sexual thrill of dread tingles in her breasts, her thighs, when she thinks about these possibilities. To be raped, murdered . . .

Such a thought has never crossed her mind before. She never used to wonder what direction they were going, whether this or that route was the shortest. But, *before*, she rode with John, relied on John's infallible sense of direction, was convinced that he knew as well where they were as if he were in the cockpit of his own airplane, checking airspeed and altitude and compass reading on his own instruments.

They are approaching the tangle of roads at the entrance to the airport. Which way you want to go, lady? His accent is heavy, Middle Eastern.

I don't know, she said. The shortest way. The least traffic.

You want to go by Triborough or Fifty-ninth Street?

Whichever way is cheapest, she said.

You're in charge. Which way you want to go? You got to pay toll on Triborough. No toll Fifty-ninth Street.

He's trying to trick her. Go by the Triborough, she said.

As the traffic whirls by, she stares out at cemeteries, at

narrow winding roads giving access to acre after acre of gravestones, a whole city of graves under bare trees and evergreens, and then at acre after acre of high-rise projects as gray and cold as if they were gigantic mirror images of the gravestones, only without the possibilities suggested by the roads—a knoll beyond that curve where, in the spring, one might spread out a blanket, lie on the grass under a warm sun. How many millions of people are buried in these graves, these ghettos? She thinks of Rome, of Paris, of cities where two thousand years, not just two hundred, of accumulated bones lie buried.

They are approaching tollgates. Are they going in the right direction? Is this the Triborough Bridge? Didn't she see a sign back there for Long Island? Where are they? She sees him looking at her in the rearview mirror, scornful, calculating.

Bastard.

She is flooded with terror, a fear as causeless as if she thought she might see a gigantic spider squatting on the seat next to her, a spider that would begin spinning its web around her, throwing coils of silky steel about her body, attaching her to the shining strands of its web. She sees herself pulsing and struggling there.

But she will not countenance this abjection. She says again, as she did when she was eavesdropping on Andrew's telephone conversation with Sarah, What difference does it make? I don't care. I simply don't care.

In front of her apartment building, the driver turns, gazes at her, smiles. See, Lady, he says. Wasn't nothing to worry about. I got you here OK, didn't I?

Has her terror been so obvious? Yes. And now he is happy—it gives him a feeling of warm male superiority to recognize her fear, to let her wallow in it. Only he had the power to reassure her and he waited until the last possible moment to speak.

It's beginning to snow. All last night and all today snow has been moving eastward across the country. This morning in the Atlanta airport where she changed planes, she picked up a *New York Times*, read that the preceding night an elderly man in a small Ohio town dropped his door key into the snow on his front stoop (temperature ten below, windchill factor forty below) and froze to death before he could find it.

That was in the paper. But how could anyone know such a thing? Who was there to see him groping in the snow? Maybe he had a heart attack. She shrugs, pays the waiting driver.

Blizzard coming, he says as she hands him the money. You're my last fare.

The facade of the building is grimy, scrofulous, yellow-painted brick; the rusted fire escape hangs askew. She stumbles past a line of battered garbage cans—chained to the iron guardrail as if they were precious objects apt to be stolen—and up three concrete steps to the gnawed and splintered doorway, unlocks the door with one of the three keys her friend has sent her, and steps into a dark hallway, bitter cold, smelling of burned food, stale cigarette smoke, and damp plaster. Evelyn rented this apartment years ago for a daughter who lived here only briefly. Then, when the daughter married and moved away, she and her husband kept it—cheap enough with rent control to make it worth keeping for her husband's monthly coast-to-coast business trips. Now, even though the landlord has let the building deteriorate, he has raised the rent on one apartment after another as old tenants have moved out and new ones have moved in. He would like nothing better, Evelyn has written, than to force them out and raise the rent on this apartment.

The carpet on the hall floor is tattered, filthy, the stairs narrow and dark. Would the keys to the apartment fit? Would the door open? Would something dreadful . . . ?

It doesn't matter, her companion says. You're a fool. You've just said it doesn't matter, haven't you?

In front of the apartment door, she dropped a key, fumbled for it in the dim light. Which lock did it fit? Would a hairy drunken man in a raveling sweater open the door across the hall and smile at her? She found the key, opened both locks, dragged her suitcase in, secured the dead bolt. The telephone was ringing.

It's Evelyn saying that she has worried all day remembering that she failed to include in her letter instructions about the location of the key to the burglar bars and access to the fire escape outside the window. The place would be a death trap in a fire, Evelyn says. But look there in the bowl on the bookshelf, out of reach even if someone smashes the window and puts an arm through. You can see it from where you're standing by the phone—OK? And don't put it any closer to the window—be *sure* not to put it where someone can reach through and get it. Leave it right there unless you have to use it.

Yes, Cornelia says.

This doesn't seem to be the right answer. Are you all right, Cornelia?

Yes, she says. Of course. I'm fine. Happy to be here.

But it's cold, isn't it? I mean cold. The landlord is supposed to leave the heat on all the time, but he knows we're not always there—that we just use it off and on. Nothing to do except give him a call. If you're cold, call him in the morning. His telephone number—Mr. Canizaro—is on the back of the Manhattan directory. Be sure he knows you're a guest. We could lose our lease if he thought we were subletting, even for weekends or overnight.

I don't think I'll risk calling him, Cornelia says. I don't want that to happen. And besides it feels quite warm. I believe the heat's on. She's lying. She hasn't taken off her coat, so she is reasonably comfortable, but she can see her breath in the air.

She put her suitcase on a luggage rack, opened it, hung up a dress, took her cosmetics into the bathroom, put her tooth-

187

brush and toothpaste on the basin, the Valium on the middle shelf in the medicine cabinet. Then she got out a bottle of whiskey, went directly to the kitchen, and fixed a drink. She walked back into the bathroom, flushed the toilet, returned to the bed-living room, and looked around at the battered sofa bed, fire-sale chest, canvas sling chairs. The greenish walls were covered with unframed posters. A Mexican basket full of old theater programs and dog-eared magazines sat on the floor next to the sofa, a Mason jar full of pens and pencils on the mantelpiece. She walked to the front window and looked out. The snow was still coming lightly down. She drew her coat about her and stood, sipping her drink, gazing into the street as the dusk deepened and snowflakes, caught now and then in a gust of wind, drifted and whirled, then settled into a heavier, slanting, eastward-driven pattern. Cars passed slowly, following funnels of headlighted snowflakes. Streetlights came on. She walked to the kitchen and fixed another drink.

Standing in the tiny hallway opening on one side into the kitchen and on the other into the bath she felt that the air was noticeably warmer here than in the front room. Why? In a corner, she saw an exposed pipe running from floor through ceiling and touched it lightly. It was warm, must carry steam to some more fortunate tenant above. She brought a chair into the hall, turned on the overhead light, sat down beside the pipe, and tried to read the *New York Times*.

First I'd better . . . Deli on . . . Where did Evelyn say . . . ? Eighty-third Street? Eighty-second? And down from there, a reasonably good restaurant. But I'm not going to a restaurant tonight, and if there's a blizzard. . . .

Without warning, without reason, as it seemed to her, Purvis's thin face and white thatch surfaced in her mind. There he is, the face first and then the rest of him, standing with his hands on his hips like Errol Flynn playing Captain Blood. Not Andrew on a vine cut from its root by his father, but Purvis swinging down on a rope from the rigging of a pirate ship, standing arms akimbo on the slanting deck and then knocking the pirate captain aside just as he raises his dagger to stab the ringletted, kirtled heroine in . . . She smiled at him.

Ah, *ma vieille,* Purvis says, *Courage! Courage!*

Purvis, Cornelia said, you don't know French.

She laid aside the unread *Times.* Yes, she said, I'd better get some food in.

Why bother?

But she went out, tramped south and then west, head down in the now-driving snow, seeing only legs, blown skirts, emerge from whirling snow, pass and vanish, found the deli, bought milk and butter and eggs, fruit, coffee, bread and cheese, and a pastrami sandwich and a piece of cheesecake for her supper. Next door at a liquor store she bought wine and brandy and bourbon. The wind blew, whipped her coat, drove snow into her eyes.

What am I doing here?

Inside her head a swelling and vibration, but no one answered.

She fumbled with a numb hand for her keys, scurried up the dark stairs, down the dingy hall. Something behind her?

The dark!

She feels a crawling weight of darkness moving nearer at her back, for a moment sees Tweet's face close to hers, hears her voice: Evil out there. I be a fool not to know that.

The dark. Yes. When? Had she been eight? Nine? When she would come running down the stairs. . . . Why had it been so dark? Yes, a light switch at the head of the stairs for the upstairs hall, and no e at the foot, so that you had to . . . Yes, she'd imagined the darkness as alive, as losing its power slowly. One had to scuttle down, get beyond its strength into the lighted living room. And if you left it on . . .

Mother: Go back upstairs, Cornelia, and turn off the lights. We don't waste electricity. Go upstairs. And come down slowly like a lady.

And later, in bed: Night-lights are for cowards. You don't need one.

But, Mother . . .

Silly. Don't be silly, Cornelia.

Mother's bulk blocks out the light from the hallway through the open door, and then she is gone. The door closes, thunk, the strong darkness falling heavily on the bed weighing me down, and . . . The old house breathes, springs groaning, walls popping, floors creaking. . . .

I won't hear all this, I won't, Cornelia said. I will not.

If you don't listen, her companion says calmly, your head will explode.

Oh, God, Cornelia said. I hated her. If she were alive, I would kill her. She slammed and double-locked the apartment door behind her.

I'm afraid, Tweet says. Nevertheless I go. I go to the turn-row and listen. I make myself strong to listen. I have to be strong to give way. Like this, she says. My grandpa might be singing this: What set Paul and Silas free is good enough for you and me. Keep your hand on the plow, hold on.

But John, oh, yes, he did, he took me away from . . . And I never—all those years we never . . . Our children, we never, to them . . .

She's lying in bright sunlight on a towel spread out on a sandbar, the children playing in a scooped-out pool left behind by the spring rise, clear green water, brown sand, light all around them. . . .

My God, he was *alive* . . . always so . . . *there.*

He rolls toward her, takes her hand in his, brushes away a speck of sand from her forehead, kisses her temple, his lips touch her skin above the shadowy hollow where the pulse throbs.

Now, he's standing knee-deep in the pool, fly casting, and she watches him, his attentive stance, his competent hands flipping out the line, skipping the fly across the water.

The line snaps taut, a bass leaps into the air. But then he turns toward her, as she thinks, to hold up the caught fish, and she sees his face, his eyes are bulging, his tongue extruded.

I didn't say that, John. I didn't. Oh, I didn't.

Yes, he says. You did. I brought you out into the sunshine, we climbed down the ginkgo tree together. I loved you, he says. All my life I loved you. And you said that to me and now you can never take it back.

Alone and locked in, she took off her hearing aid, put away the groceries, opened and made up the sofa bed. She unwrapped her sandwich, allowing herself to think only of the small operations: Eggs in the egg rack. Slice the pickle—where is a knife? Another drink? Wine with my supper? After she had eaten, she sat down in the hall by the warm pipe with another drink. Once, she got up, went into the bathroom, opened the medicine cabinet, took out the full bottle of Valium. But she put it back on the shelf and fixed another drink. By nine o'clock she was in bed, heavily asleep. At one or a little after she woke, lay staring at the square of light in the window. She was very cold. She got up, found in a bureau drawer a heavy old comforter that smelled of dust, spread it on her bed, put on her robe and socks, and crawled back in.

She observed that although she was cold, she was not shivering. Everything inside and out was still. Earlier, alert, as deaf people are, to vibration, she had been vaguely aware of the continuing traffic, the slight felt punctuations of slamming doors, footsteps, sensed in her own feet, her body. But now everything was still.

I am dying, she said aloud. This football in my chest is my death growing inside me.

A curious faint light filled the room, cold and clear, as

if the apartment had filled up with wholly transparent ice, the ammoniated block ice of her childhood that came from its bed of sawdust in the ice wagon, clear and veined as spring water.

She turned on a lamp, got up again, padded to the window, looked out. The window ledge, the street, the air were white, the air filled with flakes, large and light as the ginkgo leaves that whirled round her window at home in the autumn wind. The street was empty. She picked up a month-old magazine from the basket, went back to bed. Her eyes followed the print down column after column. Toward morning she slept uneasily for two or three hours. When she got up, the snow was still falling, thick and light. In a drawer she found a straightedge, opened the window and measured the cushion resting rounded and puffy as a risen loaf on the window ledge. It was already fifteen inches deep.

After she had drunk coffee, huddled by the steam pipe in the tiny hall, she turned on the hot water full force in the tub, and when the bathroom was warm and steamy, got in, bathed quickly, and dressed. By now it had stopped snowing; but her boots were inadequate for this weather— high heeled and thin soled.

You can stay here. No reason to go out.

Keep your hand on the plow, hold on.

She set out walking. A couple of blocks west and three or four to the south she went into a shoe store and bought fleece-lined, flat-heeled boots. Across the street in a women's clothing store she found socks, a scarf, and a knit hat.

Outside now the sun was shining, snowplows were clearing the streets, although everywhere there were cars buried in drifts, and piles of already packed and trampled grayish snow made the crossings almost impassable. She walked south on Lexington.

After all, it's a perfect day—the sun . . .

Perfect for what?

She stepped on a grating in the sidewalk from which clouds of steam were rising, stopped to warm herself, spread-

192

ing the skirt of her coat around her. In the building beside her a door opened: I smell garlic. Garlic and olive oil.

She is standing in the stairwell of a pensione where she and John stayed one year in Rome. She looks down, as if she might see the stairs descending, the paisley carpet on the treads, the doorway at the foot opening into a kitchen where something marvelous is always cooking.

But as quickly as it had come, the scene, the piercing joy of recollection vanished. The wind raised a swirl of snow. Snowflakes melted on her collar and icy drops trickled down her neck.

I don't care. I don't care, she said aloud, and set out walking south at a great rate, turned west at the first corner, and crossed over toward Fifth.

It clung heavily, dragged heavily at her shoulder, whispering, voice stridulous (yet silent), vibrating soundlessly against the barrier raised inside her head, inside the blocked ear canal, by frozen hammer, anvil, and stirrup.

Wire vibrating inside my head.

Listen. Stories. Stories about betrayal, about helplessness and cruelty, about guilt and innocence.

I'm cold. The wind is blowing. This crosstown wind . . . And I have to watch my step every minute or I'll fall down.

Listen.

Cornelia put her foot on a slanting icy mound, slipped, recovered her balance.

Now Tweet speaks. I commence running, she says. Run as well as I could to Martha's house. Seem like my feet was made of stone.

Cornelia sees her running ahead, wrapped in Grandfather's old coat, the tails dragging in the snow, feels a twinge of envy at her agility.

What's that you got on your shoulder, talking like it got sense? Tweet says.

Stand still, Cornelia. Stop wiggling.

Sound like your mama to me.

Who is that disgusting illiterate colored woman?

She don't know I went to the eighth grade.

I want to tell you about Nabokov—where is it? In *Speak, Memory*? Do you remember he wrote that when he was a child he could manipulate huge figures in his head, instantly find squares and square roots, multiply ten digits by . . . ?

Never heard your mama talk like that, Tweet says.

No, it's not . . . not Mama.

How he had a fever, was delirious, felt his head swelling, filled to bursting with numbers?

Last night, Cornelia says. Yes, I was thinking last night it felt as if my head were too full, as if it might burst. Not full of numbers though. . . . Of . . .

I can make your head burst.

Tweet turned. Listen to *me*, she says. I'm too polite to say, but I notice you don't hardly ever ax a question, and sometimes *seems* like you're listening—you put on listening —but you ain't. Seems like you think you don't need to ax, don't need to listen, you already got answers, or else you don't want to hear none. But where are all them words, if you don't ax, don't tell, don't answer? They might be out here in the world. Or they might all be shut up in your head, waiting, making your head swell up. You thought about that?

Cornelia continued to plod into the wind.

Or here's another thing, Tweet says. You right it ain't your mama. But sounds dead to me. Dead voice. Heavy. You carrying a dead body on your shoulder. You don't bury it, you got to carry it.

Body? Body?

Hold on. Hold on, Tweet sings. Keep your hand on the plow. . . . and so forth.

The buckle of Cornelia's shoulder bag dug into her shoulder. She shifted the weight.

Listen to *me*. Listen to *me*, Cornelia.

Sometimes it ain't *hold on*, it's *let go*, Tweet says.

The two of you, Cornelia says, you can say anything you please, ask anything you like. Who's left for me to listen to except you?

Look out! Right there by that next pile of snow—right in front of you. Dog shit. Whoa! I'm trying to see after you.

Had she ever heard Julia use that word—shit? If she had she could not remember it. Thank you, she said.

Here's a question, Tweet says: How do you hold on and let go at the same time?

Do you know what became of Tweet's money after she and Nig and the girls moved to town?

You better answer, Tweet says. Whoever tis. Maybe you heard once and didn't listen. I know it, but that don't matter—

I'm not sure, Cornelia says. She . . . She must have spent part of it on the house. Yes. She bought that house. But she only had to put down five hundred, and then she and Nig paid out the rest over . . . They may still be paying for it.

And?

She . . . she must have helped Cynthia and Charlene with school, and then, when they went on their own. And . . . I'm trying. You know how money goes. A car? Clothes? Julia loves clothes. I've . . . She means to say, *I've forgotten*, but she does not. Now she is standing, back to the wind, at the bus stop on Seventy-sixth and Fifth. Beyond the low stone wall, the park stretches away, its vistas mounded with un-blemished snow, its paths deserted. Snow lifts from the mound tops, whirls up, limbs shake off their loads, whip through the air like catapults released. The wind scissors through her coat as if through gauze. She winds her scarf around her head, covering her mouth and nose, thrusts gloved hands into her pockets, seems to herself to be cold beyond shivering. Two old women stand nearby, their heads bent toward each other. She sees their lips move.

You think I'd throw away my grandpa's money on clothes? Tweet says. That sweet sticky money that was more than money? Him still out there talking and singing to me?

No. You wouldn't even have bought a car with it. Helped Cynthia and Charlene, yes. But not a car.

This is what happened to Grandfather's money.

Wait, Cornelia says. This is heavy. Too heavy.

You got that purse on your shoulder, Tweet says. If it ain't a body, maybe it's a talking purse.

Julia . . .

You think you know heavy? You hadn't drug a cotton sack twelve or fourteen hours a day, have you? Carried a load of somebody else's wash on your head. Carried two buckets of water from the cistern? That's heavy.

Whatever this is, it's heavy, too, Cornelia says.

If it's wash, carry it home, wash it and iron it. Get you a red wagon and a basket and carry it back. Hold on, that's the message. Keep your hand on the plow, hold on. If it's water, drink it, wash with it, cook with it. If it's a cotton sack, hmmmm. . . . My advice, if it's a cotton sack, go get you a better job. Let go, let go, let go.

Tweet joined a church when she and Nig moved into town—a church in their neighborhood.

Don't she talk stiff, Tweet says.

She got interested in the choir, the preacher . . .

Got interested! Tweet says, What do you know about *got interested*? I'm singing. Can't get along without singing. Redeemed . . . Redeemed. Sing it! (Oh, I can't sing solos like that Puddin Greene, but I can sing.)

Interested in the choir, the preacher, fund-raising, putting a new roof on the church, buying a new piano. Before long, even young as she was and new to the church, she was vice president of the choir, organizing the drive to get the new piano. . . .

Some say you got to stick to one or the other, Tweet says. Church music or the devil's music. Not me. I sing it all.

Spoonful, spoonful, spoonful. One little spoon of your love is good enough for me. . . .

And the president of the choir was—you remember?

That story she told me—that may have been nonsense. She may have made it up to entertain me. I never believed . . . Cornelia gets on the bus, drops her change into the funnel. She's out of the wind, sitting comfortably in her place, staring out at the . . .

Look out *right now* for that next pile of snow—there—in front of you. Dog shit. Whoa! I'm trying to . . .

We're on the bus, Cornelia says. On the bus, Tweet. There isn't any dog shit. Not on the bus.

You saying you don't believe what I tell you? You don't listen to what I tell you?

At the next stop, an enormously fat woman boarded the bus, staggered into the seat next to Cornelia, crowding her against the window, turning as she settled herself, shaking snow from her collar, folds of flesh draped below her chin, at her wrists. She looks like a fat bulldog, chin whiskers like . . .

Cornelia felt a pounding deep in her ears, a swelling inside her skull, pain in her temples, managed to say: No. It wasn't nonsense. I'm sorry, Tweet. I know it was true.

Mrs. Greene was president of the choir. A young woman, younger than Tweet, married—Marie Adele Greene.

Lemme tell this story, Tweet says. This is my story. I can tell it better. Yeah, she had a fancy name. Name, she say, for her grandma, suppose to be French, but she call herself Puddin. So, to begin with, we was all in the same church. That is, me and the girls was in that church, because Nig never went to church—hadn't been save, still hasn't. But he'd take me and the girls, and then he'd go on down to Blaze Street, look for somebody to pass the time with until church was out. But time all this happen, the girls are grown, Cynthia's off at nursing school.

One Sunday he carries us to church, and she—Puddin

Greene—comes up to the car and starts talking. She's a beautiful brown color, skin smooth as a child, little bitty waist, shakes her tail like a bird, got gold earrings in her ears. So she's talking to me about the choir. The piano this, the piano that—we need a new piano so bad. But we hadn't got the money—maybe we can pay it out on time with the music store, maybe go to the bank and borrow the money. I know Lawyer Quinn, maybe I can go to the bank and talk to him about a loan.

But all the time she was talking, she'd look at me and then she'd look at Nig, smile at Nig. I saw it. It was after that day he begun to come to church every Sunday, begun talking about getting save, maybe he would get save before the next time they baptize.

Oh, Lord, Tweet says, she could play the piano. She could sing. I have to admit I never a heard a soul in this world sing "Redeemed" like she could. And she was young and kind of shy, her voice strong and sweet and—I don't know—you have to hear it. But she'd get scared sometimes when she was singing her solo and it would shake—her voice would—make her seem that much younger—like she's still modest, scared of men.

That was in nineteen fifty-one or fifty-two, before Tweet came to work for you.

Year after I had those risings scarred my face so bad.

Beside Cornelia, the bulk of her seatmate shifted, unyielding as a block of ice. Icy water dropped from her sleeves, soaked into Cornelia's coat, cold against her skin.

Tweet told you Nig wouldn't sleep with her, wouldn't even lie in the same bed with her all that year she had the risings. As if she were so repulsive to him that . . .

That fat lady feature your mama, don't she? Tweet says.

Disgusting! the fat woman says. Disgusting.

Talking about me, Tweet says. She giggles. Lord, ain't she fat!

No, Cornelia said. Yes. But I . . .

She hasn't got no power over me. I know her. You think

I don't know her? I heard her talk. You think I hadn't heard her? Saying them risings come from dirt and ignorance. Ignorant niggers, that's what she say.

Julia—Tweet—she never . . . Never in front of you. But . . . Yes.

I hate her, but she ain't my mama. You hadn't got around to beginning to hate her yet.

To continue, Tweet says, twas like somebody had put a spell on me that year. Nig didn't want none of it to rub off on him. Didn't want to . . . Ugly. I was so ugly. Seem like nobody would ever love me again (not counting Cynthia and Charlene).

Disgusting!

She did it, Cornelia says. Mrs. Greene—Puddin. She did it.

Is that what you say? You think she put a mojo on me?

No, Cornelia says. No. I don't mean . . . Her head is swelling. She takes a deep breath. Inside or outside, it's all the same, she says. Then: Tweet, she says, you and I . . . You and I . . . We . . . The bus shuddered to a stop. The fat woman rose, made her way down the aisle. The door opened for her with a hiss and she floated with a light swaying fat walk down the steps and was gone.

Go on, Cornelia says. And then they . . . I want to *hear* it.

That's the ticket, Tweet says. And I never will forget it.

Coming home from work—I was working for that lady had lead poison that year —waiting one day at the bus stop there by the entrance to the park where she lived, and Elder Robbs (in our church) sees me standing there, stops and offers me a ride. He's getting off his shift at Chicago Mill. Little after three in the afternoon. Nig's on the night shift at the Gypsum Company that week. Sleeps all the morning. But I know he might or might not be up and gone time I get home. We take the short way down Calhoun and Farish Streets. Bus doesn't go that way, so Nig wouldn't expect me to be passing by. And there, at the corner of Farish and

199

First, across from Nasser's Superette, I see Nig's car parked in front of Puddin Greene's house.

Just let me off here at the Superette, Mr. Robbs, I say. I got to get some things for supper. Not but two blocks from home, I can walk the rest of the way.

I went over to her house running, Tweet said. Busted in without knocking—nobody locked doors in them days— and there they were, setting up in the living room, got all their clothes on, setting there conversing.

Excuse me if I don't knock, I say. Seeing Nig's car here, I thought maybe something had happen to him. Give me a turn.

He was as cool as if he was buried in the shade and I just dug him up. Cool as the root cellar in January. Well, I had a flat tire, Tweet, he says, right here in front of Puddin's house, and she was kind enough to fix me a glass of lemonade when I had done changed it.

Sure enough there's a pitcher of something or other— lemonade, gin, whatever—setting on the table between them, and he's got a glass of it in his hand.

She gets up, twittery. Hops around like a little flycatcher. Shakes her tail.

Sit down, Miss Tweet, she says. Let me pour you a glass. *Miss* Tweet!

Thank you, I say, but I got to go over to the Superette, *Miss* Puddin. Nig, you can wait and drive me on home.

So that's what we did. And as soon as we're in the house, I say, I done forgot something at the Superette, gimme the keys, Nig. He doesn't want to give me those keys, no. But he chances it. I go out to the car and open the trunk and take a look at the spare and it ain't any flatter than the ones on the ground. Charlene coming up the walk, coming home from work.

I see this flat tire you talking about, Nig, I say. I see how flat it is.

So that's how I found out he's fooling around with her, Tweet says. He nor she wouldn't admit it. He says he made up that about the flat tire because he knew what I'd think. But the truth is, he says, he had just happen to see her in the yard and stop to speak and she had invited him in for lemonade. Would I leave my car park right in front of her house for you to see? he says.

As for Miss Marie Adele, she keeps on being sweet as cream to me, always calling me Miss Tweet, asking my advice about the piano and all that, but it continues to go on. Every day I'm throwing fits—feeling so awful—my face all scarred and . . . Nig won't say nothing. He's hardly talking—gets up and leaves when I start in on him.

Cornelia reaches out. She wants to touch Tweet, to comfort her. The bus is crowded now and they are south of Fiftieth Street. She had meant to get off at Fifty-third. Was that where the fat woman got off?

You ain't begun to hate her enough yet, Tweet says.

Inside her ear now, again, that vibrating wire. On her flesh the dragging weight: When Tweet told you about that, when you thought about her with boils on her face, about Nig, so faithless, so callous to her suffering. That was when you thought about firing her, wasn't it? You never wanted to have to look at her face again.

But I didn't do it, Cornelia said. *I did not fire Julia.*

And now there comes into Cornelia's mind another scene. The year is nineteen sixty-seven. Rosa has brought her dying husband, Robert, to live with Tweet and Nig. He's been through a local clinic, has been diagnosed as having an inoperable cancer, and the two women have joined forces to look after him.

A minor crisis in the unfolding drama of his death has brought Cornelia into the house. The old man—in his late seventies, considerably older than Rosa—has bedsores, and Cornelia has brought a sheepskin for him to lie on, and advice, and boric acid powder to sprinkle on the sheets.

Here the three women are in the bedroom that used to be Cynthia and Charlene's, now given over to Rosa and Robert. They are surrounded by Rosa and Robert's belong-ings—suitcases and boxes, folded towels, stacks of adult-size diapers, a bedpan, a table crowded with bottles of pills, chairs stacked with sheets and quilts, draped with coats and sweaters, on the mantel, as on the living room mantel, a clutter of pictures, bills, china figurines, small glass bowls filled with odds and ends of costume jewelry. Cornelia sees the room, and it brings with it the scene between her and Tweet the day of Martin Luther King's death: clutter, disorder, pierced through with sorrow and mystery. She sees the three of them—herself and Tweet and Rosa—gathered around the bed on which Robert lies, inert, silent, watching them consult over him. She and Tweet are lifting and turning his long emaciated body. She sees his legs, polished sticks of walnut, his grayish calloused feet, the hospital gown rucked up around his thighs. Rosa stands at the foot of the bed, nervously rubbing her hands together. Cornelia and Tweet look at each other, businesslike, detached as two nurses might be. It seems to Cornelia that they act as one, their intimacy and mutual understanding is perfect. They lift and turn the old man, pull the nightshirt up so they can inspect the bedsores on his buttocks. They slide the sheepskin under him, and when they turn him again, she sees sparse white pubic hairs, dark scrotum, penis flaccid against his thigh. She glances up and sees him gazing at her, his long face grim, then smiling in a kind of ironic acknowledgment of the helplessness of illness, the sexlessness, racelessness of death. She smooths down the nightshirt.

Heels, Rosa says.

Tweet is humming. Then, Oh, Lord, ohh, ummm . . . she sings in a voice so low Cornelia scarcely catches it, distorted, metallic, through her hearing aid.

She examines the sheet burns on Robert's heels, sprinkles boric acid powder on the sheets. She sees herself turn away, face the mantel. She is looking down into a green glass bowl filled with baubles—rhinestone earrings, a necklace of glass bead, a gold barrette. Then she turns back,

202

moves toward Rosa and Tweet who stand together now at the foot of the bed. You need to turn him every hour or so, she says.

Did all this happen? Yes.

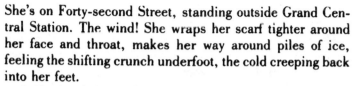

She's on Forty-second Street, standing outside Grand Central Station. The wind! She wraps her scarf tighter around her face and throat, makes her way around piles of ice, feeling the shifting crunch underfoot, the cold creeping back into her feet.

And now she's inside, wandering the concourse, jostled by crowds of people. What is she doing here?

She finds herself, inexplicably, on a commuter train. Where had she meant to go? Had she intended to catch the shuttle to Times Square, to wander there, as she and John had done dozens, hundreds of times, watching the people—whores resplendent in thigh-high golden dresses and black net stockings (not real people, surely), fake cripples, pimps with shining pointed shoes, young girls with lank hair and round granny glasses, long-haired boys wearing gold earrings, chains, fringed jackets, tourists like themselves deciding what show to see, what spectacle to gape at. Or maybe she'd meant to go back uptown, perhaps to the Cloisters, where in the empty hours of a snowbound day she could drift almost alone from room to room, gazing at unicorns, virgins, at the stations of the cross, at tombs with marble knights lying asleep on their lids, hands folded over swords.

Perhaps it's another day. Did a whole day—two days, or three—vanish almost without her knowing where it went? Did she eat, go to a movie, wander through Saks and Bergdorf's, warming herself slowly, feeling the return of circulation to her feet and legs?

The train gathers speed, passes through the columned

darkness under the city, dim lights shining on distant pillars, ghostly engines half visible on sidetracks. Inside, the floor vibrates under her feet, the lights fade, everything is dark, then light again. Black stone tunnel walls flash by.

To continue with what we were talking about: Things between Nig and Puddin got more open, more brazen. Everyone in the neighborhood knew Nig was having an affair with Puddin Greene.

He disgrace me, Tweet says. He shame me before the church and all my neighbors. Act like he was a crazy person, running after her, howling around her house like a dog after a bitch in heat. As for her, come to find out, her husband don't even care what she's doing. He's off in the streets, running after any woman he happen to see after dark. Jicky, both of them. Wild, don't matter how much she goes to church, how good she can sing.

And then it happen about the money, Tweet says. You know I never would trust a bank with my money. When we first come to town, me and Nig figured on what to do, decide to put a false bottom in the chifforobe drawer. No more than an inch of space under it, but enough to spread the money out in little low stacks, put in the bottom, and then fill the drawer up with clothes. I kept my nightgowns and underpants in there. Hadn't moved that money since nineteen and forty-five, except for the five hundred we put down on the house and what we gave Cynthia to go to nursing school on.

So I come home from work one afternoon, come in the house, go in the bedroom, take off my uniform. I'm tired and hot. It's August. I go on in the bathroom, take me a cool bath, and when I come out, I open the chifforobe drawer to get some fresh underclothes and I can see right away, things messed up, not lying in stacks like I left them this morning. The pile of pants slid over to the left on top of the slips.

Naturally, first thing I think is: The money! I lift up the

bottom and I see it's gone. Not all of it. Some little stacks still there, but some of it is gone.

Never cross my mind nobody took it but Nig. He's got my money—and they fixing to run off.

I'm calm, Tweet says. I put my clothes on, put my .22 pistol in my pocket, thinking, First thing to find out is, Have they gone yet? They're not going to know I've already caught on to what's happening. Maybe they're still over to her house, or at least in town, thinking I'll get home from work, won't begin wondering where Nig is until up in the night—they got plenty of time.

I almost can't believe it, Tweet says. But that's the way it happens with that kind of craziness. Like you out of your senses, like you become another person for a while.

Now the train is above ground traveling northward through the ruined, the smoking city. Cornelia sees piles of rotting crossties, torn-up concrete, rusted tracks. There, near the tracks, is a fire in an oil drum. Three men stand close to it, hands outstretched. Another and another. She looks out across a chaotic burning ground, here and there an oil drum filled with fire, or a pile of smoldering debris, smoke rising, and beyond, sidewalks, steam rising from grates over which, even in daylight, the homeless huddle.

Empty buildings, graffiti-covered walls, shattered windows. In any room of these buildings one could find the shard to slit one's wrists. Flashes of icy clothing flap stiffly in the wind—a blue bedspread, yellow curtains, hanging like sheets of glass from lines of ice. At one window, behind a broken pane, she sees a face, a thatch of white hair. Purvis. He is looking out at her as the train flashes by.

She must get off, search him out, rescue him.

She is standing on a platform high above the city. All around her, rising from the whiteness, blackened buildings, their bases above the snow decorated with fat, spray-painted epitaphs, scarlet and mustard yellow and purple, outlined in black. Who lies in these graves? Ernie. Maria. Karen and Joe. Juan. Motherfucker. Derelict cars in vacant lots, overhung by walls with windows concrete-sealed. A huge sign looms three stories high on the building opposite: Conti Coffins.

She's headed down the platform toward the crossover. He's in that building and I have to . . .

At the head of the stairs she halts. A child, a black child, ten or eleven, whose face is disfigured by what looks like an old burn scar, is climbing steadily toward her, head lowered. He raises his head, looks at her with burning hatred. . . .

You're in Harlem, Mrs. O'Kelly, Tweet says. Plenty people here who'd kill you in a minute. Toss up a apple. Shoot out the core. Peel it and slice it before it hit the floor. Get on the next train. Don't even cross over the crosswalk and try to catch a southbound train. This platform's empty. Stay here and . . .

A northbound train is roaring into the station.

That's the sensible thing to do, Cornelia says. Yes. Purvis . . . Of course Purvis is at home. She sees his thin face, his secret vulnerable glance that morning on the levee. We need to go home, he says.

I'm afraid. Nevertheless I go. I make myself strong to listen.

I'm listening.

So I found the two of them at Puddin's house. They've spent the morning buying a used car with my money, got the papers and the license, and now they're packing to go.

I was hollering at them as soon as I saw them, Tweet says. You think, Nig Carrier, you think I'll stand all by myself in the woodlot, shoot into the hornets' nest, get my money off of Julius after he tries to kill me, and I'll let you take it and run? You and *her*, little flycatcher, switching her tail at you. Jicky woman looking for a jicky man.

So she commence to cry—I reckon when she seen the pistol in my hand. Tweet, tweet, she's crying, saying my name, but sounds like she might be chirping.

Gimme the rest of my money, I say, and Nig and you go sell that car. I'm going to kill you both, if I don't get my grandpa's money back.

Now, Tweet, Nig says. Now, Tweet. All your money we taken, we put it on the car. Left the rest in the drawer. Didn't you see it? I wasn't going off with all your money. And looka here, I left you the old car, too, didn't I? Bought that car with *my* money. He doesn't mind lying—knows well enough, some of my money from working went into the car. It's not his, it's us'.

Tweet, he says, I ain't coming back. No use you waving that pistol at me.

I shoot in the floor in front of him, Tweet says. Watch him jump. I can't kill Nig. That's what I think. I can't do it, much as I wished I could. But then, then I do. I shoot again. Am I aiming at his heart? Hit him in the arm, see the blood commence to stain his sleeve. As for her, before I let off the second shot, she runs out the back door, still tweet-tweeting. And now he takes out after her, holding onto his arm. He looks back and I see his face, all twisted, his hand gripping his arm, bloody. He's crying. Tears and sweat running off his chin.

I got the papers, he yells at me. You can't take that car back. I have done work ten years at the Gypsum Company for that car.

My grandpa's money! Mine, it's mine, I hollered after him.

In the yard he stops like he don't even care if I shoot him again.

Ten years, he hollers. Working in the cyclone, putting out the fires, getting a million splinters like fishhooks in my skin. Ten years, while you keep your money in the drawer. He's standing under a big old pecan tree, still holding onto his arm.

Didn't I take the tweezers and pick em out for you? I say. Didn't I? Any night you come home and ax me to. Tweet is weeping in an extremity of grief and rage.

That's when I shoot again, she says, try to hit him again, and I do, in the thigh, but it barely nicked him. I'm not sorry, she says. I'll never be sorry. I can't be sorry.

He takes off after Puddin, not even running. I go out and look at the car. I'm not going to hurt that car. Mean to get my money out of it.

The train slows down. Cornelia sees, half buried in the snow outside the window, row after row of stripped car bodies crushed flat and neatly stacked in piles of three. Where is she? What stop is this? A crane lifts a battered Cadillac, swings it across the nearest pile, drops it crashing into its place. Nearby a conveyor belt pours out shredded metal into a pile above which a huge magnet swings slowly back and forth.

Fleetwood next, a bodiless voice calls out. Next stop, Fleetwood.

At the station she got out, climbed the stairs, crossed over the tracks, bought a ticket, and sat down in the small, overheated ticket office. It would be half an hour before the next train for the city. Fifteen minutes passed before other passengers began drifting into the office. A trim elderly man, white hair brushed carefully across his bald spot, came into the room, took off his cashmere overcoat, set down a leather briefcase, gazed at her, it seemed, as if he knew her, sat down, opened his paper, hid behind it.

I'll be staying at the Roosevelt as usual. I'll leave my keys at the ticket office, in case anyone wants to use my car.

Twould've been better if he'd done something, even if it was wrong, Tweet says.

How do you know? You weren't there. Cornelia got up abruptly, went out onto the windswept platform, stood with her back to the ticket office. She stared down into the gully behind the station platform, a tiny wilderness of icy trees, piled snow, frozen-over river (the Bronx? Water still flowing under the weight of ice and snow?). She stood without moving, without turning her head until she felt in her feet the vibration of the approaching train.

This car, Tweet says. Get in here. Ain't I seeing after you? Sit down here. See? You see him sitting there across the aisle. That ain't your daddy. You daddy's in Mobile enjoying hisself. Ain't that a disgrace? And he wasn't in that Cadillac getting ready to be squeezed up into a chunk of steel, either. He could be dead, but he ain't. He could be dead and . . .

John could be alive, Cornelia said.

Yeah. No use eating your heart out over that.

It was then that Tweet . . .

Yes, I know, Cornelia said.

I went in the kitchen first and then in the bathroom, Tweet says. Can't say I didn't know what I was doing. Didn't know, maybe, what I was looking for, but I knew I'd recognize it when I found it.

Looked under the sink—Ajax, Pine-Sol, roach killer. What can you do with a can of roach killer? Nothing but kill roaches. It was in the bathroom I found it, sitting by the toilet—a can of Drano. Drano sitting on the floor, douche bag hanging on a hook on the back of the door.

Ahh, I would like to've seen her insides eat plumb up. I'd've like to hear her yell. I'd lay awake nights for a year just waiting to hear her yell.

She never used it, Tweet says. The Drano ate through the douche bag and ruint it, dropped on the floor, burnt a hole in the linoleum. She and Nig went down on Blaze to Mr. Hammond's drugstore, got his arm patched up, bought them some whiskey and got drunk. She never noticed the douche bag until the next day.

That's what Nig told me afterwards.

Tweet? (Is Cornelia at last going to ask a real question?) Tweet, did you ever forgive Nig for . . . ? Did you and he ever . . . ? Do you . . . ? Now do you . . . ?

Didn't have to forgive him. I shot him, didn't I? After that, no use talking about forgiving.

But I mean, when you had the risings and he . . . he wouldn't go to bed with you . . . ? And after that, Puddin . . .

Well, I'm telling you. I shot him. No getting around it. No saying I didn't. And that's the end of that. Now I got to say to myself, let's see what's going to happen next. Let's look around, see where we headed. That's all I can see to do after you shoot somebody.

But . . .

Look at Nig, Mrs. O'Kelly. Maybe you can't see Nig, what a—what a *man* he is.

No, Cornelia says. Yes. I see him.

Well, you ought to could see what happens next then. He ain't going to stay with that tweet-tweeting Puddin Greene, and she ain't going to stay with him. Here he comes. Says he's sorry. Says he was crazy. All like that. I *say* I'm sorry I shot him, even if I ain't. Satisfy him with that. And then, when he's nekkid in the room with me—still looking like he looks—a *man*, if he is getting gray, getting older—you think when he gets back in bed with me, I'm going to put a cold foot in the middle of his belly and push him out?

Lord, even now, to think about him, it still makes me . . . Ummmm. So, all I can say, is, Well, I can't quit you, baby. Just now and then put you down awhile.

But love, Cornelia says. Love . . .

Yeah, love: Love you, baby, but I sure do hate your ways. I say, I love you, darlin, but I hate your treacherous low-down ways. . . . That's the way the song goes.

This morning Cornelia caught a crosstown bus at Seventy-sixth Street, rode over to Fifth Avenue, transferred, and got off at Forty-ninth. The sidewalks are clear now and snow-mounded cars have been shoveled out and moved. The wind still cuts cold and wet through the cross streets, but the sun is shining and the streets are crowded. She is in a neighborhood she knows well—she and John used to come here often to wander for hours through Scribner's Bookstore, Brentano's, and the Gotham Book Mart, walk north, eat lunch at a restaurant in Rockefeller Center, watch the skaters, go on to the museum. Today, too, leaning on the parapet, she has watched the skaters, although she didn't eat lunch. She seems most days to forget lunch and then, rather than sit alone at night at a table in a restaurant, to postpone eating until she is enclosed in her apartment, then to drink until she is sleepy, eat a sandwich, and go to bed.

It was a mistake, today, to stop in the Gotham, where the two of them used to root patiently through used books, examine the new issues from Miss Stelloff's press, watch surreptitiously as Miss Stelloff, white hair flying, shoulders hunched like a witch's, brought out treasures held back for a favored collector, ordered up stacks of old *Partisan Review*s and *transition*s from the basement for some solemn and delighted scholar, or, in a dramatic stage whisper like a rapier swishing through air, disemboweled an idle employee.

John leans toward her, speaks in Miss Stelloff's hoarse furious voice: If you can't *be* busy, at least *look* busy. And under *no circumstances* bother the customers. You understand me? Under *no* circumstances!

She flees.

Now she is standing in front of a picture in the Museum of Modern Art—she's been standing here for a long time. Half an hour? An hour? Why does she stay? It's as if she's wandered into an alley, a cul-de-sac, come against a wall —not brick but paint—the gray-painted board floor and walls of the picture. She can see no way out. Never mind that there is a window in the picture looking out on mountains. There are also the faces of three mysterious men in the window, blocking any impulse of hers to escape past them, to climb to a mountaintop, where, in reverse, she'll

211

see their backs, where the window will be in shadow, the scene inside invisible.

Craziness. This is craziness. The picture has nothing to do with John's death, with Cornelia, her sorrow, her guilt, her life. It's one of those flat, inexplicable surrealist paintings, a Magritte—*L'Assassin Menacé*. In the middle ground a woman lies dead on a chaise longue that looks like a cardboard cutout, a trickle of blood running from the corner of her mouth. In the foreground her killer stands with his head bent listening to silence. On the table beside him is an old-fashioned phonograph (not so old-fashioned when the picture was painted) with a flaring horn. Perhaps, to begin with, it was the phonograph horn that attracted her attention —the enigmatic fact that what is painted here is sound— he's *listening*. But what screams to her from the picture is silence.

In the wings on either side of this tableau two men stand, one with a club, the other with a net. The title indicates that they intend to kill the killer. And then, in the background, the window with the three expressionless faces looking in.

Cornelia doesn't even like the surrealists, has always uneasily shrugged off Dali's slick melting watches, hates Balthus's paintings of lecherous elderly men and innocent girl-children, can scarcely bear to look at the elongated, fragile (no matter that they're made of bronze) figures of Giacometti, with their message from a world in which men and women are diminished, helpless, tortured out of shape.

And there is nothing here to seize her by the throat, to confront her with her own life: no fat spider mother, no gentle selfish father, no awkward, adolescent girl whirling around a dance floor where no one breaks in, no woman presiding at a dinner table where secrets are passed, signals exchanged which she cannot hear.

A silent canvas with a blaring horn painted on its flat surface and an arrangement of silent figures. No one will ever know what music, what voices come from the horn, why the assassin listens so intently, why he has killed the woman, why he is about to be killed. There is only the surface of a world of blood and violence at which Cornelia continues to look. The room in the picture is spotless, the floor swept clean. No drop of blood has yet fallen on it. Everyone is properly dressed: The murderer wears a suit, the menacers neatly buttoned overcoats and derbies. The men looking in at the window stand in a row, expressionless, undisturbed. One can imagine, too, that everything in the rest of this house is orderly: ribbon-tied stacks of folded sheets, labeled preserves on the pantry shelves, polished copper pots hanging on the kitchen walls.

How can John's death, Cornelia's sorrow and guilt, Tweet's jealousy, her passionate violent life, Andrew and Willie Belle's marriage, Purvis and Louise, the postcard from Vietnam with its photograph of a mangled dead or dying child that Andrew laid on the counter for Cornelia to look at—how can these be connected with this painting?

I don't know, Cornelia says. I don't know. All I know is my grief. I am grieving for—for John.

Give up. Sleep.

And for Tweet. For Purvis. And for Nig. Yes, for Nig, too. And for myself—my hateful self. Did I make myself deaf? Did I cement together the hammer and anvil and stirrup so that no vibration passed to the nerve? And the nerve. Did I will its atrophy?

She stumbles blindly out of the museum and I see her walking the streets of the city, taking refuge again in the crowded aisles of stores where she stands staring at piles of sale merchandise, at festoons of jewels laid out on velvet behind polished glass—until life finally comes back into her feet and she plunges again into the cold city.

That night she went to a movie at a small theater somewhere in the East Fifties, came out just at the time when, across town, the theater crowd was pouring, laughing and chattering, into the cross streets around Times Square, flagging taxis, being whirled away in limousines to glamorous parties, nights with new lovers. She tried halfheartedly a couple of times to flag a taxi and then set out walking, plodding northward in the cold silence—at some point in the movie she must have turned off her hearing aid and then forgotten to turn it on again. Yes. The picture had been subtitled. No point in trying to listen to foreign voices. But the music? She hears music badly, the quality distorted even by the finest instrument she can buy.

Now, no longer filled with vague city fears of rape and murder, she is scarcely conscious of the cold, of the silence, the dark frozen streets, almost deserted at this hour in this part of the city. It has begun to snow again.

Wandered long enough, she says. Sleep. Valium waiting in the medicine cabinet. Can't be alone, after all. No way to be alone. But I can make it all stop. She steps into the street, stumbles over a half-melted and refrozen pile of blackish slush, hails another cab, realizes that its light is off. Another. The snow is coming down more heavily now.

Watch out for that pile of dog shit! This town got more dog shit than a pasture cow flops.

The movie is dropping through layers of darkness in her mind, vanishing. Did she get up and leave before it was over? Women's faces? Curiously dislocated faces that seemed somehow to be crushed together, distorted.

She steps again onto the sidewalk, walks on, shoulder strap cutting into her shoulder. Sleep. . . . Sleep. . . . But . . .

What is it I want to tell you to make these tales plain? Again and again images have come to me of the crushing together of lives: The fat woman crowding against Cornelia on the bus; the moment when, looking through the window of the slowing train into the car graveyard, she saw huge machines lifting and dropping cars on top of each other, crushing them flat, loading them onto conveyor belts, shredding and separating and baling the shredded metal; those mysterious figures in the painting, so closely, so intimately joined, one dead, one about to die, two about to become killers, three witnesses—all of whose lives and deaths, no matter that no one knows why, must be entangled beyond extricating. And now this movie that Cornelia has just seen, in which an actress who has not spoken for six months is cared for by a young, unsophisticated, chattering nurse, a movie in which the two women, alone together in a house by the sea, seem slowly to take on each other's personalities, characters, lives, even come to look alike. I see the two of them in an idyllic scene sitting at a table under the trees sorting the baskets of mushrooms they have gathered. Their heads, shaded by sun hats, are bent toward each other. They are at one. I see them walking together on the rocky seashore. They embrace each other, enter each other's dreams. But then they quarrel. The actress strikes the nurse across the mouth. The nurse lays down shards of glass for the actress to step on, rips her face with long fingernails.

But they are not like us, Cornelia would once have said. Not at all like us. And she would have called to mind for comfort images of herself and Tweet moving and turning Robert's passive dying body, of Tweet bringing her gifts of ragged robins, flowering pomegranate blossoms, tales of the past, would have seen herself reach out to Tweet that terrible day of King's death, saying, I'm sorry, Julia. I'm sorry.

As for what she might say today, I don't yet know.

But what I want to add, what I want to say now is that *I* am here, too, I, the tale-teller, to warn you, as I have before, that I have a stake in the story. It is not only of Cornelia and Tweet that one must say: Your lives have become so entangled that you can never separate them. Not of them only.

I wanted, for example, to take Cornelia by the shoulder

and shake her when she thought of the Valium bottle and said, *I can make it all stop.* I wanted to say, You can't do that, Cornelia. It's not in your character to kill yourself in this strange city, to leave your body for Andrew and Sarah to deal with, to leave the unexplainable legacy of your death to Purvis whom you have just begun to love.

She walks slowly and more slowly, one step and then the next. Twenty blocks north she's walked, and three or four crosstown through the falling snow. Where is she? Ahead she sees a familiar corner. It's here by Gracie Square Hospital that she should turn north again toward her apartment. Almost there? Light pours from a side entrance to the hospital—a wide service entrance. A van is parked in the opening. Two men move around it, gesticulating, speaking to each other as silently as mimes, lifting and passing packages, loading them into the open rear of the van. Severed limbs? Aborted infants? Whole bodies to be delivered to some morgue or undertaker?

She is walking toward the silently speaking men in the entrance to the hospital, walking steadily toward them, thinking of cutoff legs and abortions.

Look out! Dog shit.

One of the men, working in shirtsleeves and a down-filled vest, short, heavily muscled, smiles at her shyly, looks away. He reminds her of Nig. She thinks briefly of Nig. Remembers his power. Remembers seeing him pick up a stove—a whole kitchen stove—carry it out of her kitchen and load it into the trunk of his car. Remembers seeing him move, as if they were one-by-twelves, the railroad ties she uses to raise the level of her vegetable beds. He smiles again.

The other . . . She glances at him. He's moved now, closer to the open end of the van, and Nig is tossing cartons to him from a pile inside the building. He's tall, walks lightly, as if he might be jumping from stone to stone across a creek. Curly brown hair ducks up around his navy blue watch cap. The two men work together. Through the veil of snow she sees the heavyset black man toss a carton. The tall white man catches it, swings, sets it down inside the van, turns, catches another. Something about him . . . Something in the articulation of shoulder and back as he swings the box to its place on the stack, the curly brown hair . . . Who . . . ?

She's walking in the fall woods with the comrade of her adolescence, the lad she used to hike and shoot with. That's who . . . And Mother said, Yes, such a suitable beau. I'm going to call on his mother.

No! Don't do it!

They're out skeet shooting together, standing in a pasture now, by a barbed-wire fence. Across the field sumacs flame in a long low line. The air is the clear cool air of October. She sees him beside her, turning, rifle to his shoulder, leading a clay pigeon. He squeezes the trigger and the bird explodes. His brown hair curls out from beneath a knit cap, ducks up around the folded hem.

Something in the articulation of shoulder and back . . .

Of course they're not stacking boxes of cutoff legs. How ridiculous can you get in the middle of the night? But . . .

Whatever became of that lovely boy? Lewis. Lewis Robinson. His family moved, didn't they? to the West Coast. The war . . . Was he killed? Where does he live now? He would be—her age, of course. And this man couldn't be more than thirty-three or four. Curly brown hair and rosy cheeks. And he used to wear a watch cap like that. Why didn't I . . . ? Why didn't we . . . ? A flood of love sweeps her along the sidewalk. She sees his crooked smile, ironic, self-deprecating, as he catches her hand and helps her balance along a log crossing some ravine or other. I *loved* him, she thought in astonishment. If it hadn't been for Mother, if she hadn't wanted so much for us to . . . Shrugged. If she hadn't, I would have known it—known I loved him.

217

But he . . . He was probably terrified of her—of Mother. If he wasn't, he should have been. What did she do? Did she *call*—push me at them. *Christ.* Ugh! How is it possible still to squirm at those ancient petty humiliations. Children. We were children.

I outwitted her, though, she thought with deep satisfaction. I found John. A stranger. She never touched *him.*

Now she's passing the van, staring openly at the tall man whose curly hair ducks up around his cap.

She steps on a slanting glassy patch of ice, slips, tries to recover herself, skids sideways toward the van, goes sprawling, flailing outstretched arms, strikes her head on the front bumper.

She's lying on the sidewalk. Noise blasts in her head— the sound of shouting voices. She must have struck the volume switch on her hearing aid as she fell and now she hears music and the loud distorted voices of the men as they bend over her.

Wake up, Rosie . . . Someone shouting? Singing?

. . . hurt lady? Nig is smiling down at her, an anxious shy smile.

You OK, lady?

I'm all right, she says automatically. She reaches up, touches the knot already beginning to rise on her forehead.

She feels hands supporting, lifting her gently, the pressure of male hands under her arms, against her rib cage under her breasts. The hairs on her arms rise, her nipples rise, and she feels a movement, melting, as if of ice, around her heart, a throb deep under her pelvis.

Look at her leg there. . . .

She's torn her left knee, the palms of her gloves, ground sand and cinders into her hands, but she feels no pain.

Bleeding . . .

. . . maybe need a doctor, lady? This is a hospital here.

. . . take you to the emergency . . . ?

Yes, she said. No. I mean, it's all right. I . . . I'm fine. My . . . my apartment is just around the corner.

Look at your leg, lady. That's a mess.

Music blasts from the cab of the truck: "Wake up Rosie. Tell your midnight dreams . . ."

I need to keep my hearing aid turned up higher, she says. What?

The music. I . . . I didn't know I missed the . . . You . . . you're very kind. Thank you. She is still wavering and Nig is still keeping a steadying hand under her elbow. She pulls herself erect, reaches out, intending to shake hands, but the other man takes her hand, turns it over, looks at the torn glove, the bleeding palm, shakes his head dubiously, clucks in sympathy.

Thank you, she says again. You're very kind and . . . Thank you.

You're just around the corner, lady? We're through here. I could help you to your place. OK, Larry?

Yeah. Twelve o'clock. I'll lock up and take the van to . . .

Now she's climbing the stairs toward her apartment and his arm, her curly-haired friend Lewis's arm, is still supporting her. Here he is, respectfully helping her up the stairs. She fumbles in her purse for the keys and hands them to him. As he opens the door she hears a ringing in her ears. Her head? She touches the knot on her forehead. No, the telephone is ringing. She beckons him in and crosses the room to answer. Wait a minute, she says. I want to thank you. And . . .

Cornelia picks up the telephone, holds the receiver against her hearing aid, clipped, as it always is, to her brassiere strap, concealed under her shirt, so that when she listens she seems to be listening to her own heart. She says, Hello. The man has followed her in and closed the door behind him. He turns, sees the upside-down telephone receiver, stands, hands hanging loose at his sides, watching her curiously.

The voice she hears is not Evelyn's but a stranger's, a soft, precise female voice with a trace in it of the South.

Mrs. O'Kelly?

Yes? she says. This is she. Found somewhere the old calm voice of Cornelia, full of confidence, authority.

This is Cynthia Naron speaking.

Yes?

You don't know me, the voice says. You probably don't remember meeting me, but I'm Tweet's daughter.

Cornelia sits down on the floor. Tears begin to roll down her cheeks.

The young man moves forward a step, stands with his head tilted, as if he is asking himself a question.

Cornelia covers the mouthpiece with her torn hand, looks detachedly at him. I'm crying, she says, I can't seem to help it. Then, to Cynthia, Yes, she says, of course I know you, Cynthia. I saw you—met you—when you visited Julia and . . . and Mr. Carrier in . . . Yes.

I wouldn't be calling so late, but I've been trying to reach you off and on all day, and all tonight. You must have been out at a show or something.

Cynthia. It's Cynthia.

I was. I just walked in the door. Cornelia covers the mouthpiece again, draws a gasping breath, feels a sob begin to rise in her throat.

The reason I'm calling, Tweet is sick.

Cornelia is weeping uncontrollably, sobbing.

He glances around the tiny apartment, sees the small kitchen at the back, walks lightly in, picks up the bottle of whiskey off the counter, pours some into a glass from the drying rack, adds ice from the refrigerator, takes it back into the living room, and hands it to Cornelia. He can hear the voice at the other end of the line.

Mrs. O'Kelly? Are you OK, Mrs. O'Kelly?

Cornelia takes the glass. Thank you.

What? What's that?

I'm sorry, Cornelia says to the phone, gulping the whiskey, gasping. I . . . I fell down. I just fell down outside the apartment, and it was so late, and I hurt my leg and . . . and then I heard your voice and . . . It's all right. I mean, of course it's not all right. Tweet's sick. What's the m-m-matter?

She's been in the hospital—we've just brought her home. She had a seizure of some sort a couple of weeks ago—passed out standing over the stove stirring a pot of greens —and she must have fallen forward onto the stove and . . . Well, she knocked the pot off and . . . Fortunately my dad was in the house, heard the noise. Anyhow, she got scalded pretty badly on her arm and leg—second- and third-degree burns all down one side.

The young man crosses the room to the window and stands staring out into the snowy night.

. . . she was in convulsions, I think, when he got in the kitchen. (That's what it sounds like.) So it wasn't just the burn. Something else was obviously wrong. Anyhow, she's been in the burn unit at the hospital and also they've been doing some tests—they called in a neurologist. The voice is cool, neutral, controlled. They released her yesterday. The reason I'm calling—Rosa insisted that I let you know. I got your number from your daughter today.

Cornelia is still struggling to control herself. She draws a deep breath, pulls off her glove with her teeth.

Are you all right, Mrs. O'Kelly?

Yes. I'm all right. I didn't mean to . . .

How badly did you hurt yourself? The voice at the other end of the line is severe, businesslike, the voice of a nurse with a potentially hysterical patient. Do you need a doctor?

No, no. I just scraped my leg—nothing serious. A . . . a friend is here with me. I'm trying to think. Rosa? Rosa wanted you to call and . . . ? But—neurologist? What's the matter? Is Julia . . . ?

She'll be all right, Cynthia says. We've got everything

under control. And I would certainly not have bothered you if Rosa hadn't insisted.

I'll come home, Cornelia says. I'll see if I can get on a flight tomorrow. If I can't, surely . . . Tell Julia I'll be home as soon as I can get a flight.

It's not necessary for you to do that, Cynthia says. I don't think there's anything you can do here.

As she put the receiver in its cradle, he turned, looked doubtfully at her. You're pretty upset, he said. Are you sure you don't want to see a doctor? I can take you back to the hospital. There was a detachment in his voice, an impersonal concern that reminded her of Cynthia's voice on the telephone.

She shook her head, got up. I'll be all right, she said. I'm not hurt, really. She's at work, bringing herself under control. And I'm—well—leery of New York emergency rooms. I'd have to be in worse shape than this. It was just the phone call. A friend of mine is sick. Tomorrow I'll have to go home and see about her.

You ought to clean up that mess on your hand, he said. Your knee, too.

Yes, I will. But—thanks, she said. I wanted to thank you, but I don't want to keep you. You'd better go, hadn't you? It's snowing harder. She's staring at him. You don't really look like him, she said. It's just your hair—and the watch cap.

What?

I feel a little dizzy, she said. She sat down on the couch.

Here, wait a minute. Are you going to faint? Put your head between your knees. He sat beside her, gently pushed her head down.

I've never fainted in my life, Cornelia said firmly. I'm not going to faint.

Let me take a look at your hand. OK? You don't have to be afraid of me. I'm—all right.

She sat slowly up. I know, she said. But in any case, it wouldn't matter, would it?

He said nothing.

She held out her hand briefly, then took off one boot and rolled down the knee-length sock. It's not so bad, she said.

Look at the dirt and cinders. You've got an infection waiting to happen. He got up, went into the bathroom, opened and closed drawers and cabinets, turned on the water. Come in here, he said. I'll help you.

When she came, he held her hand under the faucet and washed it. She winced. I know it hurts, he said.

No, no. It's OK. Are you a nurse? What were you doing throwing boxes around in the middle of the night?

I'm on the night shift, he said. No. Not a nurse. But I've been an orderly, among other things. He helped her put her leg over the basin and washed and washed her knee, until all the cinders and dirt were washed away.

Thanks, she said. Now—you'd better go. Where do you live? It's going to be a mess getting home in this.

But he paid no attention. You're deaf, he said, as he dried her leg. That was odd, seeing you hold the receiver to your breast. And then I saw the button in your ear, and the cord, and realized you were deaf.

The music, she said. I had the hearing aid turned down, and then, when I fell, I must have hit the volume switch and . . . and I thought you were shouting at me: Wake up Rosie. Tell your midnight dreams . . . but you never can, can you?

What?

Tell your dreams. On the truck radio. Tell your midnight dreams.

Oh. He laughed. Maybe. Sometimes. He opened the medicine cabinet—empty, except for the Valium bottle, a half-used bottle of shampoo, and a few rusted pins. You don't live here, he said.

No. It belongs to a friend who uses it now and then, and I . . .

I was looking for an antibiotic—bacitracin, maybe?— and gauze pads and adhesive, but . . .

I think there is a first aid kit in my suitcase, she said. Maybe there's a tube of bacitracin in my makeup case. Here, on the counter. She drew it to her, found the ointment, limped into the other room, found adhesive tape and gauze, and they contrived a dressing for her knee.

Well, he said, you're OK. Right?

They're standing face-to-face in the cold shabby little living room. He's picked up his coat and watch cap and is smiling at her, that smile of impersonal reassuring kindness.

Curiously, Cornelia is filled with the same reckless confidence she felt on the long-ago day in the tower when she said to John: *I'm not afraid. I've been climbing trees and swinging on ropes all my life.* It's almost as if she feels herself swinging from the rope as John pulls her from the tower to the ginkgo tree. Now, instead of thanking her rescuer again and seeing him to the door, as she fully intended to do, she delays.

Why in the world did you go to so much trouble to help me? she said.

He shrugged. I don't know. Somebody needed to give you a hand. I . . . just generally do the next thing—whatever it is. Sometimes it works out and sometimes it's a disaster.

Well, snow or no snow, maybe you could—would you? —stay a little longer. Please. Have one drink with me before you go.

Sure, he said. Didn't I say I did the next thing?

You'll have to fix it. She gestured toward the kitchen with her bandaged hand.

When he came back, she'd brought a blanket from the closet and wrapped it around her shoulders. I fell because I was staring at you, she said. I thought you looked like a

friend of mine. I was staring at you there by the hospital
and . . . But you must be ten years younger—too young to
be him, too old to be his son. And of course you don't really
look like him. I just . . .

He is sitting, holding his glass, watching her.

I just went flying through the air, because I was remembering him—this boy—shooting skeet on a . . . a sunny
afternoon a long time ago, and . . . She broke off.

Yes? he said. And?

And all of a sudden . . . Years ago it was, years ago. We
were children. All of a sudden I knew I'd been in . . . in
love with him and hadn't known it, had been *asleep*. So—
thinking about the way he looked leading the pigeon, and
looking at your back, your shoulders, there by the hospital
—have you ever shot skeet?

He shook his head.

Anyhow, I wasn't watching for the slick places, she said.
His name was Lewis Robinson.

How long ago did you . . . ?

We were in high school together—kids. Twenty-five, thirty
years ago.

Well, he said, I'm not Lewis Robinson.

I know, she said. I've been . . . She drew a deep breath.
I feel as if I've been wandering in this city for months, she
said. The light from the lamp is shining on her chestnut
hair, her pale skin. She shakes her head slowly and he
watches her hair move softly on her shoulders. My husband
died a few months ago and since then things have seemed
. . . I don't suppose I'm myself. She broke off. Listen, she
said, please, have another drink with me. Stay with me a
little longer. Tell me who you are.

I'm not Lewis Robinson, he said again. No, thanks, I
don't want another drink. But I'll stay awhile if you want
me to. As for who I am . . . Are you sure you want me to
stay?

She nodded.

He'd grown up, he told her, everywhere. His father was

225

a journeyman printer and a wanderer, moving from job to job wherever the money was best, sometimes taking his family, sometimes not.

No, not married at the moment, although . . . No, no children yet.

He'd been a wanderer, too, working at this and that, doing his stretch in the army, going off and on to night school and eventually picking up a degree in English, but never settling down to anything. Lately he'd decided it was time to be serious (or as serious as one can be, he said) and had gone back to school, working at night, going to classes in the daytime. He intended to teach history. He shrugged. It seems a relatively harmless, perhaps even a useful thing to do, he said.

Then you need to go home, don't you? Need to get your sleep.

Tomorrow is Saturday, he said. He smiled at her tentatively, reassuringly touched her shoulder.

Cornelia felt again the melting and flow of her body, as if . . . as if . . . She got up, walked over to the window, gazed out into the thickening snow. It looks as if there's going to be another blizzard, she said.

Now he has joined her, stands beside her looking out.

It reminds me of a story, she said. You know—"The Dead"? How does it go? *Snow was general all over Ireland. . . .*

He laid his hand on her shoulder. *. . . falling on the treeless hills,* he said. *Falling softly upon the Bog of Allen and, farther westward. . . .*

I'm forty-five years old, Cornelia said. I've . . .

Shhh.

He drew her to him and they stood a while in silence.

And now they are moving toward the couch and opening it out and the hinges are groaning, and they are lying against each other, clothed and shivering, and then under the covers, naked.

226

And John stayed where he belonged and so did Tweet and Mother and Father and Purvis and . . . All. They all stayed silent for a little while.

It's not a dream, he said afterwards when he saw how she looked at him. We're both in the world.

I'm forty-five years old, Cornelia said again. I've never had . . . never slept with, had sex with anyone but my husband. Oh, my God. I'm alive.

And?

He's dead, she said. But I'm alive. I can't help it. I'm alive. We're all alive. She sat up, stretched, drew the blanket around her. And I'm hungry, too, she said.

He got up and pulled on his slacks and sweater, puttered around in the kitchen and brought them cheese and bread and an open bottle of wine, and they ate and drank and made love again.

I'd sing you a song if I could sing, he said early in the morning before he went away.

I think you did, she said.

SIX

S tanding in the doorway, the old woman beckons her in.

Hello, Rosa. Cornelia does not offer to touch cheeks with that dark forbidding face.

Just keeps on setting there, Rosa says. Hums to herself some. Don't say a word. Can't talk. Mind's gone. Cynthia tell you that?

Cornelia felt her skin draw as if a cold wet wind had blown against her neck.

I'm the one told Cynthia to call you. Seem like the right thing to do.

On the porch the swing chains creak. I brought the children with me, Cornelia says. Do you mind if they sit on the porch awhile?

Rosa shrugs. Cold out there. To Cornelia Rosa's voice sounds loud, slightly distorted.

They'll be all right, she says, for an instant holds her hand in front of her breast. She has set the volume of her hearing aid higher than she used to. The sounds of the house and street are tinny, she hears an occasional echoing wowww. But she *hears:* the rasping creak of the swing chains, the children talking, the faint brushing sound of her blouse moving against the microphone clipped to her brassiere strap, and now, inside the house, from the radio the voices of a gospel group above a driving piano accompaniment.

> Yes I do, yes I do, yes I do.
> Yes I do, yes I do, yes I do.
> Yes, yes, yes
> Yes, yes, yes. . . .

Acutely aware of sound, unable to assign every vibration its proper place in an aural order, she is like a woman long blind and suddenly seeing again, who has lost her mind's capacity to sort, must ask herself at every moment: Is it near or far away? Large or small? Am I moving or is the train moving? She even consciously hears from the kitchen the noise of the refrigerator fan and the faint continuous hiss of the glowing gas heater near which Tweet sits in a canvas and aluminum wheelchair.

But she resists the temptation to turn down her hearing aid, instead, to rid herself of the confusing brush of cloth on mike, she fishes it from inside her blouse, clips it on a pocket.

I'm the one told her to call you.

Yes, Cornelia says. But she didn't tell me how . . . how . . . She turns toward Tweet slumped in the wheelchair, her right hand and right leg swathed in bandages, her left arm in her lap, fingers trembling against her thigh.

> Yes, yes, yes,
> Yes, yes, yes,
> Every time I feel the spirit
> Moving in my heart, I sing

A shawl lies across Tweet's shoulders, slipping down on one side. Rosa puts it in place. Seems like she's cold. Shivers a lot.

You don't need to talk so loud, Rosa, Cornelia says. I hear pretty well. Then: Julia? Tweet?

Didn't I say she don't say nothing? They want to cut her head open. Say they see something in there, think they'll take it out. A bubble. A *bubble!* Say it might be getting bigger in there, squeezing everything up. Might bust. Cynthia, she says, Go ahead—cut it out.

Rosa! Cornelia is staring at Tweet, who appears to be unaware of their presence.

Nig, he can't make up his mind. Goes first one way, then the other. What I say is: Them doctors looking for somebody to cut on like they cut on dogs—only it's people. Find out what's in there, how it works. They always done niggers that way. Don't need to be no bubble in there for them to want to cut on her head.

Rosa, Tweet's *here.* You'll scare her.

Ain't I told you she don't know nothing? Anyhow, they say it ain't cancer.

But . . .

If she knew, she'd talk, say something. I ax her often enough. But she just sits there. Sometimes she hums. Hums till it drive you out of your mind. And then, seems like sometimes she listens to the music. Music quiets her down —blues and gospel. The rest she don't pay no attention to.

On the porch the swing creaks. Inside, the gas hisses, the refrigerator hums.

She always did like Aretha—and the Wolf, Rosa says. But I tell her she do better now to forget that Howling Wolf. Think about Zion.

Wolf? Cornelia says. Wolf?

Seventh Son and all that. But she can eat. Wants to eat. You can tell when she's hungry. Does me good to see her eat.

Rosa, this is so hard on you all. My God. It's so hard. What can I do to help?

Nig and Cynthia, they do the heavy work. Help her get in and out of bed and all. She can walk if you steady her. Cynthia bathes her. Nig, want to know the truth, he's scary. Don't like to be around sick people. Rosa laughs. Reckon he thinks he'll catch that bubble—catch Death? His age, he might.

What can I do? Cornelia says again. Tweet? Hello. She moves closer, takes the shaking hand in both of hers, squeezes it, separates the fingers, gently massages the palm. I'm home, she says. I've come to see you. Hello. Tweet? Hello. We'll—all of us—we'll find a way to help you, she says. We'll make you better. Do you hear me?

Tweet's face is expressionless, lids drooping slightly, as if she drowses.

The swing continues to creak on the porch. Louder now: Purvis is pushing it higher and higher. Louise is squealing with pleasure. A car door slams. Voices talking.

Here come Cynthia, Rosa says. She been to the store. You can ax her what she wants you to do. She seem to be in charge here. Ha! She might be a nurse, but nemmine that, *I'm* suppose to be Tweet's mama. *Me.* She ain't even her true daughter. But ax her. She knows everything.

Cynthia opens the door, still talking to the children. Slow the swing down, honey, she says to Purvis. You're going to throw that child out. Who are you children, anyhow? Who . . . ? She breaks off.

Cornelia is holding open the screen, follows her into the kitchen. My grandchildren, Cynthia, she says. I found them visiting when I got home. My daughter's keeping them while my son and his wife are on vacation. She closes the kitchen door, speaks in a lower voice. What can I do? she says. You didn't tell me on the phone how sick she is.

I wasn't expecting you to come back, Cynthia says. No use to upset you. She sets down two crackling brown paper grocery bags on the kitchen table. They say she has an aneurysm. A weakness in an artery. It's been leaking, they say. You understand? Caused this—what looks like a stroke. And the seizure. Pressure from this bubble causes seizures.

Can they . . . ?

They say they can take it out, fix it. It's possible she

could talk again. Maybe she wouldn't have the seizures. But they say they don't know for sure. It's always dangerous going inside somebody's head, messing with the wiring. But, if they don't—well, it's like a time bomb ticking away in there. No telling when it might burst and kill her. It's worth a try. They advise it. They say at her age, young as she is, it's worth a try.

But . . .

They advise it. Nig says, No. I say, Yes. Charlene agrees with me.

What about her? Have you tried to explain it to her?

She'd be better off dead than like she is.

Does she . . . ?

She doesn't respond, Cynthia says. I don't think she understands anything about what's happened. I haven't been able to get even a look from her, a shake of the head, a nod, yes. And Nig: Nig's a superstitious old man, if he is my daddy. Bad as Rosa. They both say there isn't anything in there: It's just an excuse. Say the doctors will kill her, just to see how her brain works.

But Cynthia, maybe she understands everything—or anyway, some of what's going on around her. I hate to see Rosa—It's none of my business, I know, but anyhow, please. . . . Rosa ought not to . . . Suppose Tweet understands?

Cynthia gave her a cold look. I'm here, she said. I'm aware of what goes on.

I shouldn't. I know. I'm sorry. Cornelia sat down at the kitchen table, put her head in her hands.

I don't know whether she understands or not, Cynthia said. She hasn't given us a sign. But if she does, she's tough, she can handle it. I tell her when I'm putting her to bed at night and when I'm changing the bandages that I know how tough she is, I know she can handle it. I remind her of things she's done in her life. I talk to her like she's —*in there*. But I don't know—I explain it to her and ask her what she thinks about it, but—nothing.

I can come and sit with her, Cornelia said. I can't think what else. Is there anything else?

We don't have to make a decision for a while, Cynthia said. This leak—they say—*they say*—has stopped. They want the burns to heal. Want her as strong as possible. She began to unpack the grocery bags, to move about the kitchen, putting things in cabinets, in the battered icebox. I'm going to have to leave, she said. I have children at home and a job. Charlene is going to try to get a leave and come in a couple of weeks for a few days. If we decide on the operation, I'll come back. She shrugged. I'm going to do everything I can to persuade them to it. I keep thinking it'll sink in on them after a while that if there's a chance to make Tweet better, we should take it. She stood in the middle of the kitchen with a can of tomatoes in each hand and looked at Cornelia.

Cynthia, maybe things will get better by themselves. Sometimes the blood vessels, you know, they accommodate. I've read . . .

Cynthia shook her head, put the tomatoes on a shelf, folded an empty bag and put it in a drawer. With a stroke, maybe, she said. But we're talking about an aneurysm. Things are going to get worse, not better. Only the burns will get better.

In the living room, Tweet is alone now. Rosa has put on a coat and joined the children on the porch: Y'all better come on in now. Too cold out here. . . .

Music from the radio, opening piano chords.

Cornelia draws a chair close to Tweet's and sits down. But Tweet does not look at her. Her right hand lies bandaged in her lap. Her left hand now seems to beat a shaky tattoo on her thigh. She raises it, pecks at the chair arm with her fingertips. One, two, three, four. One, two, three, four.

From the radio a fresh young tenor voice sings out, We are Soldiers. . . . Cornelia gets up, walks around behind the wheelchair, lays her two hands firmly on the smooth dark skin of Tweet's neck, massages her neck and shoulders gently, leans close to her. I love a massage, she says. Don't you? John used to massage my neck and shoulders like this. Do you like it? She stops a moment, keeps her hands resting on Tweet's shoulders, feels under her hand a slight tremor. Tweet has lifted—shrugged?—her shoulder.

We are Soldiers. In the Ar-my. . . .

I remember when—especially after the children were born, you know, when I was still sore—I'd lie in bed on my stomach and he would . . . I could do your back, you know. If you were lying down, I could give you a real massage. Sitting so much, lying down, I know your back gets tired. We'll . . . She lays aside the shawl, moves her hands along Tweet's upper arms, gently squeezes and manipulates the muscles.

Tweet continues to beat a tattoo on the chair arm.

Relax, Cornelia whispers. Re-la-a-a-x.

Cynthia is moving about the kitchen. On the porch the swing chains creak. Cornelia no longer hears Rosa's voice, feels herself concentrating herself in her hands as she strokes Tweet's arms.

Purvis and Louise are singing in time to the creak of the swing: The eensy beensy spider climbèd up the waterspout. . . .

Cornelia keeps one hand on Tweet's arm, skin touching skin, sits down again, takes the drumming hand in hers.

One day I get so old I can't fight any more. Gonna stand there and fight anyhow. . . .

Cornelia squeezes Tweet's hand. I'm coming to see you every day, she says slowly and clearly. Do you understand me, Tweet? I'm coming every day. Rosa and Cynthia may need to attend to business, and you and I can sit together and visit. I can give you a massage. We can talk. I have some things I want to tell you, to talk to you about. You don't know it yet, but you've . . . you've been *with* me—I mean in New York. I've been in New York and you were —there. Oh, it's hard to tell about, but you were. I *heard* you. Like you used to say your grandpa talked to you—

237

remember? But you're not dead. You're alive. We're both alive.

Slowly Tweet raised her head, looked into Cornelia's eyes. For a moment it seemed to Cornelia that she saw a look of such rage and hatred there, it ran through the air like fire through a wick, joined their eyes together, pierced hers like a fork of lightning. Then, again, the eyes were blank. Tweet lowered her head, looked at her lap.

Now Cornelia raises her own hand, touches Tweet's cheek. You were. You were there. Is it too hot? Your face feels hot. Are you too close to the fire?

Tweet shivers slightly.

We are soldiers . . .

OK. I was just checking. Listen, Tweet, I saw how you looked at me. I saw it. OK? I can't worry about that. We have to think about *you*. Gently she touches Tweet's cheek. We can't worry about it, she says again. Listen, I see what a mess you're in here. A mess. But . . . We can start doing something. We'll work on it together. OK? Think about it before I come back. We can have talking lessons and listening lessons and . . .

Tweet pulls her hand away, turns her head to the side, lays her hand on the arm of her wheelchair. The hand begins to tremble, then to drum again. Her lips tremble. *Ah*, mmmm, *ahh*, hmmm, she hums. *Won*-ahh, *shhoom*-ahh. *Shhhomm*-ahh, *Shhomm*-ahh.

Rosa opens the front door. Them children going to freeze. Don't you want them to come in?

Wom-ahh, *shhon*-ahh. . . .

Cornelia lays her hand again on Tweet's shoulder. We have to be going, she says. Tweet? I promised the children I'd take them to a puppet show at the library this morning. She looks at her watch. We'd better go.

Mmmmm-ah, shmmm-ah, hmmm-ah, shhmmm-ah . . .

See what I'm talking about? Rosa says. She'll set there and hum. . . .

Cynthia comes in from the kitchen.

What I wanted to tell you—all of you—Tweet? You, too. . . . Cornelia breaks off. She is swallowing now, opening her eyes wide and then blinking. She does not want to weep, feels she has no right to shed easy tears.

Hhhhmmm-ahh, Hmmmm-ahh. . . .

Tweet? I can help out, if you'd like me to. I mean, Rosa, I know you and Cynthia have things you need to do. So. I could come every day for a couple of hours and sit with Tweet. May I, Tweet? Would you like for me to do that?

. . . eensy beensy spider climbed up the waterspout. . . .

Tomorrow, say. Sunday. Rosa? Cynthia? Would you like me to come and spend tomorrow morning with Tweet and let you two go to church—or whatever you wanted to do?

Well, that would be nice, Cynthia said. We'd appreciate that.

Do you recall that a long time ago I wrote, "I want to remember that every act in a human life has layer upon enfolded layer not only of imagining, but of circumstance, beneath it"? I was thinking then not of Tweet or of myself, but of Cornelia, of her refusal to plunge down through those layers, to lift them apart, even to admit their existence. And later, I said that she skimmed like a skier over the surface of her life. Now—now that Cornelia seems willing to look, now, as I struggle with my own difficulties, with the near impossibility for *me* of grappling with these events—I think that perhaps—no, certainly—I am the one who is skiing, who cannot acknowledge or express the complexity of all those layers of circumstance and imagining—in all our lives, but particularly in Tweet's. I thought I was at home in Tweet's life, that when she spoke, I heard her speak with her own authentic voice.

But of course I never heard her speak, *except to Cornelia*. Does that trouble you as it does me? Again and again I have

239

turned aside, shied away from knowing how she spoke at home, in bed at night with Nig, sitting in their crowded little house, the gas heater pulsing, with Robert and Rosa and their friends and neighbors. I wrote nothing, for example, of Martin Luther King's death, except that Tweet turned away from Cornelia's gesture of sympathy. What tangle of snakes have I been skiing over?

I think back to the moment when I invited your "absentmindedness" about "these ludicrous and dreadful matters." About race. Cornelia and Tweet, I wrote, might have other, more complex business with each other.

Other business, yes. Sometimes. But surely not more complex business. I made the routine disclaimer. *They* were not absentminded, I said. But the truth is that there is no way Tweet could present herself so that *you* would be absentminded. No way. She is black. Cornelia is white. She is servant. Cornelia is mistress. She is poor. The measure of her poverty is that she considers Cornelia (who thinks of herself as modestly well-off) immensely wealthy.

Two moments keep coming back to me, moments that I must have written of for a reason, a reason not yet clear to me. One is on the occasion of Cornelia's call at Tweet's house the day King was murdered, the other on the occasion of her attendance at Robert's deathbed. Do you remember? Each of these scenes justifies Cornelia, gives substance to her courage and generosity of spirit. But something else—remember? In each there is something about clutter and about jewels. A bowl of Mardi Gras necklaces and doubloons sits on the coffee table. There is costume jewelry on the mantel—earrings, a braided gold barrette. At the time I wrote those words, described the rooms, I meant them to give you a sense of the richness and poverty, the clutter and crowdedness and human closeness in Tweet's house.

But the strings of beads still lie tangled in their green glass bowl, reflecting spikes of light, the gold barrette still glints at me, first from the coffee table, later from the mantel, as if there is another reason for its being there.

And now, I think of Tweet, sitting in her wheelchair, occasionally moving about the house (to the bathroom, to her bed) with Cynthia or Nig's help. She can walk now, could probably walk alone with the help of a cane, but they are afraid to trust her. The burns are healing, no longer draining. The new skin is an ugly strange pinkish color. Her hand is drawn and clawlike where muscles and tendons were damaged. She is silent. She sits in the living room close to the gas space heater, silent—she whose voice has echoed in my ears, spun its tales in my head for so long.

It's as if some dark magician has cast a spell over her, over us all, has snatched away the voice with which, all these years, she's given us the gift of her life. What can I do to break the spell?

Cornelia comes, again and again.

This is her fourth visit. Last time and the time before, they sat alone together in front of the fire and Cornelia talked. She talked of her grief and guilt, of her wanderings in the city, of ghosts and magic, her past and Tweet's past, Grandfather, her own mother and father; she even told Tweet about the child who was afraid of the dark, the fat woman on the bus, the commuter-train ride to Mt. Vernon. In Harlem you made me get back on the train, she said. And—dog shit. You kept telling me to look out for dog shit.

Tweet as usual appeared not to be listening.

And then, Cornelia said, that last night, I fell down in the street—late, late, in the cold and snow on the icy pavement. And this man—I saw Nig and this other man—and they picked me up and he—the other man—helped me to my apartment, and something happened, Tweet. I fell apart. I turned into—Me? Not me? We had sex—yes, *sex*—made love, and . . .

Tweet was silent.

Oh, *listen* to me, please, Cornelia said. It's about coming back into the world.

Tweet sat and stared at the floor, retreating, visibly, as it seemed to Cornelia, deeper inside herself. Sometimes her eyes moved as if following the dream of a play or battle or dance that acted itself out in her head. Almost always, even while Cornelia talked, she hummed, and when Cornelia turned the volume down on the radio, Tweet pounded the arm of her chair until she turned it up again.

> I'm the one, I'm the one, I'm the one
> They call the Seventh Son—
> Heal the sick, raise the dead,
> Make little girls talk out of their head. . . .

Cornelia stood up, sighed. Here's Rosa—home, she said, and I have to go. She took Tweet's hand in hers, stilled its beating. I know you're in there, she said. How can we persuade you to come out?

Rosa stood holding the door open, expressionless, waiting for her to leave.

Andrew and Willie Belle are still away, have treated themselves to a two-week holiday in the Caribbean, left the children, as they thought, with Sarah, but now, of course, with Cornelia, too.

Two *weeks*? Cornelia had said to Sarah when she got home and found them there. Two weeks? What about school?

They needed to get away, Sarah said. She didn't add, after six months of trying to deal with you. It was the only time Andrew could get loose in the next few months.

But, out of school?

Sarah is forbearing: Mama, you know Willie Belle is not one to let rules and regulations get in her way. Besides, what harm can it do to miss two weeks of the second grade—or even the fifth grade? Especially if you're as bright as Purvis and Louise.

But—what have you been doing with them?

Sarah looks frazzled, thin, her chestnut hair pulled hastily back and done in a thick plait, jeans faded and in need of mending. She's been trying to run a bookstore and a press as well as to look after the children. Sleeping with Louise, for one thing, she says. She misses her Mama. But . . . There are plenty of kids in the neighborhood. They watch TV, go to the library. Purvis keeps up with his homework.

But . . .

Mama!

.You're right, Cornelia says hastily. You're right. Some things I say because I haven't any better sense than to keep on saying the same things I used to say. You know?

Sarah doesn't know, but she nods.

And I've left you to struggle with all this. Well, I'm better. I'm going to be—do—better.

So she's spending time with Purvis and Louise. Today on her visit to Tweet she brings them along. Children, she thinks, maybe the children . . . She has explained to them ahead of time what she is doing: Every time I go to see Tweet, I try to do and say something different—take something or somebody different. Last time I took flowers—burning bush—only thing I could find in bloom. And the time before, a new dress. She loves so to wear pretty clothes. And today—y'all. You two are better than clothes or flowers. Remember how she used to like you, how she'd take up her time telling you stories?

I guess so, Louise says. Sort of.

Of course you do.

Driving from the wide boulevards and green expanses of winter grass in her part of the city to the narrow streets and frost-grayed ditches of Tweet's (children playing Kick the

Can along the side streets, men lounging behind the steamy windows of street-corner cafes), she finds her way automatically, her mind on what she is saying.

She used to bring *me* flowers, Cornelia says. And all sorts of things. So, today, you two. OK? You don't mind, do you? And if we do something different every time, maybe, hit or miss, we'll find something that'll bring her out.

Out of where? Purvis says.

I think she's kind of buried herself inside herself, Cornelia says. You know how, sometimes when you're sad, you want to go in a closet and never come out?

No, Louise says. Closets are dark.

Well, yes. Yes, darling, you're right. Who would want to stay in a closet? So what we have to do is show her that she wants to come out into the light.

Louise has brought her crayons and a coloring book and now, in the backseat, she is already at work. There isn't any purple in this box, she says. I need purple.

This is something important you two can help with, Cornelia says. I'm hoping she'll try to talk to you.

I need purple. This dress is suppose to be purple.

Try putting red on top of blue, Cornelia says, or blue on top of red. Now listen, both of you. She—Tweet—talks funny. Or rather, she doesn't talk. She makes noises sometimes, but she doesn't say words. It's nothing to be scared of. You're not scared when a baby makes noises, right? She's like a baby. She's going to have to learn to talk again.

Purvis, sitting beside Cornelia, has been listening intently to all this. What about? he says. What can we talk about?

Red on blue works, Louise says. I like it.

Anything that comes into our heads. School, football, TV, whatever. Have you been listening to me, Louise?

I guess. Sort of.

Cornelia has put the sponge-rubber ball in Tweet's hand and is gently squeezing it, with her own hand over Tweet's.

244

The two children stand in front of Tweet, timid, unsure what to do with themselves. Louise makes her best effort. I know a riddle, Tweet, she says. Why did the chicken cross the road?

Cornelia hears the hiss of the gas heater, the sound of cars passing outside, the radio murmuring. Tweet humming. Rosa has moved the television set into her own bedroom. She won't let me play it, she told Cornelia, and I got to see my soaps.

Won't let you?

Gets mad. Beats on the chair arm.

Why, Tweet? Why did the chicken cross the road?

Silence. (Squeeze, squeeze. Squeeze, squeeze.)

Because he wanted to go to *Memphis*!

That's a weird riddle, Purvis says. Listen, Tweet: Knock, knock.

Silence. (Squeeze, squeeze. Squeeze, squeeze.)

You've got to say, Who's there?

Silence. (Squeeze, squeeze. Squeeze, squeeze.)

Who's there? Cornelia says.

Dwain.

Dwain who?

Dwain the tub, I'm dwowning, Purvis says, waits for a laugh. Listen, I've got a book of those at home. I'll bring it next time. OK? And listen, Tweet, Louise and I have been watching this great new show on television. Do you know about it? It comes on in the afternoon and it's got this huge yellow bird in it that talks. Not a real bird. And puppets—this frog and . . . You'd like it, Purvis says. You ought to get your mama to bring the TV back so you can watch it.

Tweet is humming again, ahh-mmm, ahh-mmm.

Squeeze, squeeze. Cornelia hears the hissing of the gas heater, feels the throbbing heat against her cheek, feels all through her body the rhythmic tap of Tweet's free hand on the chair arm, matches the squeeze squeeze of the ball to the beat she feels. It's hot, hot, as if the heater is expanding, sucking in the room. They will be drawn against the glowing tiles, consumed. . . . She masters her. . . .

No. She doesn't *master*. Something else happens. She lets go of Tweet's hand, the ball drops to the floor, rolls away. She puts her hand on Tweet's warm skin, begins to stroke the poor scarred twisted fingers, falls into a dream of stroking, touching, hardly knows that the children have given up, turned away.

Ahh-hmmm, ahh-hhhmmm, Tweet hums.

Now the children are sitting on the sofa, subdued by illness, misfortune, unfamiliarity, their own failure—but still curious about this sick silent lady. What will she do? Will she ever speak? Purvis is turning the pages of the book he has brought, Louise is coloring. Cornelia massages Tweet's neck and shoulders, never lets her hand break the touch of skin on skin. The skin under her hand, warm and supple, seems to yearn against hers. The gas hisses softly. Cornelia whispers tunelessly to the rhythm of the tattoo Tweet continues to beat on the chair arm: one-an, two-an, one-an, two-an . . .

Yes, yes, yes, Lord. Yes, yes, *yes*. I know the Lord will make a way.

A shiver goes through Tweet's body under Cornelia's hand.

Shh, shh, shh, she sings in a whisper. Shh-t, shhh-t, shh-t.

From the radio: Yes, yes, yes.

The children are restless. Purvis stirs the bowl of dusty Mardi Gras beads and doubloons on the coffee table. I'm a pirate chief, he says to Louise. OK? And you're a rich lady—a princess. I captured you and sank your ship. Here. He begins to drape strings of beads around her neck. Play like I captured your ship and . . . He catches her heavy dark hair back with the round twisted gold barrette.

Yes, he will, Yes, he will, Yes, he will. Yes, yes, yes. Yes, yes, yes.

Shh, shh, shh, Tweet sings. Shh-t, shh-t, shh-t.

She raises her head, stares at the children. Shh-t, shh-t, shh-t.

246

Louise looks at Cornelia, rearranges the strings of beads around her neck. Tweet sang, Shit, shit, shit, she says.

Cornelia, matching the rhythm of Tweet's body (Yes, yes, yes) under her hands, pays no attention.

Tweet sang, Shit, shit, shit, Louise says again, louder. She did, Purvis. Purvis? It's OK to say *shit* at home. Well, not *OK*, because you might get in the habit. And you have to be careful to remember *not* to say it at school, because the teacher doesn't like it and people get in trouble.

SHIT, SHIT, SHIT, Tweet sings, pounding the chair arm.

Now Purvis is listening, too.

Yes, I do, Yes, I do, Yes, I do, from the radio.

Noah dough, noah dough, noah dough, from Tweet.

No, I don't. No, I don't. No, I don't, Purvis sings.

Under her hand Cornelia feels a shudder. Tweet raises her head, looks straight at Louise, leans forward in her chair. SHIT, SHIT, SHIT. SHIT, SHIT, SHIT, she sings. She turns her head, looks at Purvis, waits until she hears *Yes, I do* from the radio again. Ahhh, she moans. No, I dough. No, no, no. No, no, no. Pounds on the chair arm.

She's singing *No, I don't*, Purvis says. Tweet can't talk, but she can sing.

Cornelia lifts her hands from Tweet's shoulders, stands still, still. The memory of the beat throbs in her body like the pulse of her blood. She drops to the floor beside the chair, drawing her hand along Tweet's arm, taking the twisted claw in hers. You're singing, she says. Oh, Tweet, my God, you're singing. All the time, all the time I've been here talking and talking, you've been singing.

Shit, shit, shit. Tweet pounds the chair arm. Shit, shit, shit.

They are all three staring at her now. Louise begins to cry.

No, Cornelia says. It's all right, darling. It's all right. Don't cry, don't be afraid. Purvis is right. Tweet's singing because she can't talk. She squeezed the burned hand.

Arrrhh, Tweet screams. Shit, shit, shit.

Oh, Christ, my God, I'm sorry. I didn't mean to hurt you. Listen. We'll . . . we'll listen to you sing, OK? Then we'll understand and—and we'll practice singing together. Don't cry, Louise. You're the one. You're the one who heard Tweet. She laughs. You're the one who is the Seventh Son. And now we have to figure out what to do, how to go about . . . She turns to Tweet again. She's the one, she's the one who is the Seventh Son. . . . And wait, let's see. . . .

Shit, shit, shit, Tweet sings. Shit, shit, shit. No, no, no.

I know you can, Cornelia chants. You can talk. Yes, you can. Yes, you can. Yes, you can.

Shit, shit, shit.

Oh, listen, Tweet darling. Listen. She has put her hand now on Tweet's good hand. Listen to . . . to Grandfather. We . . . you and I . . . We heard him singing in New York, remember? We'll sing like *him*. What was it? She's chanting. Been calling Roberta five long years. Yeah. She don't answer, yeah. Wonder does she hear. Like that. We can say anything, anything, like that, and make it fit the music.

Shit, shit, shit.

Cornelia reaches over, cuts off the radio. *NO.* Listen: I be so *glad*, uh huh, When the sun goes down. Remember? Can we try it? I be so *glad* . . .

No, I wo, no, I wo, no, I wo.

Oh, please, let's try it. Please? Try it like him. Be so *glad* when the sun goes down.

Ummm, yay, Tweet hums. Ummm, yay.

Like this, Cornelia says. We can do this: We can *sing talk*. Listen: You can tell us when, yeah, when you're hungry again. See? You can tell us when, see, when you want to pee. Try it, please? Try it with me? She chants: You can tell us when, yeah, and on the repeat Tweet joins her: an mm hungy gain hmmm. An mmm hungy gain. AN HMMM HUNGY GAIN.

When you want to pee.

an ahhm aun ta pee. Yay.

You can tell me why you're mad at me, Cornelia chanted.
Damn, damn, damn, Yeah, Tweet chanted. Damn, damn, damn.

When Cornelia and the children got home that afternoon, even preoccupied as she was with Tweet's triumph, Cornelia observed that the children had forgotten to return her jewelry. She unfastened the barrette from Louise's dusky hair, gathered the strings of beads, and asked Purvis for the doubloons he carried in his pants pocket. After she had unclipped the barrette, she looked at it for a moment, turned it over in her hand, traced the delicate ropelike twists of gold, turned it over again, looked closely at the smooth back next to the clip, and saw engraved there in tiny almost invisible letters: 18k. Then she went to her bedroom with the barrette in her hand and sat down and looked at it for a long time. Afterwards, she found a small box for the beads and doubloons and barrette and put them in it and put the box in a drawer and closed the drawer.

Tweet, at home, is chanting. She chants blues and gospel and all Grandfather's old hollers. She chants with Aretha and Mahalia and the Wolf and with Cornelia and Cynthia. Even Rosa, grumpy and suspicious, began to respond to her chants. And Nig, although he may have feared for his own enchantment, listened sometimes and halfheartedly responded.

She chants and talks and talks and chants. Before Cynthia leaves to return to her family and job in New York, Tweet has chanted, No, no, no, Lord. No, no, no, to the surgery on her head.

What do them folks know, yeah, she chanted, What do them folks know how my head wired up?

Bubble done gone, yeah, she chanted. I shrunk it down.

And still, when Cornelia came, she sometimes looked at her with fury in her eyes.

During those passing days Cornelia did a great many things besides talking and singing with Tweet and spending time with the children. She opened the closet door—John's closet —and kept it open. If anyone passed and closed it, she opened it again. After a few days, she opened his suitcase and took out his clothes. She called Sarah in to help and together they opened his chest and took out everything that Andrew might not want or need. They folded the shirts and slacks and the old seersucker robe and put them in boxes. They wept together as they worked, and then they gave the boxes away.

Every day she went down to O'Kelly's Books for a while. Some days when she went into the store, she felt such a strange inexplicable surge of joy that she thought she must be crazy. Sometimes she went to the washroom in the back and wept.

Sex, she said to Tweet one day when they were sitting together. Like, today. . . . There was a man—an old friend of John's and mine—in town from Atlanta, and he stopped by. We had lunch together.

I'm crazy, she said. I had us courting and married before dessert. Problems. Would Sarah and Andrew like him? Would I want to move to Atlanta? What about the business? Should we close the store and just keep the press? Or . . . Maybe he could move here. Why should the woman always take it for granted that she's the one who will move?

Tweet found nothing to say to this.

Can't someone else search for the end of this story? Discover where it is leading us?

No. It has to be me.

* * *

250

Three months have passed since those strange days in New York. Cornelia and Tweet are sitting together again in Tweet's living room. Nig has returned the wheelchair to the rental agency—Tweet gets around the house easily with a cane, even walks around the block. The burns on her leg and hand are healed, although the doctor tells her she needs plastic surgery to gain more mobility in the hand. She almost always has the sponge ball in her hand, squeezes it steadily.

Today, as they sit together, doors and windows are open; it's one of those beautiful early summer days that bless the South, the heat not yet oppressive as it will be in July and August, the air sweet with fragrance from the mock orange at the corner of the front porch, pungent with the odor of tomatoes swelling and showing color on their vines. The morning sun strikes through the east window of Tweet's living room, slants across the table where the bowl that held her jewelry still sits empty.

Tweet has been humming. Sometimes when she is tired she lapses into her chants again, although most of the time she speaks in a normal voice, stops once in a while, searching for a lost word, pounds the chair arm, plows ahead. Now, she raises her head, looks with those strange eyes, concentric circles of blue, into Cornelia's face, and begins to speak a sentence in a normal voice. Those children took . . . she says. Stops. Those children took . . . She shivers, can't find the word. Took—took—took. She breaks off. Uh, *huh*, she chants. Them children *took*, yeah. Took all my *beads*. I say: Them children *took*, yeah. They stole my beads.

Cornelia sits very still for a minute. Then, Beads? she says. Beads. No. It's my fault. I forgot we had them. I'll go get them.

Yeah, Tweet says. I want my beads.

Wait, Cornelia says. She gets up, takes up her purse and keys, and without another word leaves the house. Within half an hour she is back. She sits down again across the table from Tweet, opens her purse, takes the box out, and empties the jewelry into its bowl. Here they are, she says.

251

I just—forgot. Not like me. She is quiet a minute, then, Yes, it *is* like me, she says.

Cornelia is sitting on the sofa, Tweet on a straight-backed chair. They look at each other across the bowl.

If the children were here, they'd say thank you for letting them play with them, Cornelia says. They'd be sorry they forgot and took them home. In fact, they wouldn't even remember they had done it, I feel sure. They thought I'd returned them. But I forgot.

Tweet says nothing.

Purvis hopes to grow up to be a pirate, I think, Cornelia says with the shadow of a smile. And Louise—of course she wants to be a princess.

Why you talking so stiff? Tweet says.

Cornelia shakes her head, shrugs.

Tweet hitches her chair closer to the table, picks at the jewelry, sparkling green and blue and scarlet in a shaft of sunlight. Andrew and Sarah give me them beads when they come back from—stops, pounds the chair arm. . . .

Mardi Gras? Cornelia says.

Yeah. Them fake dollars, too. Don't know why I kept them. Luck? She laughs. The other stuff—dime-store beads my daddy and—and—Clar*ee* brought me. I keep them to remind me of—evil. And that—she points to a pair of earrings. Nig give me those to distract me when he was going out with *Miss* Puddin.

Maybe you ought to throw them all away, Cornelia says.

That's what you'd do, huh?

I don't know. . . . Maybe not. I didn't say I was sure. She pushes aside two or three strings of beads, picks up the gold barrette, turns it in her hand, holding it between thumb and forefinger, looks at Tweet, lays it back on top of the pile.

I could give them back to—to—Purvis and Louise.

If you want to do that, why did you tell me they'd stolen them?

Now Tweet shrugs.

The sound of a car door slamming outside. Steps on the front porch. Nig comes in. Morning, he says to Cornelia. After all these years, he has still not decided what to call her.

Good morning, Mr. Carrier.

What you doing home? Tweet says.

Car broke down over in front of Nasser's Superette. At least, I went in there and when I come out I couldn't start it. Battery's dead. I stopped in the Gulf station, checked it out. They say ain't worth putting a charge on. I got to go get me a battery. He pulls a watch from his pocket. Suppose to work a shift today—three o'clock.

Look, Tweet says. Look—look at Nig's watch. The Gypsum give him a gold watch for twenty-five years. What you think about that? Ain't that *fine*? she says in a furious voice. I'd put it in with them other—other *jewels*—if he'd give it to me. She has an idea. Might buy him a watch myself, she says, get him a watch for—for—for Christmas, throw that one against the wall.

Now, Tweet, Nig says. Now, Tweet. You talking foolishness. What you want to talk like that for? Cornelia sees him following Tweet across Mr. Lord's backyard that cold December morning the year they moved to town. Now, Tweet. Now, Tweet.

I might. You look out. Some night you're asleep I might get it and throw it against the wall.

Tweet, Nig says, all I want to do is tell you I caught a ride out to Sears to get a battery. All right? I be late for dinner.

Ahh-mmm, Tweet hums. Ahh-mmm. Can't quit you, baby. Just now and then set you down a while. She rocks back and then forward in her chair. Go on, she says. Go on.

After he leaves, the two women sit together in silence, the table between them.

Finally Tweet says, Yeah, it's yours. Belong to you. Yeah. I know.

I know you know. But you never missed it, did you?

No.

You got four, five them gold barrettes. Naturally, you wouldn't have missed one.

I would have given it to you, Cornelia says.

Yeah. Didn't I say you wouldn't have missed it? Why not give it to me?

Why? Cornelia says. Why did you steal my gold barrette?

Tweet laughs. Evil, she says. I'm evil. Then, Right is right, yeah. Uh huh, And wrong is wrong. People don't do *bad* by accident.

Why did you do it?

Maybe your hair was caught in it? You think maybe I took your hair? Make a mojo? Fingernail clippings? Blood, too, like blood from old used Tampax, Kotex? I throwed out enough in my day. From your panties when you—when you—fff-flooded? Washed enough of them. Shit? Cleaned enough of your toilets.

Cornelia moans. She feels as if her joints are being pulled apart, as if a jackhammer is sending its vibrations all through her body.

Hated you, Tweet says. She rocks back, leans forward in her chair. You ain't got *sense* enough to know I hated you. I hate you all my life, before I ever know you. When you making them Christmas cookies in Mrs. Lord's kitchen, when you saying to me about Wayne Jones: Oh, Tweet, he's just *like* that; when you sitting at the S.O.B. desk in the bank building: when you fixing them blue hy—hy—hydrangeas in the living room, saying, *That's just right*. Every day, every hour of my entire life from the day I'm born. Hate you when you acting like you the only woman in the world ever got sorrow when her husband die. I hate you, hate you, hate you. And I steal that gold barrette to remind me of it, in case I forget. She laughs. Sometimes I forget, she says.

Damn you, then, Cornelia says. I hate you, too.

Talking all that shit about me being with you in New

York. You ain't never *seen* me, *heard* me in your entire life and you talking that shit. I wasn't in no New York. I was down here falling on the stove, getting my hand—cook—cook—cooked. Having fits, shrinking that bubble.

Yes, you were. Yes, you were, Yes you were, Cornelia chants. You were there, yes you were.

Shit, shit, shit.

You can't help it, no. Not what you've done for me or what I've done for you, Cornelia says. You can't take back what you've told me. It's here. It's mine. Mine, mine, mine. Not just yours. Listen to this: I'm afraid. Nevertheless I go. I make myself strong to listen. That's mine. Mine, too.

I hate you, Tweet says.

Fuck you, then. Fuck you, then, fuck you, then.

Shit, shit, shit. Tweet rocks back, tilts back in her chair. Shit, shit, shit. She thumps down on all four legs again.

Neither of them has heard the car door slam or the steps on the porch, and now Nig is standing in the open doorway, looking in and backing away at the same time. Jesus have mercy, Tweet, Nig says. What are you doing? What are you saying?

Oh, Lord, Tweet sings, Here's that man again. Where he come from? Where he been? She throws herself back in her chair. She's teetering and rocking on the back legs of the chair. Cornelia half rises, reaches across the table, puts her hand on Tweet's knee, thumps the chair down. The bowl of beads goes skittering across the smooth glass surface of the table, falls to the floor, the jewels scatter.

Nemmine, ladies, Nig says. Nemmine. I thought I had done forgot something, but I'll come back and get it later.

Now Cornelia and Tweet are on the floor together, picking up the strings of beads, the plastic doubloons. Tweet picks up the barrette, hands it to Cornelia, who drops it back in the bowl.

Well, Tweet says. Well. She reaches out, touches Cornelia's hand. Lord, what I'm talking all that foolishness, she says.

Cornelia laughs. What can we do, she says, when we've shot somebody? Look around? See where we're headed? That's all I can see to do after you shoot somebody.

Cornelia is leaving now, walking down the sidewalk toward her car. She turns, looks at Tweet, who is standing on the front porch, watching her go. Tweet sings out suddenly: Oh, I love you, baby, but I sure do hate your ways. She's laughing and singing at the same time. I say, I love you, darlin, but I hate your treacherous low down ways.

That's how the song goes, she calls to Cornelia.

Sing it, Tweet. Yeah. Sing it, Cornelia. Sing it.